THE BROTHERS OF THE SNAKE
THE COMPLETE CHINATOWN CASES
OF JIMMY WENTWORTH, VOLUME.3

THE BROTHERS OF THE SNAKE

THE COMPLETE CHINATOWN CASES OF JIMMY WENTWORTH, VOLUME 3

SIDNEY HERSCHEL SMALL

ILLUSTRATED BY
JOSEPH A. FARREN

COVER BY
LEJAREN HILLER

POPULAR PUBLICATIONS · 2025

TABLE OF CONTENTS

THE BROTHERS OF THE SNAKE

Jimmy Wentworth Knew That Even the
Threat of Grim Reprisal Would Not Stop
the Killers of the Fiend, Kong Gai

1

RAIN SLASHED AGAINST the west windows of San Francisco's Hall of Justice. It was cold outside, and growing colder. Kearny Street, below and westward, was slippery and wet with winter, but the cobblestones of the narrower street leading up to Chinatown were washed almost white. The car tracks and slot between glistened like the blades of long N'ing-po swords. A bazaar at the top of the rise gleamed yellowly. All of the smaller shops were dark and seemingly deserted.

In the warm office of the captain of detectives the radiator hissed comfortably. Captain Dunand, smoking the final two inches of his after-breakfast cigar, felt so pleased with himself that he said:

"Jimmy, why walk your Chinatown beat today? The tongs are at peace. Take the day off, and tomorrow—"

"And tomorrow I can have a look-see at the body of your spy, captain, and count the knife-holes in him," Wentworth said.

Dunand stared at him.

"Who said anything about my spy?" he growled. "Who let it leak out?"

"At quarter past seven, sir, Wang Chen-po telephoned me. He said, 'Sing Mi'u and Gon Yee La'ang just passed my window. A white man was with them. What's up?' And if Wang knows it, so does the rest of Chinatown."

"Wang's a friend of the Department. He just happened to guess, that's all. I'm not worried."

"It's your spy who ought to be worried," Wentworth said, reaching for his black slicker. "I know how anxious you are to nab Kong Gai, chief, but you can't do it white-man way—"

"This is a number-one scheme," the gray-haired veteran grunted. "It's in the bag. By night we'll have our arrests made. Including your friend Kong Gai. He won't be The Evil One when we get hold of him. Now what do you say?"

"I just hope your spy's still alive," Wentworth said grimly.

Captain Dunand chewed the bitter end of his cigar. "Nonsense," he said finally, looking out at the driving rain, at the blackening sky. "If you didn't think like a Chinaman, Jimmy, you'd see just how good my plan is. I figured it out the moment we picked up this man, Gregory, yesterday afternoon. Don't say, 'You would!' or I'll send you out to the Sunset district, where the most exciting thing is a drunk on Saturday night. Well?"

"I haven't said anything, chief," Wentworth told him quietly. "Hadn't I better get up to Chinatown?"

"Wait!" Dunand's ample gray hair began to rumple itself into the air. "This man Gregory is a godsend to us. He's dealt with the Seattle dope ring. In Portland. He's on the inside. We grab him on advice from the Federals, and we get him without anybody knowing it, too!

"Here's what we're doing right now. Gregory goes into Chinatown—for us—to make arrangements to deliver a big ship of hop. He says he's got to meet Kong Gai himself. He refuses to talk to anyone else. He'll make a date to see

Jimmy had no time to draw his gun
The hatchetman was at him again

Kong Gai, maybe this afternoon, maybe tonight, and when he does, boy, we'll be there!"

"I know where you'll be," Wentworth said.

"Where?"

"At your spy's autopsy."

"Nonsense! What's wrong with the plan?"

Jimmy Wentworth wanted to say, "Everything," but remarked only, "You've done it, sir; what's the use of arguing?"

"This was figured out, Jimmy, by a departmental conference—"

"By men who know as much about the Chinese as I do about afternoon teas."

Dunand's eyes narrowed, although he said steadily enough, "I know you want 'hands off' in Chinatown, sergeant. However, this Kong Gai business has been going on long enough. It's time we all took a hand. Kong Gai is to be caught, and we're going to get him."

Wentworth pulled on the shiny slicker.

"You might tell the newspaper boys that, when the body of a white man is found in the bay, it will be Gregory's," he said softly.

Dunand leaned a big elbow on the table. "There are four men on Waverley Place right now," he snapped. "Good men. Keepin' Gregory in sight every moment he's on the street—"

"And informing Kong Gai what you're doing."

"Don't you think my men'll keep out of sight?"

"No. I'll bet there are a hundred Chinese right this minute who could give me a perfect description of them, sir, and tell who and what they are."

"Don't believe it! No, Jimmy. I don't. Just the same, Gregory's safe as if he were in his own bed. Have you forgotten that Si'u Sing, or whatever his name is, and Gon Yee La'ang are with him? Respectable Chinese. I told 'em if anything happened to Gregory I'd have 'em walk the thirteen stairs themselves so fast they'd be out of breath. And I'll do it. They whined, but agreed."

WENTWORTH FASTENED THE clasps of his slicker high about his throat, and picked up his cap. "How," he asked, "did you happen to pick on Sing Mi'u—that's his name—and Gon Yee? Because they're on probation for being implicated in importing that slave girl?"

"No. Funny thing. After Gregory was picked up, they offered to go his bail. I'm not dumb, young fellow! I knew they were in the mess somewhere—"

Wentworth's words were out before he could recall them,

"No, you aren't dumb, chief. Nobody knew you'd nabbed Gregory, didn't you say?"

Dunand leaned far back in his chair. He looked at the end of his cigar, and with a restrained gesture placed it on his tray. "They don't make a good cigar any more," he said. Then, because his sergeant in charge of the Chinatown detail had picked the flaw in his plan, he began to shout: "Even so! It don't make any difference! I said, 'Boys, you like go jail long time?' They say no, so we come to terms—"

"Sing Mi'u and Gon Yee. Bazaar owners. I never cared for 'em, sir."

"D'ye think I kissed them, lad? I told them both that if anything happened to Gregory, anywhere, I'd see that they were jerked up to their heathen gods over at San Q. And that their bodies wouldn't be shipped back to China, either. I made 'em like it. They've got to play ball. I told 'em if anything happened to our man I'd have false testimony sworn to, and string 'em up. They knew I meant it."

Wentworth thought it might work at that. The question is, who do Sing Mi'u and Gon Yee fear the most? Our kind of swift death, or Kong Gai's torture for betrayal? They're avaricious. They'd think if Kong Gai were caught, they themselves might control the drug trade. He said, "Chief, is Gregory to be depended upon to reveal Kong Gai's whereabouts, if arrangements are made for a meeting to deliver the hop?"

"He came clean. He's a white man, and I know when a white man's wishful to go straight. He can be counted on absolutely."

"Then," the youthful sergeant of detectives said, slipping his hand into the slicker pocket to make certain that he could reach through the inner slit and get at his gun, "I'll be going to Chinatown and… see where his body is, if I can."

"You won't find it! Or, if you do, I'll keep my promise to those two Chinese! We're going to get Kong Gai! Listen, boy! They go to Kong Gai, with Gregory, and their story is that he comes to them offerin' a prime number one lot of poppy. They refused to deal with him, insisting that Kong Gai's the fellow to do the buying. So all three of 'em go to see the Evil One—"

"They were willing to do this?"

"Sure."

"Then you can count on it that they are brothers of the snake. Servants of Kong Gai. Cobra-men. Otherwise, they wouldn't dare go to visit him!"

"No? Not if they wanted to curry favor?"

Wentworth shrugged. "I'll go look for the body," he said again.

The Chinatown detective sergeant was so coldly positive that Dunand's assurance began to be shaken. He covered this with sharp words.

"He isn't going to be killed, Wentworth. Not while he's shadowed by Johnsen and Maginnis and Haight and Timmerson. All good men. If he goes into a building and doesn't come out, I'll frame Sing and Gon Yee. They know I'll keep my word! If they are mixed up in the Snake Society, Kong Gai's got to protect 'em—"

"Or lose face with the other Chinese," Wentworth nodded.

"Good! Gregory's safe, I tell you. The only thing Kong Gai can do, if he's suspicious or wise, is to have his hatchetmen and 'binders try to trap us when we surround the meeting place named. Of course he might refuse to meet Gregory. We can't help that. But if he agrees—and sends his 'binders, we'll give the Snakes a taste of hot lead comin' out of the chopper that they'll remember. I'll civilize 'em, Jimmy! And, besides that, I'm positive that..."

The gray-haired captain of detectives was talking to himself. Sergeant James Wentworth had quietly left the office.

Dunand stared at the growing storm. It must have been growing colder outside, for although the rain had lessened, coat collars were high and hats pulled down low. The sky was black, ominous, with winter Pacific Coast storm. Far westward, lightning flickered palely. Low thunder rolled over the ocean, dim and distant. The wind, from the west also, was steady and chill as it blew toward the roiled water of the Golden Gate.

"I hope he gets damn good and wet," the captain of detectives ejaculated angrily. "Even if lightning hits him, that thick skull'd be protection. If Jimmy were not so all-fired young... and such a good detective... and if I didn't like him... I'd make him stay in all day and go over records. 'Twould be discipline. And good for his soul."

The gray-haired official began to drum ceaselessly on the top of his desk. No one could have guessed what he was thinking, until, alone in the empty office, he said aloud, "Have I sent that poor devil Gregory out to his death? Have I?" It was a full minute later before he added, "Jimmy said, 'I'll try and find his body.' He's sure Gregory'll be murdered. If the man's killed, I'll keep my promise to those two fat Chinos! If human hands kill Gregory, I'll see that Sing Mi'u and Gon Yee swing, because, no matter what

they say, they'll know how it was done, and be accesso-
ries...."

With that he went to the window, just in time to see the
slickered body of his sergeant climbing the long hill into
Chinatown.

2

THE ONLY PERSON Wentworth saw until he reached the principal street of the Oriental district was a tattered beggar—a *kao hou tze*—crouched in a dark doorway, wet to his scrawny hide, his teeth chattering as he offered impossible gifts to the storm demons. The shops were all dark and unopened now, for did not every Chinese know that the snake of the sky, the dreaded lightning demon, was crossing the ocean clear from the Celestial Kingdom, bringing vengeance and death? Who dared defy the devils of heaven? Not even the mission-educated second generation, nor even the university graduates of the third. When devils were abroad, wise men burned incense, made promises in return for safety, and repeated as many prayers as they could remember.

Wentworth knew perfectly what was going on behind the shuttered windows. His boyhood had been spent in China; he spoke a dozen dialects like a native. The Chinese knew him as the patrolman who paced from the old cathedral down to the edge of the Barbary Coast, to meander back up dark alleys—Waverley Place, Fish Alley, along that terrible portion where women of every color, black, brown, yellow and white, and every shade between, waited for trade—until he reached again the walls of the church, and gazed up at the clock, to see the comforting

"Son, Observe the Time
And Flee from Evil"

carved in letters of gold against a black-painted ground.

The flower-girls' snake-bellied *san-hi'n* were all silent now. No food-coolies ran about with hot morning rice. There was not even a few *bo' how doy*—highbinders, hatchetmen—lounging restlessly before tong headquarters. In a crate, two bedraggled ducks quacked mournfully. Edible snails floated soft-side upward in a tank of murky water before a meat shop. The shop itself was deserted.

Although the bazaar at the top of the hill was lighted, the door was closed, and the interior empty. Standing against the corner of the building was a patrolman, staring uncertainly along the street.

Wentworth approached him at once, and as the man's fingers moved to an involuntary salute, Jimmy said, "Easy, Riley. I'm just another bull up here, you know. You waiting here in front of the Gon Yee bazaar on orders?"

"Johnson says I'm t' wait here until Gon Yee an' another Chink an' a white man come back."

Jimmy thought, too bad the boys didn't carry a sign telling what they were up to! They think the Chinese are stupid. If they only knew! All he said, however, was, "Right. Where'd Johnson go?"

"Down Dupont, sergeant. Turned off at Clay. I dunno where he went after that."

"Thanks. How long ago?"

"A good hour, anyhow. Maybe more." As thunder rolled again, a little nearer, the patrolman rubbed his hands together. "We're in for a tough day, sarge."

Wentworth nodded. "Anything happen here, Riley?"

"Quiet as th' grave, sergeant."

"Anybody watching you?"

"Not a soul."

Wentworth said softly, "Next time you turn, southward, take a look up. Third story. Window with china lilies in a blue pot. You'll see that the bottom part of the shutters aren't closed like the rest of it. That's where you're watched from, Riley. If there's any trouble—I don't think there will be, not here, anyhow—take a shot at that window for luck."

"Watchin' me? An' me never knowin' it! 'Tis devils they are, Sergeant Jimmy! Gives me th' creeps—"

"Don't forget what I said," Wentworth told him, and, with that, started not down the street, but up, southward also, toward the cathedral. Riley's honest face showed bewilderment, and the patrolman almost called after his superior, but was too anxious to get a squint at the china lily window to do anything else.

Wentworth reached the cathedral. He paused, whirled, saw that he was not being followed, and then began a curious business. At first he walked sedately enough, but each time he was out of observation, of spots he had learned were look-outs for the tongs, or possibly for Kong Gai's cobra-men, he ran swiftly. He was alert, and cold of mind. He felt that something was happening, or would happen shortly, and wanted to arrive on the probable scene of action as soon as he could, but without going directly to the place.

He did not believe Gregory's life could be saved, if, indeed, the man were still alive. To get hold of Johnson and the Headquarters men, and batter down doors going after Gregory, Sing Mi'u and Gon Yee, was not only instant death for Gregory, but death for them all, with nothing accomplished. Gregory might be saved from torture, but—unless he did it from sheer cruelty—Kong Gai had little to learn from the newly appointed spy. The whole matter could be explained by the Chinese with him, and then Kong Gai would plan the proper way of disposing of Gregory, and at the same time protecting his brothers of the snake.

The easiest, most likely scheme, Wentworth figured as he started northward again, was for Kong Gai to hack the life from the white man in his toils, and for Sing Mi'u and Gon Yee to disappear, and become respected merchants in Seattle, or San Diego, or even New York... and never be apprehended.

Yet this was hardly Kong Gai's way. The King Cobra, knowing that all Chinatown was watching, would certainly attempt to kill Gregory as a faithless person, and strengthen his grip on Chinatown by having Sing Mi'u and Gon Yee go free, despite the warning and promises of the police. That was the sort of thing Kong Gai would delight in doing!

In what diabolical way would he bring it about?

AGAIN THUNDER ROLLED, deeper, dangerous, nearer. This time it followed the crackle of lightning more closely, spaced fifteen or twenty seconds later.

What a scene for terrible death! The narrow, dark, deserted streets of Chinatown. The storm, coming nearer every minute. Between the roaring of the thunder, the Oriental district was very still; so still that even through the walls of a house Wentworth could hear the nasal whine of a grandfather reciting the Thousand Words of Perfume, which the sky-demons cannot abide. Death was in the air. The Chinese felt it in some uncanny way. Wentworth knew it. Death rode in the sky; death stalked a white man, attempting to patch the pieces of his life by serving his own race in a valiant effort to remove the awful menace of the Evil One, Kong Gai, leader of the cobra-men.

The rain had stopped; the air was heavy, pregnant with the coming outburst. In the west the ocean-bred storm raced nearer, cloud on cloud.

With the rapidity of lightning itself, every thought save one vanished from the detective sergeant's head. Somewhere, under the ground, high in a building, behind steel doors, silk-clad 'binders must be doing a white man to death, a white man who was trying to square himself with the world.

Wentworth's first duty was to find some way to catch the Evil One, but he forgot that also. Plans, caution, everything disappeared, overwhelmed by a blind and blazing fury. He broke into a run in the darkening street, his slicker hissing and crackling like the approaching lightning.

A voice rose somewhere in excited Cantonese. The rumble of thunder, and the sound of his own feet on the pavement, together with the singleness of purpose in his own mind, kept the meaning of it from Wentworth. Another voice, ahead of him, answered the cry; a door opened, and a gigantic black-clad *bo' how doy* peered out, to retreat instantly.

Not until the white detective raced past did the hatchetman leap, crying:

"Vengeance from the sky! Vengeance for Kong Gai! Vengeance for the brothers of the snake you have killed!"

In shouting, the yellow killer made his one mistake. He might have leaped on Wentworth's back, and borne him down to death. Instead, the white man sprang to one side, at the same time whirling about. The 'binder's wide sweep with his assassin's blade missed its mark.

Wentworth had no time to draw gun, for the hatchet-man was at him again. He might have continued running, and outdistanced the cobra-man, but rage seethed in his head. As the 'binder—the largest Chinese Wentworth had ever seen—tried to rip upward at the white man's middle, Wentworth drove a lean hard fist at his jaw, landing too high.

Without hesitation Wentworth grabbed at the knife-wrist, and as body met body the two rolled over the cobbles of the street.

The 'binder's long black-pointed nails were horribly busy. His teeth ripped at Wentworth's slicker, tearing it voraciously. Then the *bo' how doy* gave over his useless chewing and set his jagged fangs in the hand holding his wrist. Jimmy attempted to crush the big Asiatic beneath him, while pain from his gnawed hand ran through him. He had a glimpse of the fiendish face of the Chinese, and suddenly knew what the yellow man intended. Inch by inch, between the locked bodies, the 'binder was working his free hand, to get at a second knife.

Wentworth was half sick with agony as he ripped his hand from the 'binder's teeth. He felt searing pain somewhere as the knife reached him.

Somehow, he was on his knees, while the 'binder shrieked with triumph, his blade high in the air.

"I have him, oh snake-brothers," screamed the hatchetman. "Keep away! Here is vengeance from the sky!"

THE KNIFE NEVER descended, save in a long arc, ending in a clatter on the stones. Wentworth had caught the other arm of the Chinese, seized him tightly, and then jerked his body close to his own lean powerful frame. Astonished, the 'binder tried to yank himself away from this man who fought back instead of protecting himself, and in so doing dropped the knife.

The hatchetman was not crying out now at all. Wentworth had him in the desperate grip Captain Dunand had taught him. One hand about an arm. The other around the waist of the big Chinaman. The 'binder was twisted in a half-circle, held upright by the arm about his waist, twisted to the side by the grip on his arm. He was unable to do anything more damaging now than attempt to set his teeth in Wentworth's shoulder.

Fierce cries echoed in the street, urging the big Chinese to tear the white devil limb from limb, that his body might be fed to the dogs. The Chinese watching from behind barred windows were unable to determine what was actually taking place. Since the powerful 'binder was not crying for help, they supposed he was finishing off the hated enemy of the cobra clan by throttling him.

Wentworth put desperate pressure in his two-way grip. A wrench at the arm. Waist held tight and firm. Another grim twist. There was a sudden snap. The Chinese's body went limp, without a sound coming from the thin lips. Bone had snapped.

As the white man rose swiftly to his feet, a lightning flash revealed to the blood-thirsty onlookers what had really happened. A voice screamed savagely. A short heavy knife was hurled. It missed Wentworth's body, and buried itself deep in the unconscious form of the highbinder.

Wentworth's gun was out now.

His anger had cooled. His head was cold again, as if the physical combat had made him a reasoning man—a calculating, quiet member of the detective force, the sergeant in charge of Chinatown. Certain that his words would be translated, he called out loudly in English:

"I'll shoot the first man I see on the street!"

He heard the words changed to nasal, sputtering Cantonese.

Then the thunder crashed again, loudly, and seemed to shake the sandy foundations of Chinatown.

Words pelted down: "Judgement... from heaven. Big Mun To' Ying... must have been... traitor. Gods... did not protect him..."

Knowing the Chinese, their customs, their fears and superstitions, Wentworth knew that not a hand would be laid on him.

Not only would the Chinese believe that this big hatchetman should have been protected by the venomous and deadly lightning-gods and devils, but all of them would think twice before venturing out into the storm. For it is considered a great disgrace, Jimmy knew, and an obvious punishment of sin—and what member of the Kong-Gai society had not sinned a hundred times?—to be struck by lightning. In addition, lightning destroyed a man's very soul, and the body became that of a vampire.

When lightning struck the earth, was it not because there was the body of an evil person buried there, perhaps centuries ago, and was not the coffin and body struck and destroyed, even to the last bit of bone? Every Chinese knew the story of Li Pao, evil emperor, who, after death, was struck as his cortege was passing under the South Gate, and utterly destroyed except one tiny bit of pure jade? *Hai-ya!* A knife might be hurled again at the white man, but none of the Chinese intended to venture into the street.

One blade must have been poised, because as Wentworth started along the black alley he heard, "Ae-ee! What is the use? Did you not see how the blade turned aside before, and went into the body of Mun To' Ying? The devils are protecting the White One!"

"There is another white man who is... not being protected," someone shrilled.

"You lie," came the answer. Wentworth tried to walk softly, so he could hear, between the banging of the thunder, what might follow, and he was rewarded. "You lie! I heard that even Kong Gai does not dare..."

So Kong Gai hardly dared to put the lives of his two henchmen, Sing Mi'u and Gon Yee, in jeopardy! Dunand's threat was a powerful one! Gregory might still be alive, might have a chance for life. Wentworth was glad now that he had for a time gone berserk, for he had learned something of real value. Kong Gai could find no method of removing the ex-smuggler of opium without losing his two Chinese merchant henchmen. There might be hope yet.

Wentworth managed to restrain his haste now. He knew that he must not mess matters up by racing to the scene of the meeting between Gregory and Kong Gai. He had to happen along.

Riley, the relief patrolman, had said that Johnson had turned off the main street at Clay. Wentworth knew that Gregory must have been taken by Sing Mi'u and Gon Yee to one of the side streets. Waverley Place or Fish Alley. Somewhere near, Jimmy was positive he would find Johnson and the Headquarters men. So calmly he marched along. His gnawed hand throbbed with pain.

The thunder followed the zigzag flashes of lightning like the rolling beat of drums, urging him forward. The heavens were black as the pit. Thunder brayed without pause as the storm raged into the city. Forked lightning illuminated every crevice of Chinatown.

The rain still held off, but the air was stiller, colder, than before.

3

TWO MEN IN black slickers were working at the cable slot, greasing the roller over which the cable ran. They were seemingly intent upon their labors, appearing to be the regular street car company crew. Wentworth, crossing the street, said to them above the bellowing of the storm:

"Which house, Johnson?"

" 'Lo, sarge," answered Officer Johnson, not looking up. "Fourth house. They been there a long time."

"Where're Timmerson and Haight?"

"Other corner, sergeant."

"Doing what?"

"Haight's sellin' an order of cigarettes at the Chink cigar stand. Timmerson's leanin' against a telegraph pole like a guy makin' up his mind to hit th' Coast. O. K?"

Wentworth saw no reason not to pass the time of day with the supposed street car workers. He often paused to talk here and there, in his role as beat patrolman. So he asked, pulling his cap closer over his eyes, "Who's watching you?"

"Don't get you, sarge."

"What Chinese are shadowing you and the others?"

Johnson said, swabbing grease on the roller, "Heaven knows."

"You mean the devil," Jimmy Wentworth muttered.

"Anyhow— Man! What a crash that was! Must've hit something!"

The terrific burst of lightning seemed to shake the ground beneath them. Thunder came instantly after it, showing that the storm was directly above them, and perilously close. Someone began to beat a gong furiously, to frighten away the devils of the sky, and the *bong-bong-bong* mingled with the howling of the storm.

"Worst storm I ever saw here," shouted Maginnis, "and I'm a native son. Sarge, she'll come down buckets in a minute. Wow! There's another flash!"

Thunder crashed again, terribly. The flimsy frame structures in Chinatown shook. Somewhere a woman's voice rose in terror, shrilly.

"We'll go down to th' next openin' in th' slot," Johnson said phlegmatically. "See you later, sergeant?"

"I'll walk past that fourth house," Jimmy told him.

If Gregory was already dead, if his body was on the way to the bay, where the tide would wash it into the ocean, if Sing Mi'u and Gon Yee were already leaving the city, there wasn't much to be done. Wentworth knew how useless it would be to have the ferries and trains watched. Two Chinese could slip away in machines, and, for all anyone knew, be on the way to Mexico unmolested. What was happening in that black fourth three-story structure? What awful acting was taking place, in deadly earnest, with the storm as the fearful chorus?

Wentworth thought, thinking of the lone white man attempting to become a decent citizen again by serving his community, "Poor devil! But what can I do?"

To burst into the place was utterly useless. There would

be steel doors. Hidden passages. Tunnels leading to other lairs of the venomous Kong Gai.

Gregory had only one chance of life: did Kong Gai intend to protect his two henchmen, who were not only wealthy, but must be valuable to him? If so, it would be difficult for the Evil One to murder Gregory, and still have Sing Mi'u and Gon Yee able to conduct their businesses in the city without being captured by the police. On this thin thread was Gregory's life. And Wentworth, knowing Kong Gai for the fiend he was, feared the worst.

It was really almost impossible to think coherently. Overhead the storm raged with ever-increasing intensity, as if it intended to blast Chinatown from the sandhills upon which it was builded.

The combat of the elements seemed to dwarf every effort of man; it was almost as if Kong Gai were able to summon the demons of the sky, headed by the snake-bodied lightning god, to do his bidding. Unconsciously, the lean young detective sergeant shivered, and then his lips resumed their tightness.

His eyes appeared to be watching the slippery pavement beneath his feet, but at every flash of lightning he managed to get a good look at the silent black house across the street. It had barred windows. A blank front door, probably wood backed by steel. Into that door had walked the man Gregory....

And as Wentworth looked, the door opened.

Every muscle in his body tensed. For a split second he was forced to fight for self-control, lest he go tearing across the cobbles of the street and attempt to get inside. Which, reason told him, would do absolutely no good. There were other doors. Hatchetmen guards, asking nothing better than to hack the life out of a white policeman. There would be trapdoors in the floor, opening into pits with up-thrust spears to impale the enemies of the Evil One....

The door opened. Wentworth's heart leaped. In that first moment he believed that Kong Gai had been unable, for the moment, to devise a way to kill Gregory, because, standing in the doorway, looking up at the sky, was the fat, oily figure of Sing Mi'u.

The well-dressed Chinese thrust out his hand, palm downward, testing the air for rain; he turned, and cried something to someone inside.

An instant later, in the moment of a flash of lightning, Wentworth saw, inside, two other figures. One was the familiar form of Gon Yee La'ang. The other, Jimmy was able to determine in the moment before blackness made it impossible again, must be the white man, Gregory.

Wentworth's hand was through the slit in his slicker pocket, and on his gun. A shot would bring the Headquarters men. And yet Kong Gai would never kill the white man now. All must be well! Yet, so great was Jimmy's hatred and understanding of the evil King Cobra that every sense was alert. The nearness of Kong Gai's presence made the hackles on his neck rise, and tensed the muscles of the hand about the butt of the automatic.

One of the two men inside, either Gon Yee or Gregory himself, lit a match, hands cupped to protect the light from the gusty wind. Again Wentworth saw the face of the white man; not clearly, of course, but so he could have identified him as being no Chinese.

Then, shaking the ground under Wentworth's very feet,

as had happened before in the raging storm, there was another terrific flash of lightning, and a shattering crackle of thunder. Wentworth blinked. And then his eyes opened wide, and he was tearing across the street, gun out.

WHAT HAPPENED WAS almost too rapid for the human eye to follow.

The doorway had been terribly bright for a fraction of a second, as, indeed, had all of the street, all of Chinatown. In that brief bit of time, despite the automatic shutting of his eyes, Wentworth had seen the white man stagger, and saw a form fall forward—almost leap forward!

Smothered by the brawling of the thunder, Sing Mi'u and Gon Yee had screamed; Gon Yee was leaning against the doorway, but Sing Mi'u had fallen to the street. Not as far as Gregory, for it was the white man Wentworth reached first.

Johnson and Maginnis were pounding down the street; Haight and Timmerson were rushing up, all with drawn weapons.

As Wentworth, gun covering Gon Yee bent down, the horrible odor of burned human flesh came to his nostrils.

Why couldn't the lightning have struck the Chinese, instead of the white man? That was Wentworth's first thought. He snapped at Johnson, "Don't let either of 'em get away! Send for the wagon—"

"I—saw it—happen," Johnson yelled above the storm, as Haight ran down the street toward the call-box. "Couldn't see—who was what. Bang! Just like—that other stroke. Right in—this street—"

"I saw it too," Wentworth muttered. What capital Kong Gai would make of this! He'd tell his brothers of the snake that the snake-god himself, the dreaded lightning from the sky, had struck down a spy, had killed one who attempted to withstand the King Cobra.

Gon Yee was whimpering loudly. Sing Mi'u picked himself up from the pavement, wiping blood from his nose.

"Ko' tik! Tin fo ho! Kong! What terrible lightning!" And, seeing Gregory's body, he wailed, *"Hai-ee!* A dead man? No! I made a promise to the official-with-gray-hair! He cannot be dead! But what a sight!"

"He may be only stunned," Wentworth snapped in English.

"How fortunate!"

Lightning flashed again, showing the police clearly the broken body of the man who had tried to help them. The clothing was ripped and torn. There was a lacerated, charred wound on the side of the man's neck. Even the shoes seemed to have been jerked apart. Here and there the flesh of one arm, revealed by a tear, was badly singed. The fingers of the other arm, the right, were distorted and broken.

Wentworth looked up wearily. He took his hand from over the man's heart.

"He's dead," said the Chinatown detective sergeant soberly.

"Aee-ee! Oh, miserable man that I am!" This was from Gon Yee, recovered from his apparent fright. "My poor family! My unfortunate self! Now I must suffer the vengeance of the white man! *Ae!"*

"Shut up," growled Johnson. "We said you'd catch hell if anything happened to this man—but this is different."

Gon Yee refused to be comforted, and continued wailing.

Each recurrent flashing of the lightning illumined the white, dead face of the man on the pavement.

Wentworth's head was working fast. He was forced to admit the testimony of his own eyes, even without what the other Headquarters men had seen. Gregory, beyond any question of a doubt, had been struck by lightning. He himself had seen the flash. He himself had seen the body hurtle to the street.

Also, the evidence before him was not to be questioned. Seared flesh. Ripped clothing, mute proof of the curious action of lightning. The stroke must have hit Gregory on the side of the neck, killing him instantly. A better death than Kong Gai would have granted him! And, ironically, dealt him at the very moment he was out of the Evil One's clutches!

As if contented with its deadly work, the storm began to swing southward, rapidly. Rain pelted down again.

Johnson said, "Any sense holdin' these two Chinks, sergeant? They're scared out of ten years of their lives."

"Keep 'em here," Wentworth ordered.

Why had he said that? Merely so they might tell their story to Dunand, as to what had happened inside the black house? Of course Dunand would want to hear about the meeting—a tale all lies, since Gregory, poor chap, could no longer give his version.

Over the rumbling of the disappearing storm came the shriek of the ambulance siren. Tearing along ahead of it was a police car. In moments the alley was filled with grim bluecoats, looking to Wentworth for orders.

4

THE AMBULANCE SURGEON'S stethoscope was out and over the silent heart of the dead man. "Death by shock," he said capably. "Here's one case that can't be elaborated upon by a post mortem."

"No need, doc," growled Johnson. "We saw him hit. Eh, sergeant?"

Jimmy nodded briefly.

His understanding of the diabolical ways of the Evil One, made him say, "We'll do a P.M. anyhow, doctor. For— er—poison."

The doctor shrugged.

"As you say, sergeant," he agreed. "But here's a perfect case of death by lightning, considering the fact that you all saw it happen. The lesions would have proven it anyhow, even if unseen. Wounds. Fractures. Burns. Singeing. Once it was supposed that death from lightning prevented rigor mortis, but that's been shown to be false. And medical men formerly thought the blood underwent a change. False also. Of course the cavities of the heart may be empty, but that doesn't prove anything."

"No," said Jimmy. "Er—no other way he could've been killed, doctor?"

Wentworth, as he spoke, was told by some sixth sense that Sing Mi'u and Gon Yee were listening. Yet, why shouldn't they? Was he becoming completely nutty about the powers of Kong Gai? Why, Gregory had been killed before his very eyes. He had seen him die. So had Johnson, and the other Headquarters men.

"According to one of the authorities on lightning, sergeant, you can't ever be sure a body found dead after a thunderstorm was killed by stroke. Death might be due to cardiac syncope—fright, you know. But here we have the burns and the singeing and the torn clothing, and all the rest."

Here and there windows were being opened, and slant, bright black eyes peered forth. The storm was lessening as it swept south. Shutters were being removed. To the west a patch of ragged blue sky appeared, and sun slipped slant-wise down to the city.

Then Wentworth heard that which he dreaded—a thin, nasal, mocking Chinese voice: "The vengeance of the snake-demon! Kong Gai has called the very devils down to kill those who would betray him!"

Utterly at sea, Jimmy said bitterly, "He might have been wounded, burned, tortured, before he was killed—"

"You saw him die, didn't you?" Johnson demanded.

"Did I?" asked Jimmy.

"If you didn't, I did!"

Wentworth pleaded of the doctor: "There's a lot at stake! You're positive?"

"I'm a surgeon," said the other. "I'm never positive, sergeant. If there were arborescent marks—like ferns, you know—burned on the arms or legs, or up the back, that would be absolute proof. But it happens rather rarely. Don't attach the slightest importance to the torn clothing. That almost always happens—"

"I know," Jimmy said. "I've seen plenty of that sort of thing in China—"

"And it's really difficult to determine death because of lightning. Why, sergeant, I've seen a case where the man's jaw was broken, and his teeth driven into his tongue; you'd have sworn the chap was killed in a fight. Yet he was shocked, numbed, and recovered, and said he'd been entirely alone under a tree, and had been struck by lightning. If it hadn't been for his own testimony, the police would have been positive he'd been murdered."

"Then a post mortem will not prove a thing?"

"I'm sorry, sergeant. No. Unless, as you suggested, the man was poisoned, and the lightning hit him after that."

"I don't know what to think," Jimmy Wentworth said.

The sergeant of detectives in charge of Chinatown was standing very straight now. His brother officers stared at him curiously. Johnson was saying something involving Wentworth's good sense, and Jimmy didn't blame him.

Gon Yee and Sing Mi'u, surrounded by officers, stood waiting.

Wentworth knew only too well what this would do to further the already powerful standing of Kong Gai. The leader of the cobra clan would be omnipotent in Chinatown. Not even the Six Companies would be able to stand against him. Every hatchetman and 'binder would flock to his emblem—the hooded, striking king cobra. Unless something could be done, Chinatown was in for dire trouble.

Johnson, coming up to his superior, and sorry for his

sergeant, said softly, "It's no go, Jimmy. Let's get on back to Headquarters."

A gong beat inside some building, and a shrill flute wailed. The nasal voice of a priest began to chant to the glory of the snake-gods. More fuel for Kong Gai's power! Even the priests were acknowledging the Evil One's control of the elements. Kong Gai would boast that he had commanded the lightning-snake to come clear across the ocean from the Celestial Kingdom to strike down an enemy.

Because he could think of nothing else to do, with the officers standing about waiting for his word to return to the Hall of Justice, Wentworth reached under his slicker and drew out his watch. He looked at it a long time, and then began to tap the gold metal. He was frowning now as he stared at the time-piece.

He said sharply, but very low in voice, to the surgeon:

"Doctor, what happens to metal when a man's struck by lightning?"

"What? Always magnetized, sergeant. Should've mentioned it. One of those things so elementary that we forget 'em...."

Wentworth was bending over the broken body already, his hands capably searching the tattered clothing. Without difficulty, he was able to find Gregory's watch, key-ring, coins, fountain pen with metal clip—"

"You think we rob him?" Gon Yee demanded, as if insulted. Only Wentworth was able to catch the taunting lilt in the Asiatic's question.

The surgeon and the sergeant were examining, testing the bits of metal.

Wentworth's voice sounded suddenly clear in the China-town alley.

"No, Gon Yee," he said. "You didn't rob him! It would be better if you had. For I arrest you and Sing Mi'u as accomplices in the murder of this man!"

"AE-EE! YOU SAW him hit by lightning—"

"I saw lightning! I saw brightness in the hallway—whether lightning or not nobody'll ever know. I saw him fall to the street! But, Gon Yee, he was tortured and killed, and it was all planned so you could say no human hands killed him. I—watch them, men! Get the cuffs on! And look out for trouble!"

The police drew together.

They did not understand as yet the importance of Wentworth's discovery—that none of the metal found on Gregory's body had been magnetized by lightning—but they obeyed orders. Guns were out. The driver of the police car lifted up a machine gun, and held the chopper so it might spray death anywhere on the street.

Sing Mi'u, suddenly fearful of what was hidden to him, screamed in Cantonese:

"Brothers! *Hai-ee!* Brothers of the snake! Oh great Kong Gai! We fear the vengeance of the white man!"

"Let 'em try something," growled Johnson, who, if he did not understand the words, was beginning to realize the sort of death Gregory must have died—a death by searing, burning and shock. "We've taken no chances, sergeant. Got two squads hidden within gun-sound. If it's war these devils want, we'll give it to 'em."

"Kong Gai probably knows where your men are, and how many are in the party," Wentworth said. "Nothing may happen. Just the same"—lifting his voice—"keep your eyes open, men. And let's start. I'll go in the car with you, and take Sing Mi'u and Gon Yee. Some of you go along with the ambulance. We don't want it attacked. Set? Let's get going!"

From a housetop a Chinese voice applauded:

"Well acted, Sing Mi'u! Fear was in your voice. Well done, snake-brother. The white men think you are really afraid."

"I fear indeed," wailed Sing Mi'u. "These white men have discovered—"

Laughter and gleeful shouts brayed him down. What a joke this was, on the white officials; what fools they all were.

None of the police had heard a sound at the house, but the door leading into it had been closed again. Giving the place a final look, Wentworth almost fired at the insolently shut door. He had no intention of attempting to go inside. He would find nothing, and knew it. The Evil One, careful in all things as he had been in torturing and killing Gregory in such diabolical manner as to save the threatened skins of his henchmen, would never be caught by obvious attack. Jimmy realized how easy it would have been for Kong Gai to put a bullet through his heart, but that was not the Evil One's way. First torture, and then some lingering death....

All Chinatown, save the honest merchants of the Six Companies, jeered as the police drove away.

But that same evening Chinatown learned, to its complete surprise, that Sing Mi'u and Gon Yee were charged with murder. The Asiatic district began to wonder how the white men guessed that human hands, and not the demons of the upper world, had killed the man Gregory.

At the same time Kong Gai, forehead to a crimson and gold rug, was bowed before his personal altar of the King Cobra, swearing fearful vengeance. Incense rose about his shaven head. Big black rats in cages waited to be fed to enormous cobras, whose venom had killed enemies of the snake brotherhood headed by Kong Gai.

"Oh, brothers," chanted the demoniac Chinese. "Hear my prayer, oh, snakes. Give me the live body of this white policeman. First I will feed you his eyes, one by one. Next I will slice an inch from his body daily, and give you the delicious bloody morsel. He will pray for death, but he will be long in dying! Speed the day, little brothers!"

Up in the Hall of Justice, in the office of Captain Dunand, Wentworth knew nothing of this, although he was well able to imagine Kong Gai's fruitless rage. The District Attorney was also in the office of the gray-haired captain of detectives, and he was saying:

"All in all, sergeant, you're to be congratulated, even if you were lucky. It is as good a case as I'll ever ask. I know that the Chinese's attorneys will put you and Johnson on the stand, and you'll swear you thought Gregory was killed by lightning—and there'll be a dozen Chinese witnesses ready to swear the same thing—but the testimony of the magnetized metal—the watch and keys—can't be contradicted. I've had five experts examine them, and they all agree Gregory was not killed by an act of God. I say you're lucky, because no autopsy could possibly reveal how Gregory met his death; you saw him apparently struck by lightning, and still doubted the testimony of your own eyes. Do you mind telling me why?"

"I'll tell you," Captain Dunand rumbled. "He wanted to prove me—his superior—a liar. Eh, Jimmy?"

"No, sir," said Jimmy Wentworth. "When I was a youngster, in China, my *amah*—my nurse—gave me a little piece of a broken metal pipe to play with. We didn't have toys, you know. She showed me how it'd pick up bits of iron; she said it was because it had been touched by gods from the sky. My dad took it away. He knew it had been on the body of a Chinese hit by lightning.

"I never thought about it until I looked at my watch. Then I wondered if the murdered man didn't have a watch also, and if it would be magnetized. It wasn't. The doctor knew it would have been, had Gregory been struck by lightning. That's all there is to it."

"Giving us," said the District Attorney, "an ironclad case."

"And giving me something on my conscience," Captain Dunand muttered. "I sent Gregory to his death—"

"He must have known what he faced," Jimmy Wentworth said slowly. "He was willing to die that way, sir, rather then continue as he had been. You said he had a family; that he wanted to be able to look them in the face again. The boys'll want to take up a collection for them, sir. And we'll tell his people just how brave a man he really was."

"It's the least we can do." Dunand's fist pounded on his desk. "I'll not try anything in Chinatown again," he promised. "But get me this Kong Gai, Jimmy!"

Wentworth looked out of the window.

The sky was clear now. The lanterns, blue and green

and yellow, glowed with light. The bright shop windows gleamed in a hundred tints where the porcelains and silks and strange gems were displayed. All seemed at peace, yet the sergeant of detectives knew that the brothers of the snake would be swearing bloody vengeance.

"Some day we'll meet, chief. When it happens, I'll need all the luck you can wish me."

THE BLACK COBRA

Kong Gai Strikes Fiendishly at a Great Bank's
Guarded Millions, and Jimmy Wentworth
Goes Hunting a Snake That Can Spit Death

1

GENERAL ALARM

THE THIN WHITE paper ribbon ran smoothly through the guides of the ticker in the quiet signal room of the Hall of Justice. The signal clerk, Sorenson, glanced up from the record book as if the nearing of the hands of the synchronized clock above his desk to quarter past ten had set off a signal in his own head.

It was almost fourteen minutes after ten in the morning. A spring morning in San Francisco. If Sorenson had looked out of the window, he could have seen the trees budding in the park, and the lilies blooming in the windows of Chinatown, which borders the public square to the westward. Instead, he dutifully watched the ribbon of the ticker sliding along.

At ten fifteen, without the variation of more than a second or two, the captain of the guard at the Federal Reserve Bank, a half dozen blocks away, would pull a lever, and the tape would record, under Sorenson's eyes, that all was well at the great financial institution.

The tape would read: O.K. O.K. FED RES O.K. O.K. 10.15 FED RES Xo6gg223ya O.K.

Then Sorenson would look in his record book to determine if Xo6gg22zya were the proper code signature for

*Step by step the
officers advanced into
the vault of death*

ten-fifteen on Wednesday morning, after which he might
forget about the ticker for another quarter of an hour.

The new building of the Federal Reserve Bank was said
not only to be burglar proof, but riot proof as well. Built
on made ground, set on piles, the vaults were below sea
level, and could be flooded in times of stress. A ten foot
bed of steel and concrete was below the vaults of the basement. The piles were closely set together, and were fifty foot
timbers driven into the sand. They formed the real foun-
dation of the massive structure. If it were in some unfore-
seen way possible to burrow beneath the bank without sea
water filtering into the tunnel, merely cutting through the
piles would have caused the very building itself to settle.

Nor was the human element of protection forgotten.
Guards, steel doors, electric signals, safeguarded the vaults

*On the floor of the vault
was the body of a guard*

from above. Every guard was in sight of two other guards. All were armed. All were trusted, capable men.

The door leading to the vault, left open during banking hours, weighed fifty tons, but was so delicately hung that it could be moved, or pushed shut, by a single finger.

Inside the vault were steel-barred compartments, in which gold, silver, and currency were kept. Each compartment's contents averaged in value forty millions of dollars. When the bank employees entered any of the compartments, it was necessary for three of them to insert their keys. One key would not open the compartments' locks. Only the head of the bank, and his immediate assistants, the vice-governor, carried master keys, three of them, and these were never taken from the bank at night, but were kept in three separate safes on the main office floor. When

either of these two men were in the vaults, or on their
way to them, either on inspection or to show visitors with
proper credentials the bullion and currency, every guard
was informed of this fact.

There was only one stairway leading down to the vault
floor, protected by a steel grilled door and a guard. There
was only one lower exit, where gold was received and
shipped. Here was the office of the captain of the guard
himself, a barred and shatterproof glass cage which was
an arsenal.

And yet, in addition to all of this, a hidden wire and a
private telephone ran to the signal room of the Hall of
Justice, and the captain of the guard checked in with his
"All's well" every fifteen minutes, day and night.

Should an armored truck from one of the banks arrive
at the Federal Reserve, the captain would immediately
inform Headquarters of the fact. Nor could the truck
depart without the captain's knowledge. Inside his cage
was the control button for the hydraulic lift, which was
in reality a foot thick, four foot high, section of steel and
concrete, which was raised before the outer gate leading to
the street. It took only the pressure of the captain's finger
to raise this barrier, but to lower it, an official on the main
banking floor, above, had to press a button also, showing
that the contents of the truck had been properly checked.

Rob the Federal Reserve? Why, it would have been as
easy a task to rob the Mint itself. Not one single detail had
been forgotten when the building was planned. Which was
what Sorenson must have felt as he watched the second
hand of the clock, synchronized with the Federal Reserve
time piece, move toward the quarter hour.

THE TICKER TAPE ran along smoothly, blankly. Sorenson heard a little click. That was the minute hand reaching fifteen. Fifteen past ten o'clock. Impassive, he stared at the tape. Two seconds past the minute. Three. Four. His eyes widened. He wasted two seconds tearing out his own watch. Seven seconds too long! Eight! Nine!

His orders were precise: "If a delay of ten seconds exists, communicate immediately with the captain of the guard at the Federal Reserve Bank."

Growling, "Something's wrong with th' damn ticker," but with a coldness in his heart, Sorenson lifted the telephone. The simple action would ring a gong in the captain's office.

Several more seconds passed. Then the signal clerk called, "Carpenter! Federal Reserve! Carpenter!"

Every sense was strained as Sorenson listened. His hand crept toward a button on his desk—the button he had never pressed in his years of service in the police department. Was something wrong at the great financial institution? Impossible! The ticker must be failing to function properly. A mechanical defect in it somewhere. Or Carpenter had for once forgotten to check in; the captain might be busy watching the receiving of a gold shipment… no, that, also, was impossible. Headquarters had not been told of the arrival of a truck at the loading platform.

Why didn't the captain of the guard answer the telephone? Until contact was broken by the pulling of a switch at the bank, a gong would keep ringing.

Sorenson, cold as ice, knew what would happen if he himself pressed the button marked A4. His orders, again, were explicit:

"If for any reason you are unable to communicate with the Federal Reserve Bank by telephone, upon failure to receive a properly coded signature by ticker, you are to sound the General Alarm. Use button A4 for this purpose. Twenty seconds should elapse. Exercise the greatest caution in sounding this alarm. Be positive that you are not making a mistake."

Seventeen seconds! Eighteen!

Sorenson shouted, "Carpenter! Where are you? Is anything wrong?"

For one second more he stared into the transmitter, as if he were trying to see through the telephone wire, and then he jabbed his finger down on button A4.

It might only be the ticker which was wrong, but Sorenson was obeying orders. He sat motionless for what seemed an intolerable length of time, watching the white, blank ribbon of paper run through the guides of the ticker, and then, ready as he was for what would happen, almost fell from his padded chair at the pandemonium of sound. General Alarm! Trouble at the Federal Reserve Bank!

The powerful gong on the main floor of the Hall of Justice began to issue its brazen summons. On every floor of the building other bells were shrilling wildly. In the basement the drivers of the riot cars advanced the spark and increased the gas flow of their cars so that the already warm engines roared.

The siren of the first riot car screamed and wailed. Men of the riot squad came tearing out of the next room, scrambling into the waiting machine. The car swayed out before all of them could even get inside.

Officer 1144, at the corner, managed furiously to stop traffic, and give the riot car a clear crossing.

Into the garage stormed patrolmen, detectives, bluecoated office workers. The second riot car filled in less than a minute. Officer 572, on the seat beside the driver, was fondling a chopper.

"Come on, come on, O'Toole," he growled, "Get goin'!"

"Yeah? An' be broken f'r not obeyin' orders?"

"There goes a wagon," pleaded 572. "And us waitin' here—"

A powerful voice rose above the excitement: "Let's go, O'Toole," shouted the captain of detectives, Dunand, with what breath he had left after his race to the machine. "Get in, Jimmy! In, boy! Go, O'Toole!"

Jimmy Wentworth managed to get to the running board as the car leaped forward.

General Alarm!

Back in the signal room, the clerk was pleading into the telephone. "Carpenter! Where are you? Is anything wrong? Or have I pulled a boner? Carpenter!"

When Sorenson heard the wailing of the riot car, it reminded him of his duty. He lifted another telephone, was given his connection, and then asked for the general commanding.

"Yes, sir," said Sorenson. "The department has sent riot cars to the Federal Reserve Bank. We didn't receive the quarter hourly signal, and—"

He was talking to a dead telephone. The general commanding the Pacific District was on his way to his own automobile, to see what was wrong at the government's bank. Crisp orders were given. A machine gun squad rushed to army trucks, which were soon pounding at high speed toward the financial district.

General Alarm!

2

DEATH IN THE VAULTS

"FRONT ENTRANCE!" ROARED Captain Dunand, as the riot car swerved around the corner, tires screaming.

There was no need to give an additional order. Guns were out. Two of the men were ready with high powered rifles, in case long range shooting would become necessary. The deadly department choppers, for shorter distance destruction, were in the hands of men who knew how to use them. The case of tear bombs was open. Only the gray haired captain of detectives and Wentworth, his sergeant in charge of the Chinatown detail, were not grasping some weapon.

Traffic was almost miraculously cleared from the streets along which the second riot car careened. Dunand's machine, following the course of the first riot car, made better time. As Wentworth saw the massive pillars of the magnificent Reserve Bank, he also saw the first car swing around the more distant corner of the building, heading, according to instructions, to the rear of the bank.

The two cars must have arrived at the selfsame moment at the two entrances of the institution.

Dunand and Wentworth, followed and flanked by officers and detectives, stormed up the broad steps. The car's driver halted the instantly appearing crowd, trying to keep the entrance clear.

Jimmy Wentworth, inside, saw the calm and peaceful interior of the bank. Two or three men were before tellers' windows. A guard stood at ease beside the inner door. Nothing wrong here!

The captain's deep voice boomed loudly in the stately banking chamber:

"What's the trouble?" he demanded swiftly of the guard.

"Eh? Trouble? No trouble, captain."

"No signal received at Headquarters," Dunand snapped. "Send for the head of the bank! Make it snappy! Take us down to the vaults!"

"Mr. Hoyle is in the vault now, captain. With distinguished visitors—"

"Show us the way!"

"My orders, captain, are not—"

"The vaults," shouted Dunand, patience at an end.

The head teller had hurried out; "What is the trouble, captain?" he asked. "We aren't having any here. If—"

"If you don't take me down to the vaults this second, I'll rip the place apart," bellowed the captain.

"Certainly," the head teller agreed soothingly. "This way, captain."

"Don't walk," pleaded Dunand. "Run. Come on!"

The head teller, stifling a smile, did trot more rapidly toward a heavily grilled door at the side of the banking floor. A guard standing beside the door opened it, and let the men through.

"Nothing wrong, Mr. King?" he questioned.

"These men think there is. Mr. Hoyle is in the vaults?"

"Yes, sir. He is showing two gentlemen the bank."

Dunand and Wentworth jerked the teller toward the stairway leading downward. The narrow way was very bright. They reached a second door, at the foot of the staircase. A solid door, this time. King, the head teller, touched a button near the knob. Touched it again.

He said, "That's strange. I'll open it for you, captain."

The teller's hand was shaking as he inserted his key.

"Hurry it," growled the captain of detectives.

THE WORDS SEEMED to make King's hand tremble worse than before. Wentworth himself reached forward, turned the key, and then Dunand shoved the heavy steel door inward.

A sickly, nauseous odor seeped out the moment the door was opened.

Dunand muttered, "Gas!"

And then King whimpered, "It's dark inside! The lights are out!"

Wentworth said to his superior, "The other men are at the rear entrance, sir. No way for anyone inside to get out now. But how about the people in the vaults?"

"Get masks," commanded Dunand.

An officer began to cough. Dunand himself, nearest the partially opened door, doubled up suddenly in spasmodic agony, and Wentworth, closing the door swiftly, put his arm around the captain.

"All—right—now," choked the gray haired captain.

Someone said, "Nobody alive in there. What gas is it?"

"Mr. Hoyle's inside," muttered the head teller. "The governor of the bank! With distinguished visitors. This… this is awful!"

"Who're the visitors?" Dunand asked, standing straight again.

"Very important people. Came with letters to us—"

"What's the matter with the masks?" Dunand snarled. "Why aren't they here? Why can't those men hurry? Here we're standin' waitin'—"

"I hear th' boys on th' stairs, captain."

"Who'd you say the visitors were?" Wentworth asked again.

Two officers rushed down the stairs. Masks were distributed, masks carried in the riot car, and in an instant the officers were turned into a troop of helmeted, goggled figures. Flashlights were out.

Wentworth was given no answer to the question he had twice asked.

The door was thrown wide open this time. The electric torches cut swaths of light in the black vault hall. Revealed the barred compartments, the open mouth of the vault door, the cages where gold and currency were kept… and more than that!

On the floor, not a dozen paces from the steel door itself, was the body of a guard. The man's form was doubled up, as if he had died in agony. And he was very dead. At the next right-angled corridor was the figure of another dead guard, one stiffening hand clenched about his throat. Behind the steel bars of the counting cage, where gold coins were brought for weighing, a clerk lay over his desk, motionless. Dead.

And every corner of the place was black, black as the pit. Not a light burned.

It was impossible for Dunand or any of the other men

to question King, because of the gas masks. Step by step the officers advanced into the vault room, and then into the vault itself. Through the fifty ton door, which had proven as useless as the guns of the guards—not one of which was found drawn.

The place was a tomb. Not a live person save the invading officers. Nothing but blackness, and the deadly odor which the masks prevented the police from smelling a second time.

King must have managed to conquer his horror and distress, for he suddenly stepped forward, and led the party through a different corridor.

Here the men from the first riot car were milling around. Two of their number were on the ground of the shipping area, deathly sick. Their faces were green. Other officers worked over them. The outer door, protected as it was by the captain of the guard and by two other guards—both dead on the floor now—remained open, as it did during banking hours, just as the door to the main floor was always open.

Inside the captain of the guard's room was that officer himself. He lay across the top of his chair. One hand was on his desk. Had he tried to reach the telephone, or some signal, as he died? The dead hand was actually clenched about something on the desk, and, even in death, retained its grip.

WENTWORTH'S EYES, UNDER the goggles of the mask, were troubled and amazed. The captain of the guard, protected not only by steel bars two inches thick, but also by shatterproof and bulletproof glass certainly had died from the lethal gas! But how? How could a man in a glass cage, entirely separate from the rest of the basement, be killed in the same manner as the others? Was there an air intake in the captain's room? Wentworth, looking feverishly about, saw it. On the ceiling. Unconnected with the outside rooms. Was that how it was done? Yet how could the killing have happened simultaneously with the other deaths? Or was the captain of the guard killed first? If so, the guards outside his cage would have seen him die!

There never had been such a crime before.

Dunand had pulled the door leading outside wide open. As the officers stepped out, their companions on the shipping-and-receiving platform hastily covered their faces against the fumes which sought the outer air. An officer slammed the door shut. All turned toward the gray haired captain of detectives.

Dunand pulled off his mask. While the men who were masked repeated the operation, Dunand coughed twice. Once his mouth opened as if he were about to express his horror, and then his old gray head went high.

"Wholesale murder," Dunand said clearly. "Now, men, we'll get to work. You, Crowley, and you, Henning"—to two detectives—"will get out on the street, and see if anyone knows anything about anybody comin' here from the rear. Anderson, see how air's carried in to the basement. If there's fans in the system, have 'em started so we can get inside."

As Dunand gave his orders, the men disappeared at once to fulfill them.

"Richardson, when the wagons get here—I hear one already—have a cordon thrown around the building. Hold everyone tryin' to get in or out. I don't care who he is. Or she. Nobody passes."

Corporal Richardson ran up the incline to the street, dodging past the barrier of the hydraulic lift.

IN PAIRS, DUNAND organized the remaining officers, setting them, in masks, to the task of bringing out every body in the basement of the Reserve Bank.

Then, his calm, efficient manner gone, he turned to the only department man left.

"Jimmy," he said, " 'tis the perfect crime at last. I never thought to see one. We can't keep anything from the papers. True, we came fast, and we came strong, but now that we're here, what can we do?"

Wentworth said, "Of course whoever did the job wore a mask, chief. Unless he managed to get his lethal gas through the air system."

"If it's like any I ever heard of, there'll be an air filter in it," Dunand told his sergeant. "Gas couldn't get through. Of course, if this's an inside job, the filter could have been tampered with. Jimmy I wonder what they got away with!"

The shivering head teller said, "Thanks to Captain Carpenter, not as much as might have been taken."

"How so?" Dunand snapped.

King pointed to the concrete and steel barriers, standing solidly inside the gates leading to the street. On the other side of the gates the blue-coated officers were already pushing back the excited throng of people.

"Carpenter must have thrown the lever which pushes up the barriers," said King, in a small voice. "The last thing he did before he died, gentlemen. They can't be lowered without the assistance of myself, on the banking floor—"

Dunand asked, "You knew the barriers were up?"

"I did. What about it? A dozen shipments are received every morning. I thought nothing of it. I merely waited for Carpenter's O.K. before pressing the button which drops them. And I never got it. I—"

"What time was the barrier raised?"

"A few minutes after ten. There will be a record of the time."

"The time the gas was shot in," Dunand said, half to himself.

Jimmy Wentworth's ideas died hard. For the third time he said, "About the visitors. Who were they? The men Mr. Hoyle was showing through the bank."

King managed to bring his wandering, miserable eyes to meet those of the detective sergeant. "The visitors?" he repeated. "Oh, yes. I met them. Fine gentlemen. Mr. Hoyle had me show them how we conduct business on the banking floor. Then they went with Mr. Hoyle into the vaults. Everyone likes to see the vault door. And we always let visitors see, and perhaps hold in their hand, a sheaf of million dollar treasury certificates—"

"Who were they?" Dunand asked, this time, wondering what great names the newspapers would be able to play up in the headlines, in addition to the murder of the guards and the bank people and the governor himself. "And did they come back out of the vault, eh? You said Mr. Hoyle was still in the basement—"

"He was, sir, and… oh, lord, there he is!"

A masked officer was dragging out the dead body of a well dressed man, which was placed gently on the pavement of the area. When the body of Hoyle was joined by that of a guard, brought out by the second officer of the pair, Dunand motioned for them to remove their masks.

"How about two men who were with the bank official there?" he questioned.

Officer 377 took a deep breath of air.

"He was all alone, cap," he said. "Nobody near him. I c'n show you where I found him, if you want."

"That's funny," said Dunand thoughtfully. "That's mighty funny."

"Two other men were with him," King insisted. "They couldn't leave the vaults unless Mr. Hoyle were with them. Not a guard would have let them pass! That's the rule—"

"Unless the guards were dead," Wentworth said softly.

"How could everyone be dead except the two visitors?"

Wentworth voiced Dunand's own thought: "They might have been masked for safety."

"And d'you think Mr. Hoyle would've stood there and let 'em put on masks without sounding an alarm?"

With one accord captain and sergeant bent over the body of the governor of the bank. Their swift, efficient search revealed no sign of violence at all. Hoyle must have died, so far as they could see, in the same manner that the other people had been murdered. By the deadly gas.

A blower fan was working within the vaults. Its hum was plainly audible as it beat out the terrible poisoned air.

There was now a new sound, rising above the noise of the street and the monotonous high hum of the fan; accompanied by Corporal Richardson, the general commanding the Presidio Division, with a machine gun squad in charge of a lieutenant, hurried through the gate.

Wentworth said hastily, for the fourth time, "Who were the men with Mr. Hoyle? Their names!"

"I… I don't remember. They were strange names—"

"What?"

"Yes, sergeant. Important people. They were… Chinese."

Captain Dunand's eyes flicked up to the approaching army officer, and then met Wentworth's startled eyes.

"They were Chinese," said Dunand bitterly. "And that makes it your case, Sergeant Wentworth. If you don't make an arrest in twenty-four hours, every newspaper on the Coast will be yellin' for your hide. The department's yours, sergeant, and that won't do you any good, either." His voice dropped as the general approached, and he added, in a whisper, "Was it, Jimmy? Is he the man?"

"Kong Gai," said Jimmy Wentworth.

"You know?"

"No. I guess. I'll try to make positive. If it was Kong Gai, he'll have done something to tell us."

"Or this time he's too smart! Even if he engineered it, as the Chinese visitors would seem to prove, what good'll it do? We can't find him."

"We can try," said Jimmy Wentworth soberly.

3

WENTWORTH GETS AN ITCH

CORPORAL RICHARDSON SAID, "Captain, sir, your orders was nobody was to come inside th' cordon, but—"

Before Dunand could commend his man, the general growled, "Got the barn door locked, eh, captain?"

"The horse may be dead," Dunand replied briefly, glancing down at the increasing number of bodies being dragged from the vaults, "but we don't know yet if he was stolen."

"Got any use for a machine gun detail?"

"No. The murderers are either gone, hiding inside, or dead. If the first, you can't help. Not yet. If the second, we'll get 'em. If the third, we're lucky."

"Gas, eh?"

"Yes. D'you recognize it?"

"No. Might be arsine. Smells like it. Damnable stuff. No antidote. Or prussic acid gas. Might be that. Didn't use it in the war. Too quickly fatal. The stuff's a mixture, I think. Er... how was it done?"

Officer Anderson had returned. Saluting his superior, he said, "The fans are in operation, sir. Nothing was wrong with the air system. It hasn't been tampered with. It is so situated that it couldn't have been touched."

Thinking of the dead captain of the guard in his glass cage, Wentworth said, "You're positive, Anderson?"

"I am, sir."

The roar of the blower fans increased as the last of the lethal air was sucked out of the chambers of death.

"We'll go inside," Dunand decided. "I can't wait any longer."

"Open the door and see if there're pockets of gas collected," the general suggested. "You have no clew at all, eh?"

"Clew?" growled Dunand. "We don't even know how the guards were killed! Let alone who did it. Except—between ourselves, as yet, general—the governor of the bank, Mr. Hoyle, was showing two men through. He's dead. So's everybody else, except the two men. They were... Chinese."

"Must've been important for Hoyle to be showing them around?"

"We'll find out. This man, the head teller, doesn't remember their names—"

"They were directors of the Asiatic Specie Bank," King said. "From Hongkong Their credentials will be in Mr. Hoyle's office. We don't let everyone come inside the Federal Reserve!"

"Credentials forged or stolen," Dunand snorted.

He watched the officer who had brought Hoyle's body from the vaults return with the body of a clerk; when 377 deposited his burden, he rubbed his hands together, and then jerked off his mask.

"They burn like hell," he said, without blasphemy.

"Do they?" Jimmy Wentworth asked softly. "So do mine. How about yours, captain?"

"Effect of gas," the general decided.

"Your hands burn?" Wentworth asked Dunand again.

"Mine? No. Why?"

"Let's find out." Wentworth stopped the next emerging officer, and had him remove his mask.

"How're your hands, Murphy?"

"Hands, sor? How d'ye mean?"

"Do they burn?"

"They do not."

DUNAND WAS GIVING crisp orders again: "Vaults are cleared of bodies? Phone for the wagon. King, you've got to arrange for an immediate check of the contents. Learn what's taken. Jermane, get in touch with Lucas of the traffic department. No Chinese are leaving the city. Nowhere. I want men at every dock, d'ye hear? Tell Lucas. No boats are clearing until we give the word. Tell Ingalls to hold every Chinese crossing the bay on the ferries. I want every highway out of the city patrolled. All Chinese found in cars are to be picked up and held. Do that first, see? Then come back. Harder, call the Chief. Tell him what's happened. Don't waste words. Say we want a line around San Francisco that a fly couldn't get through—"

"How much time have the criminals been given to make a getaway?" asked the army officer.

Dunand jerked out his watch.

"It's now ten thirty two," he said. "We got the alarm at ten fifteen. The murdering and robbing, if any, was done a few minutes after ten."

"Then shouldn't you've given these orders as soon as you arrived and saw what had happened?"

Dunand stared at the official: "That was automatic," he

said grimly. "When the General Alarm was sounded, every officer on the force was notified, as soon as possible, to be on the alert. Right now I'll bet we've got a hundred yeggs or ex-cons in the lock-up. It's only the Chinese angle which is new. That's why I'm giving orders about it… Wentworth, for heaven's sake quit rubbin' your hands!"

"They itch, sir," said Jimmy Wentworth.

"Mine," said officer 377, "are startin' t' burn bad, cap."

Not a mark—not even a red patch of skin, showed on either man's hands.

Wentworth said softly, "Captain, will you see that Hoyle's body is carefully examined at Headquarters? You see, Murphy dragged out the governor's body. I examined it for wounds. Murphy's hands burn. So do mine."

"Very curious," the army man said.

"Examination of Hoyle's body," Dunand agreed, snapping the order to one of his men. "Now, let's get inside. It ought to be safe. Flashlights, everyone? Or… why, the place's lighted up! How'd that happen?"

"Auxiliary system of lighting, captain," said the head teller.

Guns raised as several figures were seen inside the basement, and were lowered as a wild eyed man and two officers hurried through the vault corridor. All wore masks. The man in civilian clothes half stumbled as he ran.

He tore off his mask immediately:

"I'm Wilkins," he gasped. "The vice-governor. Good God! How did it happen? Have you caught the criminals? And Hoyle—"

"He's—"

Dunand stopped, for the vice-governor could see for himself.

The bank official turned on his head teller. "It will take days to check the contents of the vaults," he said, trying to pull himself together. "Get at it, King. Take what men you need. The police will act as guards for the only two doors, won't they, captain? I… I don't know what to do! This is a terrible thing! Our men dead! Mr. Hoyle murdered! Captain, why are you standing there, doing nothing? And"—his voice rising until it was almost a shriek—"all your men have caught is the itch! Look at that big Irishman standing there, scratching!"

The tears were running down Murphy's broad face.

" 'Tis the itch of the devil," officer 377 groaned. "Captain, me hands are that burnin' that 'tis like a taste of hell."

"Scratch where he can't see you," Dunand ordered.

Wentworth knew what the honest officer was suffering. His own hands felt as if they were slowly being consumed by a burning fire, hot, intolerable, and hardly to be stood. In addition, they itched terribly.

"First, show us where you found Mr. Hoyle's body," Dunand said. "Then you can be relieved, and get treatment you require for your hands, Murphy."

"Get it from Dr. Nye, at Headquarters," Wentworth added swiftly. "Be sure and ask him to look at your hands closely, Murphy, before he washes them or starts to put on dressings."

THE IRATE, EXCITED vice-governor beat his right fist into the palm of his left hand. "A score or more of men are dead," he said fiercely. "The Federal Reserve Bank has been robbed. Our governor has been murdered. And yet you—you police officers—are more concerned with an itch than in doing your duty." He turned to the high army officer pleadingly. "I appeal to you, general! You have the authority. Give us action! Do something!"

The general had heard what Wentworth had said before; that only Murphy, and the youthful sergeant of detectives himself, had touched the dead body of the bank governor. In a quiet voice the army man said:

"I understand how you feel, Mr. Wilkins. I've heard the captain give a good many orders, all aimed to make a possible arrest. It seems to me that the police were well prepared for this emergency. I'm satisfied, thus far, with what they are doing—"

"Standing around scratching!"

"No," said the general. "They appear to have some-sort of clew. Already the first steps are being taken. And now—"

"Now," Dunand said grimly, "we'll get inside, having had enough talk. Coming with us, sergeant, or d'ye want to check up on these bank visitors first?"

"I'll come along," Jimmy Wentworth decided. "The check can wait."

Wilkins, the vice governor, groaned. "You mean to say you suspect two respected Chinese gentlemen, bankers from Hongkong, with the highest credentials?"

"Where are they now?" Wentworth asked softly.

"Where? Why… I don't know. Were they killed along with Mr. Hoyle?"

"We haven't found their bodies."

"Find what hotel they're stopping at! Arrest them! They've got to be questioned! Don't stand there doing nothing!"

Wentworth waited for his superior to talk, but when Dunand nodded for him to reply, the Chinatown detective sergeant explained: "If the two Chinese are at the root of this disaster, sir, we won't find them in a hotel. If they're trying to get away, we may catch them. If, on the other hand, they are hiding, the best thing we can do is to reconstruct this crime carefully, so when we do go after them, we know where to go. Don't forget, sir, that it's expected that the two Chinese will be suspected by us. We must walk softly. One misstep, and we may never bring the criminals to justice."

"Sounds like good sense to me," the army officer agreed. "Lay your campaign before attacking."

"That's it," Jimmy Wentworth nodded.

"What will I say to the newspapers?" Wilkins moaned.

"As long as we've circled the bank, you needn't worry," Dunand promised the other. "No newspaper man is going to get through the cordon. We'll talk that over in a few minutes. Now, let's look things over."

4

THE DEADLY BULBS

IT WAS WITH difficulty that Jimmy Wentworth listened to the bank people's explanation of the interior of the vault. His hands, and especially his right hand, with which he had examined Hoyle's body for marks of violence, burned with increasing fury. There was no mark on either hand. Nor were they red. Yet they seemed on fire. Why? The examination of Hoyle's body should show. Wentworth wondered what Dr. Nye would find out about Murphy's itching skin.

Step by step, led by Wilkins and King, the examination of the vault continued. Although Officer Murphy had left, it was a simple matter for the detectives to determine the place where Hoyle, the governor, had been when the deadly gas seeped into the bank. One of the compartments was open. The heavy barred door, unlocked, and standing wide, told the story.

The contents of this vault were unlike the others. Instead of packages of Federal Reserve notes lining the walls from floor to ceiling, there was a bin at the end of the compartment. In it were small sacks, marked, every one, $10,000. Ten thousands of dollars, in minted gold coins. On the left wall were little wrapped packets like chocolate bars, with various denominations written on the wrappers. Sums of from two hundred to five hundred dollars. Here were the small bars of gold, sold to jewelers for manufacturing purposes, or to dentists. On the right wall were the customary packages of new currency, ranging in size from $1 bills to $20 bills.

"This is where to check, King," said the vice governor. "The gold first. Here's where Mr. Hoyle must have been. I'm surprised he opened this compartment. Usually the visitors just look in."

"Perhaps he didn't open it," Wentworth suggested.

"I'm sure he did," protested the bank official. "In addition to his master keys, the compartment lock must be turned the proper number of times before it'll open. Nobody else could manipulate the lock."

Wentworth said suddenly. "What's that on the wall here, Mr. Wilkins?"

The vice governor turned, and looked. Then he stared at Wentworth. "That's a great discovery, young man," he snapped. "Don't you know what that is?"

"Looks like a switch box to me. For the lights."

"And now the crime is solved!"

"Part of it is," Jimmy Wentworth said quietly. "Why wasn't the switch box kept or placed somewhere else?"

"Because, you damn' fool, this's where the wires lead in to the vaults!"

"I know," the sergeant of detectives said soothingly, "but it makes it too easy to snap off the lights—"

"And what d'you think the guards would be doing if the lights went out?"

"The guards were dying," Wentworth said.

"What?"

"Ever hear how the Canton-Imperial Bank was robbed, sir?"

Wilkins said briefly, "Yes. Everyone gassed. No trace was ever found of the criminals, nor how the crime was committed."

"That's where you're mistaken," Jimmy Wentworth said slowly. "A trace was found of the criminals, although they were never captured. They were German doctors. War doctors. Specialists in gases. Their companion was an electrical engineer. It's a matter of record—"

"What's it got to do with this?" demanded the army officer.

"It's similar," Wentworth said gravely. "In Canton, no proper examination was ever made of the bank premises. We won't slip up there! Somebody get me a chair. A box. Anything to stand on."

One of the detectives hurried off.

Captain Dunand muttered, "Is this a lot of nonsense, Jimmy?"

"It's straight, chief."

"Where'd you get the information?"

"Wang Chen-po—you know him; my friend in China-town—was telling me about some Chinese crimes. The Wangs lost money when the Canton-Imperial was robbed, you see. In China, if a bank loses money through theft or fraud, all of the depositors lose a percentage. We tried to figure out how it was done, Chen-po and myself. That's why I was looking for a switch box. Although it may be impossible, and I'm all wet... here's a chair. Place it near this light overhead, please. Thanks."

While all stared, Wentworth stepped up to the seat of the chair.

THE VAULTS WERE lighted by indirect-light bowls. Inverted semicircles of opaque glass, containing a cluster of electric bulbs. Wentworth looked quietly into the bowl; looked for a full minute.

Then he asked, "Only two of the lights are burning, Mr. Wilkins. Why is that?"

"Because the other two lights are on a different circuit. Half of the lights are operated from the regular source—the electric power company—and the other half are governed by our own private auxiliary system."

"I see. And they aren't both turned on at the same time?"

"Only on very dark days. The private system is for emergencies, like this morning. Why?"

Wentworth reached into the bowl, and picked up particles with a finger tip. He said slowly, looking at these: "There are three bulbs in this fixture. Two of them are burning. The third is not lighted—"

"That's strange," King cried. "I O.K.'d the regular monthly requisition for new bulbs only this morning. They were screwed into place by the vault janitor—"

"Who," said Wentworth, "was given permission to take the day off?"

"His mother died yesterday. The funeral was today."

"And he left after screwing in the new lights," Wentworth said.

King frowned. "I don't know just when he left. He said he'd be back by eleven; maybe he's here now."

"Not he," Wentworth snapped. "He's gone for good."

"Come clean, Jimmy," urged Captain Dunand. "Talk!"

"Here's what I'm positive about, sir. Electric light bulbs were placed in the bowls this morning. New ones. By a janitor who isn't coming back. While half of the lights were screwed in the sockets, the other system was kept operating. Then the other two bulbs were put in. Is that it, Mr. Wilkins?"

"Not at all," Wilkins told him. "What'd be the sense of snapping switches on and off and on and off every time each bowl was refitted with bulbs? Two guards go around with the vault janitor. One of the systems is kept in operation—the regular city lighting system. The power isn't switched off at all! Your deduction is utterly ridiculous—"

"Thanks," Wentworth said. "That's what was bothering me. I wondered exactly how it was done. Good. Now, I'll begin to guess. The janitor, with the guards carrying the bulbs, perhaps, went with his ladder from bowl to bowl, screwing in the new lights. He took out a bulb, and, with the second one burning, replaced it with another—"

"And a better one," Wilkins said. "We were trying a higher candlepower. Didn't tell the vault people, to see if they'd notice the difference."

"And that," Wentworth said promptly, "was done without telling anyone! If you'd used the same candlepower as formerly, the lesser amount of light would have been noticed, and somebody would have said something! I'll bet a month's pay the janitor suggested the brighter lights! Didn't he?"

It was King who said, "Why, yes, he did. It seemed a good idea. We were able to purchase sixty watt lights for the price of forty, with prices down—"

The captain of detectives was becoming impatient. "Shoot, Jimmy," he said. "Get at the meat of it!"

Jimmy Wentworth stepped down from his vantage point, and held out his finger. "Particles of glass," he said. "There are only three bulbs in the bowl. The fourth has been shattered. You know what happens when an electric light bulb is broken. I'm no electrical engineer, captain. I'm only guessing now. But we know that these men in the vault were killed by gas. We know there is no way they could all have been killed at the same time even if poisoned air had been shot through the ventilators. We know, by examination, that the air filter is operating satisfactorily right this minute. We know that the guards and clerks died almost instantly."

"Tell us something we don't know," shrilled the vice governor.

"Yes, sir," Wentworth agreed. "We don't know exactly how this combination of lethal gas expands and contracts under heat, nor how it would act when the temperature was reduced—"

"What on earth is the man talking about?"

"I think I understand," said the quiet army officer. "Expansion and contraction of gases. Hmm. Diabolical! Will you finish your deduction, sergeant?"

WENTWORTH NODDED.

"One of the electric light globes on the regular city circuit gave no light," said Jimmy Wentworth. "It was filled with this gas. Or it may have had something other than tungsten as a lighting medium. Only microscopic examination will tell the truth. It isn't important. But one of the globes was filled with gas. The heat of the neighboring light, or a wire of some kind inside, warmed the gas. Then, when the lights were snapped off, the gas must have either suddenly expanded, or suddenly contracted, and the shock shivered the thin glass of the bulb.

"That took place in every bowl in this basement! Gas filled every corner of the great vaults. At the selfsame instant. I'll bet there's a shattered bulb in every lighting fixture—"

"Very pretty," the vice governor broke in, "but what do you think Mr. Hoyle was doing while one of the criminals—you'd say the Chinese—were opening the locked switch-box and throwing off the current?"

"Mr. Hoyle must have been dying," Wentworth said. Half to himself, he added, "I suppose the janitor had the key to the box?"

"He did," King informed the sergeant of detectives. "And"—in a very low and impressed voice, for all the disdain of the vice governor—" he was a comparatively new man. Good recommendations, naturally. An ex-soldier, I believe. But not an old employee. Our regular vault janitor was in an automobile accident a month or so ago. Badly smashed up. He… why, I believe he said the other car was driven by… by…"

"Chinese," said Jimmy Wentworth.

"How did you know?"

"Everything pointed to it. Firstly, the Chinese visitors, probably men with forged or stolen papers. Secondly, the utter fiendishness of the crime. Thirdly, the similarity of the crime to the affair of the Canton-Imperial robbery. That, you know, was blamed by the Chinese on some devil in the electric light wire. The next day miles of wires were ripped down by Chinamen, all over Canton. And now—"

"What are you going to do?" the vice governor asked humbly. "I've done you an injustice, sergeant. I'm sorry. I'm damnably wretched about this business."

"Of course," Jimmy Wentworth said gently. "This is our job, sir. Trust us to do the best we can."

"It would seem to me," the army officer announced, "that you police people must have some shadowy idea what Chinaman would engineer this sort of crime. Perhaps the same fellow who was in with the Canton bank robbery, eh? Or the kind of chap who would learn by that experience. I'd say it took brains to figure all this out. Brains, and a good sized crew of men!"

"It did," Wentworth nodded. "The brains of the devil himself. A collection of 'binders and hatchetmen who stop at nothing, and who all take orders from one man, worshipped by them as a god. Or as a demon."

"Go get that man," pleaded the vice governor.

"I've been after him for a year. Only saw him once. And that nearly cost me my life."

"If you want help," the army officer decided, "let me know. Government crime. Glad to be of assistance."

"Thank you, sir. Now, captain"—to Dunand—"while you're talking with the newspaper boys, and seeing if the men on the street picked up anything at all, I'll go back to Headquarters."

"Do whatever you want, sergeant. Take what men you need to check up on the two Chinks!"

"What I need, sir, is something on these hands of mine."

This time the vice governor did not break out in violent

protest. His eyes left Wentworth's face, and sought the lean brown hands of the young sergeant of detectives.

"They look all right to me," grumbled Dunand. "Wish you'd talk to the newspaper boys. I won't tell 'em anything about Chinese, shall I?"

"I'd tell them that Chinese are suspected, sir. You might as well. They'd only find it out. And Kong Gai"—Wentworth's lips became a thin white line—"is so positive that he has covered all ways of catching him, or the men actually doing the work, that he used Chinese as the bank's visitors. He might have used white men. This is the sort of thing he glories in. Letting us know he did it. You know his way, chief."

"I'll say Chinese are suspected, and that the way the vault was robbed, and the guards killed, is still a mystery?"

"That's it, chief. Add that 'we expect a solution shortly, to be followed by several arrests,' and then the newspaper boys will be positive we're up a tree."

Dunand leaned close to his sergeant.

He said, in Wentworth's ear, "Are we, Jimmy?"

"We're climbing the tree, anyhow," Wentworth said softly. "When we get up high enough, maybe we can see what's going on."

5

SNAKES!

IN THE AREA behind the Federal Reserve Bank Wentworth found Officer Crowley waiting. With the riot squad policeman was a young woman, obviously excited and more than a little frightened. She kept her back toward the wall, gate, and barrier between the bank and the street. The bodies had now been removed, and the sight of the stone side of the bank must have been more comforting than the recollection of the crowded, thronged streets outside.

Crowley saluted.

"Th' young lady seen somethin', sergeant," he announced. To the girl: "Tell him, miss. Everything."

"I'm a stenographer in the Coast Company across the street," she said nervously. "I was... standing at the window. Then—"

"Tell it all," Crowley broke in. "Th' sergeant's a detective, and he's got to hear everythin', see?"

"Yes, sir. Yes, sergeant. I was standing at my window, looking out to see if my boss was just going to walk up the street, or if he was going to use a taxi and be gone quite a while. If he was, I... well, I was going to do some shopping. While I was looking out, I saw something. It didn't seem to mean anything until I heard the sirens and the police all came. It wasn't much, I suppose. A truck was standing on the other side of the street, the bank side. I think the driver was looking at his watch all the time. I could see that, from up here. I thought, 'There's somebody else isn't crazy about his job.'

"Then he started his truck. He drove up the street slowly, and turned to go into the bank. Where the gold comes in, everybody says. The gate was open, like it always is.

"I was just watching, sergeant, because I'd already seen my boss walk up the street, and I couldn't go out, and there wasn't anything much to do. No dictation at all. The other girls—"

"You were watching," Wentworth prompted. "What did you see?"

"Just as the truck went through the gate, it stopped. All of a sudden. The man jumped off the seat. He ran down to the door of the bank. He opened the door, and then slammed it. He looked drunk, honestly he did. He—"

Wentworth said, "What did he do next?"

"Went back to the truck, mister. I mean sergeant. Had a hard time getting up to his seat. There was another fellow on the seat. Maybe he was there all the time, but I didn't see him."

"Did you see anyone inside the truck? Did anyone get out and look, or talk to the driver?"

"I didn't pay particular attention," she said. "You see, it didn't mean anything until I saw the police come."

"Did anyone come out of the bank, later?"

"I don't know. I only looked at the truck."

Wentworth saw the uselessness of asking if the stenographer had seen masked men, men protected against the poison gas. He realized that the two Chinese must have left the bank by way of the rear, and that there was a possibility that someone had seen them. However, what sense was there in making any investigation of that fact? It was obvious; it was known by the police.

The girl had really told all she knew. It added only one thing to what the detective had already learned: that Kong Gai, or whoever was directing the bank robbery, had intended a wholesale theft of the gold and currency. This had been prevented by the last spasmodic movement of the captain of the guard's hand, in reaching for and pulling the apparatus which controlled the steel and concrete hydraulic barrier inside the gates to the yard.

If the truck had been a delivery machine from some member bank of the reserve system, the driver, seeing the barrier up, would have gone down to the captain's office, instead of returning to his truck and driving away.

Nor was there any reason to determine if the two Chinese had escaped in the truck, had walked away, or been driven off in an automobile. This was of no importance.

AS WENTWORTH THANKED the girl, and walked up the inclined pavement to the gate, he was already summarizing the scanty knowledge in the possession of the police. He was deep in thought as he reached the street.

The crime had, without doubt, been executed by Asiatics. It was similar to the robbery of the Canton-Imperial Bank. Chinese had been with Hoyle when the poison gas was released.

Only one thing remained to be determined; the manner in which Hoyle himself had been killed. Wentworth was confident that the governor must have been murdered a fraction of time before the guards were killed, unless one of the two Chinese had managed to open the switch box without Hoyle's seeing him and raising the alarm. That seemed almost an impossibility, unless Hoyle had been busy opening the vault to show and explain the contents. However, the bank people had said that the compartment which was standing open was not the type which the, governor ordinarily opened, since it contained a mixture of gold, coin, and currency, and was much less interesting than the other compartments.

If Hoyle had been killed, it must have been done with surprising swiftness and noiselessness. How? Wentworth looked down at his hands. The burning sensation had not abated. It bothered him less, probably because he had become accustomed to it, and because he had plenty of other things to think about.

The skin was still its normal color.

"It may mean something," Wentworth muttered. "Here's a case where a fellow doesn't dare omit a single detail."

Suppose Kong Gai and his brothers of the snake, the deadly servants of the Evil One himself, had committed the murders and robbery. What then? Where would Wentworth look? How could he find them?

There was no way to do it, and Wentworth knew that very well. The 'binders would be in some secret lair, protected and concealed. As for Kong Gai, Wentworth had only once picked up the trail of the King Cobra, and, for his pains, had barely escaped with his life.

Wentworth reached the line of officers surrounding the building. One of them, saluting, said, "Anything, sarge?"

"Not yet," Jimmy told him.

He strode to the middle of the intersection, where an officer struggled to keep traffic moving. Everyone wanted to stop in order to see what was going on.

"Can you get me a car?" Wentworth asked the officer with the winged wheel on his arm. "Want to get to Headquarters."

The traffic officer let two machines pass, and stopped the third, a powerful sedan. "Give you a good, comfortable ride, sergeant," he grinned. He said more loudly to the chauffeur, "Please take the sergeant up to the Hall of Justice. In a hurry. Go right past signals set against you."

Wentworth jumped in beside the driver, and the big machine slid expertly into gear, and shot up the street.

A voice from the rear seat asked, "What seems to be the trouble, officer? Anything seriously wrong? Somebody said a robbery was attempted at the Federal Reserve, but of course that's not possible."

Turning, Jimmy said to the elderly man in the rear seat, "I'm afraid that's what happened, sir."

"Anybody hurt?"

There was no reason to conceal facts.

"A good many men have been murdered," Jimmy Wentworth said quietly.

"Is that a fact! Any arrests made, officer?"

"Not yet," said the sergeant of detectives.

The owner of the car said, "It would be interesting to see what this chap Wentworth would do with a case like that. He's done some good work, hasn't he?"

"He's been very lucky," Jimmy smiled.

"I wouldn't say that," the other protested vigorously. "He has the young man's viewpoint. I'd like to see him let loose on a crime like this. Why, I'd be willing to bet a box of good cigars that he'd find a solution—"

The car hummed up to the entrance to the Hall of Justice, and Wentworth opened his door; he said, grinning, "I'd be tempted to take the bet, sir, but..."

"Suppose we make it one cigar," said the elderly gentleman. "Matter of fact, I'd like to hear what really happens, if Wentworth goes on the case. I'm going to request the commissioner to have him put on it. Here's my card. After this is cleared up—or if it isn't—get in touch with me, and give me the details. I don't believe what I read in the newspapers, officer."

Jimmy, stepping out, said, "I'll be glad to, sir."

"By the way, what's your name, officer?"

"Wentworth," said Jimmy, grinning again.

He ran directly inside, dashed through the corridor and down the stairs to the morgue. He demanded of the officer on duty there, "Murphy come in? Where's Dr. Nye?"

"Murphy was ordered to the hospital for observation, sergeant, and—"

"Sick?"

"I don't know, sergeant. He seemed O.K. to me. But I heard him say, after he had seen the doc,' something about snakes. Yeah. And be said, 'The good Saint Patrick preserve me,' from which I judged Murph was certainly scared."

Jimmy's eyes narrowed.

"Where's Dr. Nye?" he asked.

"He was in the morgue, sir, after he looked Murphy over. He went up in the elevator, and said he'd be in the laboratory if we wanted him."

"Thanks," Wentworth said.

He looked down at his hands again. Snakes!

6

THE TRAIL OF THE
SPITTING DEATH

DR. NYE, IN white smock, and with rubber gloves over his hands, was squinting into a microscope when Wentworth entered the shining white laboratory; he looked up, and nodded friendlily.

"Ah, Wentworth," he said. "Here's something interesting. In your line. Cobras, perhaps. Very interesting. But very puzzling. I've telephoned Dr. Heath. He's the authority here on the coast. It's too delicate a problem for me."

"How's Murphy, doctor?"

"Murphy? Badly frightened, I fear. My fault entirely. Many Irish have a snake phobia. He'll be all right, barring complications. Hardly expect any."

Wentworth said, "My own hands burn, doctor."

"Eh? And what've *you* been doing? D'you show marks of a bite? Did you see the snake?"

"I did the same thing Murphy did, doctor. Touched the body of the bank governor. I didn't know snake bites were infectious."

"Who said they were? They aren't. This… this is all very peculiar! I wish Dr. Heath would hurry! How d'you feel, Wentworth? Sick?"

"I feel perfectly well," Wentworth answered briefly. "I assure you I haven't been bitten by anything."

"Strange. Never heard of anything like it in all my experience. That's why I called Dr. Heath. I followed your orders, sergeant. Examined bits of the skin from Murphy's hands. Conducted a preliminary post mortem on Hoyle's body. Very sketchy affair. What d'you think I learned?"

The doctor, quite excited, gave Wentworth no chance to reply. He went on speaking rapidly: "Murphy's right hand skin, under a high powered lens, showed particles in no way related to skin structure. Obviously a foreign substance. Luckily, I started my tests for proteids. Found substances insoluble immediately. Hmm. Found three of them. Albumin, globulin, syntonin! The deadly three. Put 'em together, and you have cobra poison!"

"Meaning that Hoyle was killed by an injection, and Murphy and myself were partially infected by touching his body?"

"Eh? No! That's the devilish part of it. There isn't a mark on Hoyle's body. No cut. No puncture. No scratch. But he was poisoned, let me tell you! Died from paralysis of cardiac and respiratory centers, which might've happened from that damn gas, like the other men died, only Hoyle's blood fails to coagulate. I mean that it's fluid. Corpuscles are disintegrated. That's what cobra venom does. Never heard of anything like this case! Never heard of a person becoming infected from handling the body of a bitten man! And why was there poison on Hoyle's face and neck and chest? Cobra venom! You tell me that, and I'll know more than I do."

Wentworth said, "I've tried to do what investigating

I could about the king cobra, doctor. You know what Kong Gai is called. The King Cobra. But I never heard of anything like this, either."

Dr. Nye's eyes became alert.

"What am I thinking about, anyhow?" he muttered. He walked swiftly to a glass-enclosed cabinet, selected instruments, and from a drawer took a sealed package, which he broke open. "Take off your coat," he growled. "And shirt. You get a shot of this cobra anti-venin. Calmette's. Won't affect you. No need to send you to the hospital unless signs develop. Come on. Get it over with."

Wentworth felt the sharp jab of the needle.

Grumbling, Dr. Nye continued talking. "Maybe I'd better give you some American anti-venin also. Let's feel your pulse. Hmm. Normal. Here. Stick this in your mouth. You ought to have a subnormal temperature. Murphy's was. But only about a half degree. Which doesn't mean anything."

The thermometer was in Wentworth's mouth when an officer brought Dr. Heath, the reptile expert, into the white tiled room.

JIMMY SAT SUCKING on the tube of glass while Nye explained rapidly what had happened, and what few deductions he had been able to make. Then he went on to tell the parts of the matter which troubled him, and which were beyond his understanding. The snake savant asked a question here and there, but otherwise listened until the police physician had completed his tale. "What do you make of it all, Dr. Heath?" Nye concluded. "No question about the poisonous proteids. Globulin, albumin, syntonin, in proper proportions to be considered as cobra venom. The dead man shows clearly that it was snake venom. Hmm. How can one account for a skin infection merely by touching the dead man's body?"

Jimmy Wentworth, leaning forward with the thermometer in his mouth, listened keenly as the snake expert began to speak.

"An interesting case," said Dr. Heath. "Caused a skin irritation, did it? Have you any of the skin under microscope, Dr. Nye?"

"Just looking at it."

The bearded savant stepped to the stand in front of Nye's window, adjusted his own glasses carefully, and then stooped down.

He stared for a long minute into the microscope, and then lifted his head.

"Haven't seen anything like that since I left the Pasteur Institute," he announced. "Extraordinary. Someone has a real knowledge of snake venoms."

Jimmy Wentworth thought instantly of Kong Gai.

The expert's next words surprised Wentworth so much that he forgot all about the thermometer in his mouth: he took it out, and held it between his fingers as if it were a cigarette.

"You are correct in deciding that it was cobra venom," Dr. Heath said. "However, it isn't what you ordinarily consider cobra venom. That is, the venom is not from the *Naia Hannah,* the king cobra, nor from his deadly brother, the *Naia Naia,* or Asiatic cobra. He's the chap with spectacle markings on the hood, you know. I am perfectly safe in making the statement that the particles under the microscope—because of their crystalline structure—are from the little known African cobra. The *Naia nigricollis*. The black-necked cobra. Usually called black cobra. He is a terrible serpent, doctor."

The expert wiped his glasses, and then glanced at Wentworth.

"I see you've had serum infections, officer," he said. "You're very lucky to be alive. How near the black cobra did you get, and wherever did it happen?"

Wentworth said, "I wasn't near any snake at all, sir."

"Six feet away? Ten feet? Fifteen?"

"I haven't seen a snake of any kind," Jimmy Wentworth said, his eyes narrow.

"Perhaps you didn't see him."

Wentworth said, "I don't understand, doctor. I did handle the body of a dead man an hour ago. So did one of our officers, who became infected. He—"

"Skin burn, did it? Don't worry. You'll be well in no time. Lucky it was your hands, that's all."

Jimmy puffed on the thermometer. "Please, Dr. Heath," he pleaded. "I can't make head nor tail of what you're saying. I know a little about cobra poison. About the king cobra, and the common cobra. But surely you aren't trying to tell me that there is a snake which ejects poison from his fangs into the air? Isn't that merely a superstition?"

Dr. Heath rubbed his hands together.

"Not at all," he said. "No superstition about it. The *Naia nigricollis* is sometimes called the Spitting Cobra, officer. He can eject his venom a dozen feet, and more than six feet into the air. And if that poison should happen to reach a man's eves, he's blinded. If it hits his nostrils or mouth... well, he's a dead man. I can cite you a dozen cases of deaths in Africa. And one in the Institute. That's what happened to your bank governor. Somebody let a snake—a spitting cobra—eject its terrible venom in his face."

Dr. Nye muttered. "That's not possible. The men were all in a great bank, doctor. Or—"

"Or," Wentworth said, "the venom was blown into Hoyle's face, and he died instantly."

"No," disputed the expert. "He was paralyzed. His muscles became taut and tense. If he was standing up, he'd remain in that position. Unable to talk. Unable to move. But he would appear to be perfectly well. For about three or four minutes—"

"During which time," Wentworth muttered, "one of the Chinese went over to the switch box, pulled the master switch, plunged the vaults into darkness, and released the lethal gas."

"Your bank governor would have looked like a man in full possession of all his faculties," admitted Dr. Heath pleasantly. "His eyes, however, would have been filmed. His body, of course, rigid."

"The nearest guard was fifty feet away," Wentworth said. "Too far to see his eyes, even if he'd been looking. How would you say the venom was sprayed into Hoyle's face, sir?"

"Any one of a dozen ways. A simple small spray would be the easiest. Some kind of a blower. The venom, of course, was fresh from the black cobra, and naturally was yellowish and liquid. You see, unlike the venom of the Asiatic cobras, that of the spitting cobra breaks down rapidly. It is no longer toxic—poisonous—after it has been removed from the serpent. Oh, of course it retains its deadliness for a few hours. Comparatively, I meant. I do not recall the exact periods of time. You can say that for an hour, or two, or three, it is instantly poisonous—"

"Meaning that there is still, or was up to this morning, a live spitting cobra in San Francisco!"

"HE'S PROBABLY STILL alive," Dr. Heath told the sergeant of detectives. "At a guess, he is kept in a dark box. When he is allowed to go out into the light—in a glass cage, I suppose, he shows his happy disposition by immediately spitting an astonishing amount of venom against the glass. Trying to reach the eyes and face of some person he sees on the other side of the glass. Then he is prodded, somehow, back into his box, and the venom is carefully collected from the side of the glass. It is a slightly sticky yellowish fluid. This could be readily enough done."

Wentworth, his heart cold, said what he thought.

"It's Kong Gai and his brothers of the snake. No one else would have such knowledge of snake venoms. Nor use them as Kong Gai would do. Now that I know what I've guessed, I'm no better off than before."

"All you've got to do is to find the spitting cobra," Dr. Heath suggested.

Wentworth now saw what he was holding between his fingers. As his lean hands clenched, the slender tube of the thermometer cracked. A tiny stream of silver mercury slid to the floor.

"All I've got to do is find a spitting cobra," Wentworth repeated the other's words bitterly.

"And when you find him," Dr. Heath said, "you can tell him instantly by the black band across his throat. He's different from any other cobra. You'll know him right away."

Jimmy Wentworth had nothing more to say. Search for a spitting cobra in a great city! Go through Chinatown looking for a black, deadly serpent! His head dropped to his hands.

"Be careful to guard your eyes and face when you find him," Dr. Heath went on, not realizing the sergeant of detectives' dejection. "I'd recommend glasses, and plugs of cotton in your nostrils. If he spits in your face, use an antiseptic immediately, and you can avert some of the burning sensation the poison produces. That isn't dangerous. It's the one thing about the spitting cobra which is at all in his favor. Did you know that he's a cannibal, officer? Yes. Eats nothing but snakes. Has an enormous appetite, unlike other reptiles. And he won't do much spitting unless he's in good health, which means he must be fed often—"

Wentworth's head left his hands. His eyes began to brighten; the muscles about his mouth tensed.

"Has to be fed often, doctor? On snakes?"

"Absolutely. On harmless snakes. In this country, it would either be the big California garter snake, or the various Texas snakes. Probably the latter. There's a firm somewhere in Texas that makes a business of supplying zoos with snakes as food for cannibal snakes. Particularly the cobras. Only the black cobra has a voracious appetite. Er… did I ever tell you about the Horned Palm Viper, Dr. Nye? That's very interesting—"

Wentworth was on his feet, pulling on his shirt and coat. His entire demeanor had changed.

Dr. Nye said, "I didn't record his temperature. Nor put anything on the hands. Come here, sergeant, and I'll—"

"Some other time," Jimmy Wentworth said grimly. "I've got a little job to do first."

"Something about the Federal Reserve murders?"

"That's it," Wentworth agreed.

"Better be treated first," Dr. Heath told him. "Take the burning away completely."

"There's no time to lose," Wentworth said. "Not a word about spitting cobras to anyone, doctor, until the department has a chance to work on this clew."

"What clew?" persisted the snake expert. "*I* didn't hear one! You can't go about knocking at people's doors looking for spitting cobras."

"No," said Jimmy. "I'm not going to. You gave me the clew your self, sir."

"I?"

"Yes. And, following it up, I'm going to see if a shipment of harmless reptiles has been received at an express office… and where it was delivered. It's a thin thread, but it's a real one."

Buttoning his coat, Wentworth hastened out of the laboratory.

7

ON THE TRAIL

JIMMY WENTWORTH RACED through the halls, headed for Captain Dunand's deserted office. Time was the important element now, provided snakes had actually been shipped into San Francisco by express, and provided also that the shipment had been delivered instead of being called for. It was possible that Kong Gai might have had his 'binders go out into the country and return with a box of wriggling reptiles, to supply the fearful black cobra with food, but it was not probable. The Chinese did not like serpents, as witness Kong Gai's selection of the Snake of the Underworld, the cobra, as his symbol of evil.

It was a long chance, but more slender clews had been followed to successful ends. At all events, it was certainly worth trying.

Wentworth lifted Dunand's telephone. He said to Connolley, at the switchboard on the main floor, "This's Wentworth, corporal. I want you to get the highest official in the Railway Express that you can manage. Make it plain to the telephone operator at the company that this is important. Then switch me on. Thanks."

"O.K., sergeant. Hold the line."

As he waited, he could hear Connolley's demand,

politely but firmly spoken, to be connected with the highest officer of the company available. Wentworth heard the
words, but almost as if they did not register in his brain.
He was again back in the vaults of the Federal Reserve. He
saw, now, clearly, what had happened, from start to finish.

The accident to the trusty janitor. His replacement with
a tool of Kong Gai, possibly an ex-convict, addicted to
drugs, who obeyed the commands of the King Cobra. The
gas-filled bulbs placed in the sockets. The visit of the two
Chinese masquerading as Hongkong bankers, with forged
or stolen letters of introduction. The spraying of the terrible, paralyzing black cobra venom. The opening of the
switch box, either with Hoyle's master key, or with a key
given the two Chinese by the janitor himself. The escaping of the lethal gas when the lights were shut off, and the
temperature suddenly lowered. (That, also, was a matter for
the police experts to check up on, later.) The rush into the
vault, and the snatching up of gold or currency.

Waiting, Wentworth saw clearly now the reason why
Hoyle had to not only be killed, but why he had to appear
as if alive. The two Chinese needed a fraction of time, just
as the lights were switched off, to don some sort of protec-
tive mask, lest they also succumb to the deadly combination of gasses.

One of the Chinese must have rushed to the door, at
the shipping platform, to see if the truck had arrived at
the proper moment. He had probably waited there until
he saw that the barrier was up, and, not knowing how it
was raised, nor how it might be lowered, had raced back
through the deadly fumes, and, with his companion, had
pocketed whatever they dared from the vault's contents.

If the faithful captain of the guard had not thrown up the barrier inside the gate, the contents of at least that one compartment—valued into the millions—would have been rifled.

There was cause for the Chinese to hurry. They had only the time between the ten o'clock O.K. signal, which they must have known about, and the ten-fifteen signal (which the captain of the guard could not give, being dead) to complete their robbery. Some of this fifteen minutes was consumed when Hoyle was showing them about the vaults. Five minutes, possibly. Which left only ten minutes to finish the job—scant enough time, but sufficient, had the truck been able to get past the barrier.

To have carried out currency and sacks of gold to the truck, standing as it did almost on the sidewalk of the street, must have been out of the question, even for such dangerous and ferocious persons as the hatchetmen of Kong Gai.

They would have done it, had Kong Gai given the order, but, without the presence of the King Cobra, would become excited and confused, as witness the testimony of the stenographer.

WENTWORTH WONDERED IF anyone would be found who had seen two Chinese walk up the incline and leave the area of the shipping space; it was perfectly possible, but of little importance. To the average white man, one Chinaman looked exactly like another. There would be no value to the information, even if the two were seen, Jimmy felt, unless there was some distinguishing mark about either of them.

The robbery was important, because it pointed out the

vulnerability of a great bank—although the barrier had stopped a general theft—but the murders were the thing in which the police were most interested. Wholesale murder! Could the fiends be captured?

Jimmy Wentworth heard Connolley's voice:

"I have Mr. Atkins for you, sergeant. Mr. Atkins is the vice president and general manager of the Express Company."

Jimmy said, "Good work," and then, "Mr. Atkins? This is Wentworth, detective bureau. We wish some information from your company, and I'm asking you to see that it is secured as speedily as possible."

"I understand it's a matter of life and death," Atkins said. "We're at your service, sergeant."

"Good. Can you determine, quickly, if a shipment of anything live, like snakes, has been received here?"

"Snakes? We can. They are recorded separately from other animals, or anything else. Shipped to the zoo, sergeant?"

"No. Unless the zoo failed to receive the shipment—if it was stolen en route. This shipment, crate, whatever it is, would be to a private party. If it was called for—"

"We wouldn't deliver it," Mr. Atkins said. "Our franchise as an expressing agent demands that we make safe delivery into safe and secure quarters of any type of reptile, even harmless ones. Your city ordinance says the same thing, sergeant. If we received any snakes, we delivered them. I'll call you back."

"As soon as you can!"

"In less than three minutes," the express company official promised.

There was nothing to do but wait. Jimmy Wentworth sat staring out of the window at the crested roofs of Chinatown. In what cavern was Kong Gai receiving the reports of his hatchetmen? Through what tunnels did the 'binders approach the fastness of the Evil One? What terrible things took place in the underground dens of Chinatown, where Kong Gai was the master?

The door was flung open, and Dunand, followed by several detectives and the army officer, marched into the office.

"Where you been?" he demanded of his sergeant. In the same breath, "Any report from the traffic department? From the State officers? From the Coast Guard? Anything? Anybody caught?"

Wentworth, for the first time, glanced down at Dunand's desk, where several slips of paper had been placed.

He read from the uppermost report: "Sacramento reports the capture of four Japanese, suspected of being connected with robbery Federal Reserve. Time, ten twenty-seven. Taken from automobile in front of police station, past which they attempted to drive."

"Couldn't fly up in that time," Dunand growled. "Japanese! Prob'ly one of 'em had a five dollar bill in his pocket."

"Officer 894, Mission district, reports two Chinese delivering laundry. Held for questioning at Mission station. Time, ten thirty-five."

"894's on the job," Dunand grunted. "That's something. How about you, sergeant? Getting anywhere?"

"Perhaps," Wentworth said guardedly. "I'll know in a minute or so."

"IT'S ALL RATHER amazing to me," said the army man.

"Here not much over an hour has elapsed since the commission of the crime, and already you gentlemen are obviously on the trail of something. It would have seemed to me that the only thing to have done was to await reports from officers who are searching automobiles, looking for Chinamen."

"When we learn about a crime within a few minutes, as in this case," Dunand explained, "that is very often successful. Where a criminal has time to change machines, or get a distance away, it doesn't mean very much. In this affair, the criminals realized that they had very little time to work. Therefore they wouldn't make a break to get away, but would go to a nearby hiding place. You agree, sergeant?"

"I do," Jimmy Wentworth agreed. "That's the theory I'm working on."

"Wentworth's in charge of the Chinatown squad," Dunand told the man in olive drab. "It's up to him. Catching the murderers."

"Hmm. And Chinatown's only a few blocks from the bank, isn't it? Be fairly simple for the two Chinese to be there before the alarm was given."

Nodding, Wentworth asked, "Did anyone report having seen Chinese coming out of the rear of the bank, captain?"

"Not yet. Somebody must've seen 'em. That'll come. I've got a good description of the two, from Hoyle's secretary. Their letter of introduction was forged, Jimmy, and not stolen. Verified that from the correspondent bank of the China place in Hongkong."

"Again pointing to… our delightful friend in Chinatown," Wentworth said. "Not that this was needed. It's Kong Gai, chief. No question about it—"

The telephone rang; Wentworth had it to his ear instantly.

"Yes, Mr. Atkins," he said. "This's Wentworth. You did make a delivery of a crate recently? That's great! You've got the address? Good. I'll write it down… eleven one Waverley? Eleven one. Right. The crate was delivered two weeks ago? And… will you repeat that, sir?"

Wentworth listened, heart leaping, to what Atkins told him again: that the express company had received a second crate marked for 1101 Waverley Place, which was ready for delivery.

So Dr. Heath was correct! The black cobras, venomous and voracious, needed a large amount of their cannibalistic diet; needed a great quantity of harmless snakes on which to feed in order to viciously spit out their deadly yellow liquid.

"Is the crate ready for delivery now?" Wentworth asked.

"We would normally send it this afternoon. Would you like it delivered earlier, sergeant?"

Wentworth, gripping the telephone tightly in his elation, said, "Can you have it in one of the covered delivery trucks, sir? The kind enclosed in tarpaulin, front, side, and rear? You use them in wet weather, and for valuable shipments? And hold the truck at your office, or wherever it's loaded?"

"We load in the receiving department, on Howard Street, sergeant. Want it done right away?"

"Please. And give instructions to turn the truck over to the police department. We'll be glad to make delivery of the crate for you, Mr. Atkins, although we won't promise to get a receipt for you!"

Atkins must have hesitated, for it was a half minute

before he asked, "You said this was a matter of life and death, sergeant. Will you verify that in writing for us? Our regulations are strict—"

"It's more than life and death! It's bringing murderers to justice."

"That's satisfactory. The truck will be ready and loaded within fifteen minutes. I'll be at the Howard Street shed myself."

"Thanks," Jimmy Wentworth said, and hung up the telephone.

"What's all this?" demanded the impatient, eager captain of detectives. "What's being sent to Waverley Place, in Chinatown? What've you uncovered, Jimmy?"

"Snakes," said the youthful sergeant of detectives.

"What?"

"Snakes, chief. For Kong Gai. For black cobras to feed upon. We've got a chance on this case! So little time has elapsed that we may make some arrests. Don't ask any questions; I'll tell you everything while we're driving over to the express company. Now"—to one of the detectives—"go down to the Chinatown squadroom. Get my map of subdistrict A7. I want to see what place eleven one is. Who's supposed to live there. It's a shop, I think." To Dunand, "We'll want plenty of men, chief. The riot squad's not back, is it?"

"My lieutenant and his machine gun detail is downstairs," the army officer suggested. "A good lot of boys. Want 'em?"

"Are they any good at getting through windows and up walls?"

"Well, some of 'em managed to get through barbed wire over in France!"

"Fine! Drive down to the express company. The captain, a few detectives, and myself'll meet you there, just as soon as I get a look-see at the map. Then… we'll see what happens!"

8

THE NEST OF THE COBRA

LESS THAN TWO hours had passed since the O.K. O.K. O.K. failed to be printed on the ticker tape in the signal room of the Hall of Justice and the General Alarm was sounded. Less than two hours had passed, yet every means of departure from the city had been blocked. Less than two hours had passed, and hundreds of ex-convicts and vagrants and suspicious characters were being rounded up.

Less than two hours had passed when a ponderous truck with the gold painted name of the express company threaded its way through the streets of Chinatown. On the seat were the customary two figures; the driver and his assistant. Both were in the company blue and white coveralls, both wore the company caps. These were pulled close over the eyes. Also, each of the amateur expressmen wore glasses—not colored glasses, but ordinary spectacles. When they spoke together it was with a nasal twang, and unlike the soft California speech.

In the rear of the truck, which was covered completely with black tarpaulin, was the crate of harmless Texas gopher snakes, intended as a banquet for black cobras. In the rear of the truck, also, were eight soldiers, their lieutenant, the high army officer himself, Captain Dunand,

and four Headquarters men. They swayed to the lurching of the truck as it pounded along through Chinatown. None spoke. All orders had been given.

The final order had been, "When you shoot, shoot to kill. Any Chinese who runs is guilty. An innocent, or honest, Chinaman will stand perfectly still in the presence of authority."

Wentworth, sitting beside the driver—officer Seldon— had all he could do to maintain his composure. Was it going to work? Would the brothers of the snake, the servants of Kong Gai, remain at 1101 Waverley Place, after the attack on the bank? Or had they already vanished into the rat holes of Chinatown? Would they, Chinese fashion, stay to discuss the unfortunate appearance of the barrier, which had prevented a wholesale robbery? Would they burn incense and purify the stolen money, if any had been stolen? Would they say the Thousand Words of Perfume before an altar, as is proper after killing even white men?

Less than two hours had elapsed. Would they feel safe to perform the ceremonies which Asiatics insist are essential? Or… were they gone? Or, equally as bad, was 1101 Waverley Place merely a blind? Wentworth didn't think it was. The harmless snakes ought to go to the place where the live black cobra was kept. Kong Gai would never believe that such a feeble clew could be uncovered—certainly not in such a short space of time.

The very ingenuity of the Evil One, in knowing about the paralyzing effect of black cobra venom, might prove his undoing!

Officer Seldon turned the car into Waverley Place.

"Got everything straight?" Wentworth asked grimly.

"Right. We stop. We get out. Go to the back of the truck. Take out th' crate, th' both of us. Go up steps. Put down crate. I ring bell. You've got receipt book. Gun concealed under it. If Chinks let us in, it's our grief. Up to us. If they take crate, you fire a shot, and we get in anyhow. And I'm glad I'm a single man!"

"Me too," Wentworth admitted. "Slow up, Seldon. It's the next corner."

WENTWORTH, FROM HIS long months in marching the Chinatown beat, knew not the moment he had determined on which corner it stood. Two story house, containing, on the lower floor, the basket shop of Yee Y'ang Ki. No windows on the street face—Ashburton Alley. A door leading upstairs next to a dirty shop window. A door leading downstairs to a cellar, marked as 1101A on Wentworth's detailed map. The next house was built against the wall of the corner house.

A frontal attack was the one chance. If a tunnel ran beneath the basket shop, Wentworth knew there would never be time to find it. The Chinese, inside, would take to it, instead of trying to escape outside. Nevertheless, some of the machine gunners were to remain outside and shoot down anyone trying to run away. The rest, and the detectives, were to follow Wentworth inside.

Seldon pulled his brake.

"This's it, huh?" he said nasally.

Wentworth made a pretense of looking into his book, for the sake of the 'binder spy leaning against an opposite building. As he did so, he slipped his automatic under the receipt book.

"Let's go," said Jimmy Wentworth. "And, if it's necessary, keep your mouth shut, old man!"

The crate was at the rear end of the truck. Wentworth and Seldon reached inside, careful not to move the flap more than necessary lest the crouching men inside be visible to the 'binder spy, and pulled out the big box.

One man at either end, they shuffled to the steps of 1101, mounted them, and put down the crate. Wentworth pressed the bell button, and there was a jangle within the dark building. Almost at once a panel was slid back in the door, and a high Chinese voice shrilled:

"Hi! Wha' you wantchee?"

"Got a box for you," said officer Seldon. "Make it snappy. We ain't got all day."

The panel was banged shut, and Wentworth heard the Chinese pass along the information.

His heart began to pound as he heard a sweet, beautiful voice say in Chinese: *"lu ki to ch'e k'uk ni?"* Then in English: "How much is the expressage, oh L'u Sam? Pay it from your own money, and take the box."

That sweet voice! Kong Gai!

The door was slowly opened. Wentworth saw not one, but two hatchetmen standing in the dark hall.

"Where'll we take it?" asked Seldon.

"I take," said the black clad 'binder.

"How much he cost?"

"Two dollars 'nd fifty cents."

As the Chinese reached for his coin purse, Wentworth thrust out his receipt book:

"You got to sign your name in this book," he said, in a nasal voice akin to Seldon's.

The second Chinese took the pencil, and bent over the book. The one named L'u Sam counted out money.

And at that instant, when both Asiatics were busily engaged, Wentworth, every vein in his body seemingly filled with an icy flow, and thinking about the murdered men in the Federal Reserve Bank, fired squarely into the body of the Chinese signing the receipt book.

Seldon's gun roared almost at the selfsame moment as he got his hatchetman, and, side by side, sergeant and officer leaped into the hall and raced toward the light showing at the end.

Captain Dunand and the others were tumbling from the rear of the truck. The 'binder spy shrieked a warning in obscene Cantonese. The machine gunners stormed up the steps. They, too, knew what murder had already been done to white men.

Someone, in that high sweet voice, called, "Stop them, oh valiant brothers of the snake!"

HIGHBINDERS, *BO' HOW doy*, 'binders, swarmed into the hallway from the lighted room. Wentworth's gun spat; Seldon's finger pulled trigger fiercely, but the horde merely jumped insanely over the bodies of the fallen cobramen.

And somewhere Kong Gai was escaping into one of his tunnels!

Dunand's voice boomed in the hallway.

"Down! Down, Jimmy!"

Orders were orders. Not only that, but Wentworth realized the impossibility of getting through the phalanx of armed hatchetmen. He dropped to the floor, pulling Seldon down with him. Instantly the rat-tat-tat-tat of machine guns sounded. The first bullets smashed purposely into the floor before the hatchetmen, but the drug-in-flamed cobramen, intent only on protecting their venomous and terrible chieftain, rushed onward, knives waiting only to hack the life from the dreaded enemy of the King Cobra, Sergeant Wentworth.

"Hold them, men," snapped the army man.

Up came the muzzles of the little guns, and down went the 'binders like reaped grain.

Rat-tat-tat-tat....

"Cease firing," commanded the officer. "Forward!"

Wentworth was already to his feet, at the instant that the clatter of the guns was stilled. He hurdled dead and dying bodies, stumbled, recovered himself, and then leaped into the end room.

Brilliancy. Colors. Red and gold and green. Writhing incense on the altar of the snake god.

Then a mocking, sweet voice: "Ah, my friend Wentworth? And you want so badly to see me, sergeant? Look up, if you wish to see the king of the cobras!"

Wentworth's eyes raised to the ceiling.

For a moment he saw only a little pane of glass, and then behind it he made out, faintly, the features of a Chinese. As he looked—all in the same fraction of time—the face seemed to change to the head of a cobra. Then the pane of glass was drawn back, and as Wentworth's gun raised, his lips instinctively formed words which his throat shouted out for him:

"Back, everyone! Back!"

Down through the opening dropped a long, lithe, twisting serpent. Black. Black band about pulsing neck.

The black cobra.

Even as the terrible serpent was falling, it hissed horribly, and a stream of yellow venom was sprayed into the sergeant's uplifted face.

"Stand there now," screamed Kong Gai. "You will never move in life again, Wentworth. I have had my vengeance! You cannot move a muscle, but you hear what I say! This is the vengeance of the cobra. This—"

Wentworth's gun raised like a streak of blue flame. He fired his last shot at the opening, heard one frightened shriek, and then all was silent.

On the floor the black-necked cobra, half stunned, was beginning to writhe itself upright, preparing again to either eject its fearful deadly poison, or to actually spring and fasten its fangs on any human object.

Wentworth was crying, "Upstairs, men!" as officer Seldon, half fascinated by the rising, swaying, hooded serpent, slowly raised his gun, and smashed the evil head with a bullet. The black cobra thrashed about, and then, twitching with reflex action, but very dead, stretched out its full six feet on the magnificent rug covering the floor of the strange, terrible room.

Feet pounded on the stairway. Something dropped with a terrific clang, and the men returned to report a steel door stopping all progress.

"Oxyacetylene flame'll open it," Dunand raged. "Phone Headquarters! We've got the place surrounded. We'll—"

Jimmy Wentworth had been wiping drying flakes of yellow venom from his face. He said, hardly opening his lips, "I had a shot at him. May've hit him. Don't know. Doubt if I killed him."

"Why wasn't this room protected by steel doors?" said the army man.

"It is," Jimmy said. "Couple of 'em. But the brothers of the snake much prefer killing to stopping." He drew a bottle from an inner pocket, and carefully disinfected his face, neck, and hands. "Stuff burns already," Wentworth said.

Dunand shivered. "Look at the thing," he muttered, staring at the twitching black thing of evil on the brilliantly colored rug. "Without glasses, Jimmy, or without cotton in your nose—"

"He'd be where Hoyle is," said one of the detectives.

Wentworth, shrugging, pointed to the altar, before which incense burned. "Look," he said.

On the altar were several packets of currency and small bars of gold, all that the two Chinese had taken from the bank. Bits of red paper were scattered over the notes and the gold, to complete the ceremony of purification. None of the 'binders had thought to snatch up the loot.

And the detectives' examination of the bodies of the slain or wounded hatchetmen completed the last link of the affair. The switch key for the electric lights. A small nasal spray, refilled with the deadly fluid from the poison sacs of the black-necked cobra. A pass admitting one J. Besovich into the bank in his capacity as janitor....

"We got to get that janitor," Dunand said, as he listened to the hiss of the flame cutting through the steel door above, a hiss curiously like the hissing of the spitting cobra.

"Kong Gai killed him as soon as he completed his part in the business," Wentworth slowly stated. "That's Kong Gai's way. He trusts no men. Only snakes."

Kong Gai was not found. There was the hole in the floor, through which the King Cobra had looked down at the ceremonies beneath, through which he had seen Wentworth, through which he had dropped the spitting black cobra, by shoving the venomous serpent's glass cage over the hole and then pulling back the opening to the cage. This was found by the entering officers, together with a second cage containing another of the spitting cobras.

"I only hope I gave Kong Gai something to remember me by," Wentworth said.

"Even if you missed him," Dunand praised, as he glanced at the black clad hatchetmen, some dead, some wounded, "even if you missed him completely, he'll remember you for this, boy."

"And when he comes to think it over, he'll discover that he was betrayed by snakes. By the very serpents he considers his slaves, his children. The great Evil One of Chinatown, the King Cobra, betrayed by harmless American snakes! When the story is known, he'll lose face, chief. Find himself shorn of power, unless—"

"Unless he strikes back?"

"That's it, sir," said Jimmy Wentworth. "I'll try and be ready for him."

THE HEADLESS IDOL

A Dying Man, a Headless Idol and the Flight of a Bee Tell Wentworth a Tale of Frightful Crime and—Kong Gai!

1

THE MISSING CHILDREN

"AND WHAT I don't know, I can't tell you," said Captain Dunand, attempting honestly to answer the shrewd queries of the reporters as he sat behind his desk in San Francisco's Hall of Justice. He went on doggedly, "You boys seem to think I'm trying to get out of making an arrest. That ought to make you happy, because as long as the Whitcomb case remains unsolved, your papers can keep on calling me a doddering old fool—"

"Then you refuse to admit that Whitcomb and his three children are victims of a gang outrage?" demanded the *News-Call* reporter. "You refuse to admit that they are being held for ransom? You refuse to admit—"

"I'm not admitting what I don't know," persisted the gray-haired captain of detectives. "Not if you keep after me all day, boys."

The *Enquirer* man drawled, "We've been after you six days, cap, and you haven't come across with one printable line. You play with us, and we'll play with you. The public have a right to know what's being done to clear up Whitcomb's disappearance. They're pretty worked up about it, too. A man and three youngsters can't vanish without leaving some sort of clew—"

Captain Dunand stared out of the window, and blinked as the last rays of sun glinted off the roofs of Chinatown and were reflected into his eyes. He said finally, "I agree with you, Haynes. I don't want to fool anybody, except the criminals involved in the case. The department had one clew, and gave it to you."

"The fellow who came to Whitcomb's office and threatened him?"

"That's the man. Martin Cravens."

"Well," insisted Haynes, "how about finding him in time for my next edition?"

Dunand said wearily, "I told you boys that if you plastered his name all over the front pages he'd go into hiding."

"Well, how 'bout the chauffeur of Whitcomb's machine, cap? He'd do to keep our jobs for us."

Dunand was about to reply that the department was making every effort to find the missing chauffeur when he heard a whisper, followed by a laugh. He asked abruptly, "What's funny, Haynes? Let us in on it."

"I just said it was too bad it wasn't a couple of elephants your dicks were looking for, cap. They could probably find a pair of elephants, provided the animals stayed on Market Street—"

Leaning back in his chair, Dunand said, "Let's go over this thing, boys. And"—solemnly—"anything I may say isn't for publication. Right?"

The oldest reporters pledged their words with a quiet, "Shoot, captain."

"Six days ago," Dunand began, "Ronald Whitcomb left his house and went to his office. He arrived at nine o'clock, about. A few minutes later the man Martin Cravens, a

Someone drove a knife into the high-binder's throat

clerk at the Consolidated Oil, came to see him. There was an argument. It seems that Cravens had bought stock on Whitcomb's say so, and lost his shirt. Cravens said some dangerous words; he was heard to say them by people in the outer office."

"We know all this, cap!"

"Wait. Let me finish, Haynes. Cravens leaves, promising to get even. At a few minutes past ten, Whitcomb's own car takes him away.

"Then we learn that somebody telephoned his home, ordering the three children to come to Maginn-Duane's, the department store, and meet their father. The children are taken there in a taxi—"

"What taxi, cap?"

"Not the one phoned for," said Dunand, "because the maid at the house said a second cab came, a few minutes after the first one. Let me' go ahead, boys, will you? You know all this, anyhow.

"THE CAB DIDN'T go to the department store, so far as we can learn. Whitcomb is gone. His three children are gone. It looks like the work of a number of men, but there's been no demand yet for ransom. Martin Cravens couldn't do it by himself. He's only a clerk, and, as you boys've found out, a fellow with a good reputation.

"Whitcomb's chauffeur is also an honest man; been with him eleven years. So I tell you that it looks to me like the work of a gang of men, just as you fellows have been trying to get me to say, but"—his big finger waving at the listeners—"I want it to appear as if all suspicion is on this man Cravens! If he's in with a gang, I want 'em to push him forward when the time comes for dickerin'. In other words, boys, I want the department to appear dumb, and according to you fellows that ought to be easy."

"Do you realize, cap, that you've not told us a single new fact?"

"I've never lied to you, boys, and I'm not starting to do it now!"

The *News-Call* man said thoughtfully, "We've all printed stories that it looks like a gang outrage, captain."

"Sure. But the department hasn't backed up your statements."

Haynes said suddenly, "We're not blaming you, cap, but our city editors are all riding us to get some sort of story. Here's an idea. Why don't you put Wentworth on the case? It would let us print a lot of hooey, and we'd get by with it, and in the meantime put the real gang clear off any notion that they're suspected. Let us cook up a tale about the trail

leading to Chinatown! We can use Wentworth's photo-
graph, and rehash some of the stories about arrests he's
made. Be a good guy, cap. All you got to say is 'Sergeant
Wentworth has been assigned to the Whitcomb case' and
we'll do all the necessary fiction writing."

"Wentworth's only the patrolman on the Chinatown
beat," said Dunand.

"I'll leave it to the boys."

"You said it," agreed the newspaper men in chorus.

Dunand instantly attempted to retreat behind his last
line of defense: "Then I wasn't talking for publication," he
growled.

"No go," the veteran police reporter decided fairly.
"You're protected in anything you said about the Whitcomb case, but this came later. If Haynes wishes to use it,
he can. We all can, we all probably will, because we haven't
anything else to turn in. It makes a good yarn, and can't
do any harm."

"If I assign Wentworth to the case for one day, does that
satisfy you?"

"One minute'll satisfy me," grunted Haynes. "Now, call
Wentworth up here, and let us talk to him."

Dunand was trapped, and knew it. He reached for his
desk telephone, and said into the transmitter, "Chinatown
squadron. Manning? Dunand. Is Sergeant Wentworth in?
He is? Tell him I want him. Eh? Yes, I'll speak to him on
the phone first—"

There was a pause, and then the captain of detectives said, "Hullo, sergeant. I want... hullo... oh, it's you,
Manning? What? Busy? Well, let me talk to him on the

phone. There're some newspaper men here, and they want a word about the Whitcomb case."

Silence again; when Dunand said, "I'm listening, Manning. He said… what? Oh, he said that, did he? Hmm, well, well, well." A slow grin was spreading over the gray-haired captain's stolid face. "Very well, Manning," he concluded. "Just say to the sergeant that I'll wait for him here."

HAYNES WAS LOOKING at his watch. "Have him make it snappy," he said, as Dunand replaced the telephone. "I've got a suburban edition to make, cap."

"Sergeant Wentworth said he was busy," said Dunand placidly.

"Say, who's in charge of the bureau? You, or Wentworth? How long've I got to wait?"

"It takes a long time for boiling water to freeze," Dunand told him calmly.

"Meaning Wentworth said I could wait until hell froze over?"

The gray-haired captain of detectives said softly, "Something like that."

"Put into words, Wentworth isn't coming up to let us talk to him, and you are not assigning him to this case!"

"Something like that," repeated Dunand, smiling broadly. He watched Haynes scrawl a few words on paper, and then said, "And that isn't news, is it?"

"Want to hear what I'm phoning to my office? 'Dunand refuses to assign Detective-Sergeant James Wentworth to Whitcomb case. Detective bureau apathetic.' And what will the Police Commission say to that, cap?"

"I haven't refused to assign Wentworth to this case, have I?"

The oldest of the police reporters took charge.

"Captain," he said, "we aren't getting anywhere. We aren't getting any news, and you aren't getting the abductors of Whitcomb and his youngsters—"

"Who said we weren't?" demanded the captain.

Every reporter put two and two together. Several of them stood up.

"Where're you going now?" Dunand asked.

"To telephone our papers that Wentworth has uncovered a clew!"

Dunand said urgently, "Boys, he… he hasn't uncovered anything. Be reasonable!" The honest eyes of the captain clouded, and then he went on glibly, "Wentworth's only checking on some data just brought in—"

"What data?"

And so the wise chief of the detective bureau began to lie for one of the few times in his life: "We picked up a vag, just a little while ago, boys. I'll give you his name in a minute. He was standing outside the Whitcomb Building, and he saw a big green touring car with the side curtains all on, and while the machine was in front of the building he thought he heard a child cry, and then Whitcomb came down, very excited, and got in the green touring car, and…."

Three full minutes it took the captain to complete his fairy story. When he had finished, and the reporters had hurried out to get in touch with their various city desks, Dunand lifted the telephone again.

He was connected with the Chinatown squad room, and

said to his sergeant of detectives in charge of the Chinatown detail:

"I've done more lying this evening than I've ever done
before, Jimmy. It's safe for you to come up now, boy. And
if you haven't picked up a real clew—which is why I lied,
to keep you and whatever you've found out away from the
papers until we get a chance to act—I'm going to send you
out to the Sunset district where you can pick buttercups!"

2

WENTWORTH'S CLEW

IT WAS ONLY a few minutes before a lean young man in the uniform of a patrolman stepped quietly into the captain's office. It was only a few minutes, but in that time Dunand had firmly denied the pleas of two city editors, who wanted pictures of the "vagrant" who was supposed to have seen the abduction, and who promised all sort of influence being brought to bear on the captain's gray head when the requests were refused.

The Whitcomb case had been on the front page for just a day short of a week. The city was aroused, not only because of the disappearance of the wealthy Whitcomb, head of the brokerage house bearing his name, but also because of the obvious abduction of the small Whitcomb children. Rumors—terrible rumors—were on every lip. In the meantime the police were not able to produce the man Cravens, who had threatened Whitcomb the morning of the disappearance, nor to find the Whitcomb automobile and its chauffeur. There was flaming talk, aided and abetted by the newspapers, which the administration did not find pleasing. Coals were constantly being dropped on Dunand's head—and he could do nothing about it save keep after his men. Almost the entire department was on the Ronald Whitcomb case, but not a man had learned a single essential fact, nor picked up the trail of the clerk Cravens.

It was freely admitted that Cravens had just cause for anger against Whitcomb. The millionaire broker had advised Cravens to buy several varieties of stocks—or Whitcomb's office had advised it, which was the same thing—and Cravens had lost his savings. But that was not unusual. Many others were in the same fix, and through no real fault of Whitcomb's. Had Cravens taken a good punch at the broker, San Francisco would have said, "Served him right!" and laughed about it. But kidnapping three children, as well as Whitcomb himself, was a different matter.

The department was baffled. Here was what appeared an obvious crime, with the criminal known, and yet they were unable to produce the man.

All of this was in Dunand's mind as he said, "Sit down, Jimmy. I've lied hot and heavy to give you time, lad. Now, let's hear what you've picked up."

Wentworth said soberly, "Yes, sir. It isn't much, but it's a clew—"

"It'd better be," Dunand snapped. "Or the department'll be in a fine mess. I'll be the judge. What is it?"

The youthful sergeant of detectives reached into his trousers pocket, and as he withdrew his hand said gravely, "I'm afraid I'll have to be the judge, sir. It's in my line… this is it."

"That? What's that?"

Dunand stared at the object in Wentworth's hand.

It was small, no larger than an apple, which, at first glance, it resembled. A closer look showed that it was the body of an idol of some strange god, with the arms folded, and the legs drawn up. The image was of carved wood, and very old; so old that the surface was smooth, brown, and polished.

WENTWORTH SLOWLY TURNED the curious little talisman between his fingers, so Dunand could see where the head had been. Here the wood was much lighter in color, as if it had not been exposed long to the air, nor been handled much. And where the head of the idol had been severed, there was painted three tiny white flowers, no larger than the heads of matches, but delicately, beautifully done.

"That's your clew?" Dunand said wearily. "That's why I lied for you?"

Wentworth said swiftly, "That's it, chief."

"I suppose," the captain went on bitterly, "you found it in Chinatown, rolling along the gutter? Or—"

"I took it away from a *bo' how doy* who was hop-crazy, sir. If you'd seen him fight when I found it—"

"You mean fight because he was full of hop!"

"—you'd have known yourself that it was important," Wentworth finished.

The captain stared at him, and then laughed shortly.

"I'll get you a radio job, Jimmy," he said. "Bed-time stories. But tell it to me. Maybe I can give it to the reporters! It's a wilder yarn than I gave 'em, and I didn't think that was possible."

Wentworth stroked the image.

"An idol is beheaded only when a kidnapping has been accomplished," Jimmy said softly. "The kidnapper himself does it, for several reasons. It prevents the god of Life from seeing where the kidnapped person is taken. It prevents the gods of evil from enacting vengeance on the kidnappers. And, lastly, it's supposed to protect the kidnappers from capture, which, in China means they'll be beheaded with dull knives, because everyone in China wants to see kidnappers harshly and painfully treated—"

"And because of this you want me to believe that Whitcomb was abducted by Chinese!"

"I don't know about Whitcomb," said the sergeant of detectives who had spent his youth in China, "but I'll swear anywhere that the three little white flowers painted on the neck of the idol represent three children, and three white children at that."

For a long moment Dunand stared at the curious, outlandish headless idol in Jimmy Wentworth's hands, and then he snapped to action:

"What's the Chink say?" he roared. Forgetting that he knew no word of Chinese, and that only Wentworth spoke the dialects like a native, Dunand shouted, "Bring him up here! I'll talk to him! I'll find out where the Whitcomb children are! I'll… I'll… what'd he say?"

"He's dead, chief," Wentworth said.

"What? Did he talk?"

"You'd better let me explain, sir. I was finishing my beat, with an eye on Number Eighteen Eleven Waverley, because there's been hop sold there, when I heard a racket. Some Chinese were attempting to persuade another Chinaman—this one I found—not to go somewhere. He was so full of dope—that is, he wasn't past the dream stage, and wasn't out cold—that they couldn't do anything with him. He rushed out, and I thought I'd have a look-see just why they didn't want him going places.

"I stopped him—and it took a gun in his belly to do it...."

Dunand could see what had happened. Wentworth in a dark doorway. The 'binder, drug-crazed, leaping down a rickety stairway and into the street, murderous, deadly, to anyone who would confront him. Wentworth stepping before the Asiatic, gun out. A few sharp words, the flash of a knife....

"You shot him, Jim?"

"No," Wentworth said quietly. "I took his knife away from him, and intended to book him as disorderly, just as an example to the hop-joints to keep their customers inside until they'd slept it off, when some other Chino slipped up, and before I had a chance to shift my grip, he drove a knife into my man's throat... and that's hatchetman-way of saying 'Nobody talk!'"

"Get the murderer?"

Jimmy Wentworth said. "He was gone before I could get blood out of my eyes."

INTO DUNAND'S EYES crept momentarily a look of fear, the fear of the unknown, of the mysteries of Chinatown, which only his youthful sergeant fully understood.

"Ah," said the captain. And next, "The dead man, Jimmy... was he...."

"One of Kong Gai's hatchetmen? No! That's the curious part of it. My guess is that he's a new *bo' how doy*, earning his spurs, and not considered bad enough to be a brother of the snake. Some real Cobra knifed him, to make sure he didn't talk... and there's my clew."

"Put in simple words, you're trying to tell me that Kong Gai has a hand in the Ronald Whitcomb case?"

Wentworth said, "I'm telling you, chief, that the dead man had a hand in kidnapping three white children."

"Rubbish! If Kong Gai were kidnapping for money, he wouldn't take the father, too!"

Jimmy Wentworth looked out of the window. He said thoughtfully. "Not in America. But in China, chief, when ransom is demanded, one of the favorite ways of getting it is to take two people—a man and his father, for example, and… I hate to say it!… and torture the father until… the son is willing to pay any amount. And… well, you can see how this might be…."

Shivering, Dunand said, "You mean they'd torture Whitcomb's children until the father, Ronald Whitcomb, would pay? I… of course you mean it. Kong Gai! It's the sort of thing he'd do! But why should he pick Whitcomb? There are wealthier men in the city. Whitcomb's rich, but there're others with more money. Why Whitcomb, Jimmy?"

"I thought about that," Jimmy Wentworth admitted. "The only answer I can give is that shown in Whitcomb's list of customers. You had a copy of that, sir, and I looked it over. There are a few Chinese names on that list. Kong Gai might have had Whitcomb's house invest money, and have lost it in the crash, and this is Kong Gai's way of getting both money and revenge…."

"I'll tear Chinatown apart," Dunand growled.

"And scare 'em somewhere else," Wentworth said. "Not that I have anything to suggest, chief. All I can do is to keep my eyes open. And I'm grateful that you kept the newspaper boys away. One hint that Kong Gai is involved, and the lives of the four, father and children, won't be worth the price of a flower like those painted on the idol's neck…."

While Dunand's brows drew together, as the keen old captain fought to find some plan, Wentworth held the headless idol under the light on Dunand's desk.

"Look at the little tiny lines painted on the petals of the flowers, sir," he said. "The Chinese are marvelous artists, aren't they?"

"I don't give a damn what kind of artists they are! And neither should you, Jimmy Wentworth!"

"I was just wondering—"

The telephone rang sharply; Dunand answered it with his customary: "Dunand. Who's this?" and then listened.

If Wentworth had not been bent over his strange wooden idol, he would have seen his chief's face change from inattention to surprise, to astonishment, and then to fierce satisfaction. Dunand listened intently, and then said, "We'll be right there. Nobody's to see him. We're on our way."

Dunand stood up happily.

"Kong Gai," he chuckled. "Kidnapping. Baloney. Here's the end of the Whitcomb case! Ronald Whitcomb's in the Forest Park Hospital, Jimmy. Mulloy phoned. Found him 'dazed.' Blah! I'll bet his accounts are all wet, and he's been usin' customers' money. We got Whitcomb, and I'll bet he took his three children with him and intended to run off and then got cold feet about taking a trip to Peru. Dazed! Hooey! And you, Jimmy Wentworth, and your three flowers!"

Wentworth looked up, almost as if he hadn't heard the gleeful speech.

"Now, what's the matter?" demanded his chief.

"I was wondering why the petals of the flowers are

marked, veined, the wrong way. When you look closely, the tiny black lines, the veins, are painted like those on… well, on a bee's wing."

"A bee's left ear," suggested the jubilant captain of detectives. "You been taking hop, too, Jimmy? Come along with me. A breath of air'll do you good. Maybe it'll make you stop dreaming about Kong Gai."

3

THE MAN THE BEES STUNG

OFFICER MULLOY WAS standing on the fourth floor of the hospital, trying to appear as if he didn't realize that the nurse at the desk was red-headed, pretty, and Irish, and as if he had forgotten that at home there were seven little Mulloys, and Nora herself, who would stand for no nonsense.

He saluted briskly as Dunand and Wentworth stepped from the noiseless elevator, hoping that the nurse could see the breadth of his shoulders.

"Found him wanderin' on Forest Parkway, sir," he said. "Red in the face he was, and that's no lie, but whether it's drinking he was I couldn't say. He was goin' this way and that, and I says, 'Think shame to yourself, man, out on a street where th' children is playin'. But he only looks at me. At first I thinks he's far gone in a drunken spree, and then I see his eyes. And like no human eyes was they, sir! And—"

"And you brought him here," said Dunand crisply.

"No other way could he have come, sir. For he fell right down before me eyes, he did, and I stop the first machine I see, and—"

"Good work, officer. Which room is Whitcomb in?"

"The one behind me, sir. But a nurse says he's a very sick man, sir, or I'd have verified me suspicions—"

Dunand said sharply, "You aren't positive it's Whitcomb?"

Officer Mulloy drew himself up.

"And don't he live on this beat, sir? Many's the time I see him being drove home from work. I meant me suspicions about th' drink an' all—"

Dunand nodded, looking about. He said, "There's a nurse, officer. Please ask her to go into Whitcomb's room and tell the doctor I'm here, and that I want to see Whitcomb immediately."

Nothing loath, Mulloy marched to the little alcoved desk and delivered the captain's request. The nurse first telephoned her superintendent for permission to enter the sick room for the police, and, being given this, hurried across the hall. She reappeared in a moment and spoke briefly to Mulloy, who trudged back to his superiors.

"She says will you come with her to th' room," said Mulloy. "An' she says he's a sick man, is Mr. Whitcomb. And"—grinning broadly—"she wants to know if th' young felly, bein' you, sarge, is a college boy working on th' force for experience, an' I didn't have th' heart t' tell her what a tough felly you are."

Jimmy Wentworth glanced swiftly at the pretty nurse, and her heightened color told him that she knew Mulloy had repeated what she had said."

The two detectives followed her into the sick room.

On the bed lay a man in middle years. His face was gray, what little the men from Headquarters could see. Most of it, and the entire forehead, was covered with what appeared to be thick towels, but were ice bags.

One hand was visible, and Wentworth's first impression was that the skin must have been immersed in water, for drops stood out on it.

It was obvious that Whitcomb was indeed a man in peril of death.

A DOCTOR AND interne were drawing blood from the exposed arm, with several nurses assisting. The operation was completed, and the bandaging finished, before the house doctor had one of the girls strip off his rubber gloves. He said, "Have fresh ones ready. One of these broke," and then came to the detectives.

"From what the officer said, I understand this is Ronald Whitcomb," Dr. Lyle said quietly. "The hospital has already put in a call for his personal physician, but we didn't dare wait for his arrival. Whitcomb is in bad shape, sir."

"My name's Dunand," said the grim captain. "This is one of my sergeants. First thing; Whitcomb will recover?"

"Probably. Thanks to your officer, captain. By bringing him here promptly, he undoubtedly saved his life."

Wentworth asked, "What is wrong with him?"

"Heat apoplexy, I believe. You call it sunstroke, sergeant. Whitcomb's a heavy, full blooded man. They are most susceptible. Especially if they've been subjected to any kind of physical or mental strain."

"Never heard of anyone in San Francisco being sun struck," Dunand muttered.

"It isn't entirely a matter of heat, captain. He may have been wandering aimlessly about without a hat, you know—"

"Had he been drinking?"

"I shouldn't say so."

"You are positive of your diagnosis?" Wentworth questioned.

The doctor smiled. "Just about as positive as is ever possible," he countered. "The man is unconscious. Spasmodic, jerky breathing. Hands and face cold to the touch, but, as you can see, covered with excessive perspiration. Flickering pulse. Dr. Jaynes finds faint heart beats, about a hundred and thirty to the minute. Pupils insensitive to the light. All the signs of heat apoplexy. We've bled him, and packed his head in ice. In my opinion, he ought to recover."

Dunand said briefly, "Sounds logical. You ought to know."

"Has he been conscious at all?" Wentworth asked.

"No, sergeant. Nor will he be for a day or so. He will lie there without movement whatsoever. That's typical of sunstroke."

"Do any harm if I looked carefully through his clothes?" Wentworth asked in the same level tone.

"Not the slightest. I'll have Dr. Jaynes and a nurse see that his arm is not disturbed. Help yourself, sergeant."

Dunand understood what his subordinate was after; some shred of clew which might indicate that Whitcomb had been abducted, or had not been abducted. Something to tell of the whereabouts of the children. He nodded agreement to Wentworth's unasked question, feeling that the matter should be cleared up immediately.

Jimmy Wentworth stepped to the side of the high metal bed on which Whitcomb lay, covered only with a rubber sheet, which was drawn down. The broker still wore his shirt, so hastily had the hospital people applied first aid for sunstroke, and before Wentworth began his investigation he looked about for coat and vest.

"In the closet," a nurse told him.

"Please get it," Wentworth requested. No sense in

disturbing the unconscious man at all if the upper garment would reveal what he sought.

The youthful sergeant of the Chinatown squad had his hand in the inner coat pocket when he heard a strangled cry, terrible in the silent room, followed instantly by an ejaculation of surprise from one of the doctors. Wentworth turned round instantly to look.

Whitcomb's mouth was open now. His eyes were open also. A horrible rigidity had straightened his arms and legs. **THE SICK MAN** groaned deeply, and before Dr. Lyle could take the hypodermic which an attentive nurse was handing him, Whitcomb began to shout incoherently, to rave and toss his arms and shoulders about on the bed. Nurses and doctors hastened to hold him down as he struggled, and then Dr. Lyle shot the needle home. For a full minute more Whitcomb struggled furiously, crying out a jumble of meaningless words which ended in a shriek:

"No more!"

And then complete silence, as the powerful drug stopped the raving.

Whitcomb's face now was as gray as ever, and the man lay as if dead.

"Well," said Dr. Lyle. "Well. Another diagnosis gone to the devil." He growled a long string of orders, and the room became very active as the interne and nurses hurried to put them into effect.

Wentworth said quietly, "So it isn't sunstroke, doctor?"

"It is not," Dr. Lyle told him soberly. "Not when he acts in such a manner." He looked at his watch. "I wish Dr. Henderson—Whitcomb's physician—would hurry and get here. Because—"

"Because you think the man is not going to recover?" broke in Dunand shrewdly.

Dr. Lyle shrugged.

"I've done enough guessing," he said briefly.

"Will you guess what is wrong?" Jimmy Wentworth suggested.

"Don't need to guess—now," said the physician. "Not about that. I know. It's a rare case, gentlemen, and between ourselves there isn't much we can do about it. To put it plainly, Whitcomb is going to die from insect stings."

"What?" grunted Dunand. "First you said sunstroke, and now you talk about bugs!"

"Not bugs. Wasps."

"Or bees?" Jimmy Wentworth said softly.

"Or bees," agreed the medical man. "Either one. The early symptoms are exactly the same as heat apoplexy. Exactly, when there are no swellings, and that's often the case. Now you'll excuse me, please. There are a lot of things we can try, and we'll try them all, but Ronald Whitcomb is going to die without recovering consciousness just the same."

Captain Dunand stared at the dying man, and from him to Wentworth. No word was passed, but both were thinking the selfsame thing. That the petals of the little white flowers painted on the headless idol were veined in black like the wings of bees—and the image had been found on the body of a *bo' how doy*—a Chinese 'binder a killer, a hatchetman, who had himself been murdered before he could say a word to anyone.

4

THE CHARGE IS—MURDER

THE FIRST EXTRAS were out by the time Dunand and Wentworth returned to the Hall of Justice, after having left word at the hospital to be informed of Whitcomb's death, or any change in his condition. Dr. Henderson, Whitcomb's own physician, had agreed with the second diagnosis of the hospital medical men, and agreed also that chance for recovery was almost impossible. All the physicians were positive that Whitcomb would not recover consciousness, but just the same Dunand had not left until two men from the department were in the room, ready to take down any word, and, if possible, to ask the questions Wentworth had told them to ask.

The headlines just about told the story:

WHITCOMB FOUND;
CHILDREN STILL MISSING
MILLIONAIRE IN DAZE AT LOCAL HOSPITAL
POLICE REFUSE TO ALLOW WEALTHY
BROKER TO TALK

Which Ronald Whitcomb, at death's door, couldn't

possibly have done, but which held off the newspapers as to the manner of the broker's dying for a few hours.

Down in Captain Dunand's office, gray haired chief and black haired sergeant sat staring at the envelope they had taken from Whitcomb's pocket. They had already read the letter a dozen times. It was typewritten on fine paper, with the sheet cut in half to remove a letterhead or address, and said:

> The enclosed check, signed by myself, is to be honored when presented for payment by any official of the Whitcomb Investment Company. The check is to be cashed in five and ten dollar bills, and these are to be taken to whichever place is designated at a later date. If the police accompany the person bringing the ransom money, when he is told where to bring it, my children will be put to death. It is my order and wish that these requirements be exactly carried out.

The communication was signed by Whitcomb. The check, attached to the letter, was for one hundred thousand dollars.

Dunand said slowly, "Not much to go on, Jimmy. We'll have men at the Whitcomb Company tomorrow. And tap their phones. Only...."

"Only you're a man," said Wentworth, "and you don't want the children hurt."

"No. I don't want them hurt, lad. You... you still think this means Kong Gai?"

"I do, chief. Now more than ever. No one save a fiend like that Chinese would send a father with the ransom note for his children, knowing full well that he would not be able to tell where the youngsters were. And what has been done to Whitcomb will make anyone anxious to get the children out of the hands of such monsters."

"I don't understand it," muttered the head of the detective bureau.

"According to the doctors, Whitcomb was stung and stung until he became almost unconscious. Somewhere along the line he signed the demand for ransom and the letter. Then the devils allowed him to partially recover consciousness, put him in a machine, let him off somewhere near his home while—according to the doctors—he could just stagger about, but was to all intents already a dead man."

"And if he hadn't raved, everyone would have thought he'd died from apoplexy!"

"There is no perfect crime," Wentworth said slowly. "At least, not yet. Given time, Kong Gai, the Venomous One, may find it. Through his opium sales, he has his coils about some renegade physician. That's sure. That's where he must've picked up the bee sting idea. He has his slimy coils everywhere, captain! He—"

THE TELEPHONE RANG briskly, and Dunand said, "Damn reporters. Or a city editor. I hate to answer it."

He spoke gruffly into the receiver: "Dunand. Well?" and then said excitedly, "Splendid! Congratulations, sheriff! Bring him right up here!" As he hung up, he said to Wentworth, "Cravens's caught! Down in San Bernardino county! The sheriff's office kept it under cover, and they've got him downstairs now."

"And what good is that going to do?" Jimmy Wentworth

demanded. "I suppose you think Cravens tortured Ronald Whitcomb?"

"No, but he might be a tool of a gang. Perhaps"— magnanimously—"Kong Gai's tool."

"If he were, you'd find him in the bay with his throat slit."

This time Wentworth reached for the telephone, for Dunand was snapping off the desk light, and pressing another button which would cause all the brightness in the room to fall on Cravens when he was brought in for examination; the Chinatown detective sergeant answered the ring with a voice so like his chief's that Dunand was forced to smile.

"Dunand," said Wentworth. "Well? Oh, hello, Williams... you did, eh? And it checks? Thanks. I'll tell the captain."

As the door opened, Wentworth said curtly, "Williams reports that the sample of ransom letter paper we gave him coincides with paper used by the people where Cravens worked, sir."

"Very good, sergeant," said Dunand.

The captain nodded to the three deputies and the under-sheriff who shoved a thin young man into the room. Not until the four, prisoner and captors, were in the spot of light did Dunand speak. He said, "I think it's safe to take off the handcuffs, boys."

"We took no chances, cap," said Undersheriff Egan. "Not with this boy."

"Tough, is he?"

"Say! He wouldn't come across with a word! We says, 'The sooner you tell us where Whitcomb and his kids is, the better it'll be, bud,' but the punk won't open his head."

"Why were you in San Bernardino?" Dunand asked quietly of the prisoner.

Cravens lifted his head. The eyes were circled with black, with fatigue, and the young man's face was very pale.

"You wouldn't believe me," he said at last.

Dunand looked out of the window. It was black outside now. High on a roof in Chinatown a lantern glowed, like the single eye of a five-legged dragon. Dunand carefully drew open a drawer of his desk, took out a box of cigars, and handed them about to the deputies. He selected one for himself, cut the end, was about to put it in his mouth, when he roared suddenly:

"Where are the children, Cravens?"

The prisoner shivered, but his eyes met the fierce gaze of the captain.

"I don't know," he said.

Dunand waved the ransom letter in front of Cravens.

"When did you write this?" he asked.

"I didn't write it."

"It is on paper from the company you worked for!"

Cravens bowed his head, but remained silent.

A third time the telephone rang, and again Wentworth answered it. He spoke now for the first time, gently; "The charge had better be changed, captain. From kidnapping to murder, Whitcomb is dead."

Dunand shifted ground subtly.

"You can be cleared of murder," he said to the frightened prisoner. "If you will give us the names of the gang, and tell where the Whitcomb children are, I will do my best with the District Attorney."

"I didn't kill Whitcomb," said the exhausted man, "and I didn't kidnap his children—"

"Give an account of your actions for the past six days."

"You won't believe it," repeated Cravens.

"Tell us anyhow," said Jimmy Wentworth.

THE ACCUSED MAN looked at him, seeing only a fellow no older than himself, in a patrolman's uniform.

"What's the use?" the prisoner muttered.

"Because I might believe you," Wentworth told him gravely.

Cravens' head was hanging; he looked so guilty that Dunand was about to roar at him again, and then the prisoner began to speak jerkily.

"I went to Whitcomb. I admit it. I'd given him three thousand dollars to invest. He put it in speculative stocks. I wanted bonds. I told him I'd... I'd...."

"You can leave out what you told him," said Jimmy Wentworth. "Because anything you say can be used against you. Tell us why you left the city."

"I didn't leave the city," blurted Cravens. "I was taken away! In a machine. I've been kept doped. You can see"—he pulled up a sleeve—"you can see where I've been doped!"

Wentworth did not intend asking who did it, lest the prisoner say, "Chinese," and the deputies repeat it outside the Hall of Justice. So he said, "And you came to in San Bernardino county?"

"I woke up on the side of a road, and that's all I know. I never even knew who took me away! I never heard them speak. I was blindfolded after they slugged me—"

"Where?"

"Just as I came out of the Whitcomb Building! I had

walked to the curb, and turned around and shook my fist at the building. I wanted to tell the world what I thought of them all! I said something… crooks, you know… not very loudly, perhaps… and then just as I stopped, because there was a car at the curb, somebody said something I didn't catch, and I was banged over the head. That's all I remember, although I must have been yanked into the car—"

"Bull," growled one of the deputies. "Trying to tell us you were kidnapped yourself, on a downtown street!"

Wearily, Cravens said, "I knew nobody'd believe me. I remember, too, that when I shook my fist toward the building there didn't seem to be many people in sight; a couple of men and women walking the other way, with their backs in my direction, but no one saw me shake my fist—"

"One person saw you," said Jimmy Wentworth. "A person I'm looking for myself."

"You mean—you know—who hit me? Who carried me out of the city? Who got me in this terrible mess?"

"When we find him, we'll find the same man who killed Whitcomb and stole the children."

THE DEPUTIES STARED at the lithe, youthful figure in patrolman's blue. Finally Undersheriff Egan blurted, "You can't talk us out of th' reward for th' kids' recovery like that, off'cer! Cravens is guilty as hell. He threatened Whitcomb, didn't he? He wrote th' ransom note on his company's stationery, didn't he? He ran away, didn't he? We caught him, and there's a five thousand dollar reward for doin' it— and it's goin' to be ours!"

"You're wrong," Wentworth said.

"We'll see what the newspapers say about it! I kept the capture quiet to give you city bulls a chance to make some more arrests, maybe, but now I'll tell what I know. Then see where you get off if you let Cravens go!"

"We aren't letting him go," the Chinatown detective-sergeant said soothingly. "We're keeping him for his good, and for our own. If you tell the newspapers, you will excite public opinion so greatly that Cravens, an innocent man, will be hanged. You don't want that, do you, sheriff?"

"No," said Undersheriff Egan, after a long pause. "But I don't want to see the boys done out of a just reward, neither! I want some kind of assurance that you got another clew—"

"I give you my word," Jimmy said simply.

Again the deputies all looked over the slim figure in blue.

"Yeah," said Egan. "Your word. And who might you be, officer?"

"My name's Wentworth," said Jimmy.

A third time the men from the southern end of the state stared, this time in utter astonishment. Then one of the deputies ejaculated, "Wentworth! A kid like you! I don't believe it!"

Captain Dunand said soberly, "He's Wentworth, boys. Rated as sergeant of detectives—"

"Wentworth of the Chinatown Squad," muttered Egan. "Well, Well, well... I'd like to shake your hand, sergeant! If the case is in your hands, I won't say a word! When'll you make your arrests, sergeant?"

Jimmy Wentworth's heart beat more rapidly. He knew on what a slim chance he based his conclusions—little more than flowers painted on the neck of a headless idol, and what common knowledge he possessed about bees— but was convinced that he was on the right trail. At all events, he was convinced of Cravens' innocence, and that was sufficient to make him say quietly:

"Perhaps tomorrow, boys, if all goes well."

5

THE BEE'S FLIGHT

WENTWORTH HAD LITTLE sleep that night. Bees! He had to learn about bees, and with that thought in mind routed out an expert at the state university across the bay. To him Wentworth listened carefully, making notes again and again; he left with the scientist's assurance that his original conclusions, if faulty in detail, were correct in all major analysis.

These were simple. Bees were hungry little things. Bees didn't like smoke. Bees died if they did not receive adequate fresh air. Bees became angry when cooped up. Bees could get out of any crevice, and would if they had the chance. Lastly, bees would always return to their hive, or wherever they were being kept, if they had been brought a considerable distance from their original hive....

And Whitcomb had died from many bee stings, died under torture.

Only Kong Gai, the Deadly, would have thought of sending a man to deliver the ransom demand for his children. Only Kong Gai's mind would consider such a thing a joke, and something to be proud about.

Wentworth believed that the little black lines, like the markings on a bee's wing, had been made on the headless idol to further protect the 'binder carrying it from vengeance of a god or devil not even Jimmy knew—some awful being of the underworld who, in addition to riding on a dragon, in addition to breathing fire and bearing ten swords in ten hands, also could kill by stinging men to death... that must be the reason why the white flowers—representing the kidnapped children—were so painted. To propitiate the god.

At eight-ten in the morning Wentworth marched into the bowl shop of the Wangs, who had more than once assisted the department. He found old Wang Yü behind his counter, and, after bowing and hoping that the ancient's health was good, asked for the son, Wang Chen-po.

Old Wang clapped his hands thrice, and a Chinese dressed in American clothing instantly appeared. Without a word or look toward Wentworth, Wang Chen-po said, "And what are my honorable father's commands?"

"Here is our friend," said old Wang, indicating Wentworth. "I have none, except to have demanded your presence."

"Hi, Jimmy," grinned Chen-po, without apology, since he knew that his friend understood the Conduct-Toward-One's-Father. "What do you want now? Everything is quiet on the Eastern Front, so far as I know—"

"How many youngsters are there in the Wang family?"

"Thinking of adopting one of them, Jimmy?"

"It's Saturday," said Wentworth, "and I thought maybe some of them might want to earn money to buy duck's-egg cake."

"They all have the Yankee spirit," laughed Chen-po. "What do they do in order to make enough to get good and sick? They're ravenous little devils, Jimmy. They can eat you into the hospital. Shoot!"

Jimmy said lightly, "They hang around their windows, Chen-po, where the lily-pots are, and when they see a bee, they catch it and put it in a box. One bee, one dollar."

"Bees in Chinatown? Say, these youngsters aren't dumb, Jimmy! They know better than to try such a game."

"I think some of them may catch a bee or so, old man."

Wang Chen-po scratched his chin, and before he had finished his father cackled in Cantonese:

"You waste time, my son. Inform the grandchildren of Wang Yü that bees are desired, in the shortest time possible. Our white friend does not joke."

"That's right," Jimmy said, after bowing to old Wang. "And if the kids'll catch bees, maybe I'll catch…"

HE BECAME SILENT. Both Chinese knew what he meant, but neither blinked an eye. Kong Gai! Every decent Chinese hated the terrible leader of the Snake Brotherhood. No man's life was safe while the King Cobra lived.

"I'll see what can be done," Chen-po said quietly. "The kids are to be careful that they aren't seen, eh? And to say nothing about it?"

"That's it," agreed Detective-Sergeant Wentworth. "I'll go around my beat, and drop in just before lunch."

It was almost noon when Jimmy Wentworth leaned against the old bricks of the cathedral on the southerly boundary of the Asiatic district, and pulled from his rear pocket a thick newspaper. He stood there, apparently reading, but his right hand was shrewdly busy inside the paper. For Wentworth was attempting to put into practice what the bee expert had told him… would it work?

Inside the paper was a thin box, in which was a bit of honeycomb. The end of the box, fashioned that morning, very early, in the basement of the Hall of Justice, could be slid up or down, enough to permit a bee to escape. And in the box were five bees, collected by the grandchildren of old Wang as the little insects had sought pollen from the white and yellow china lilies....

Five bees!

Would the little winged workers lead the way to the venomous Kong Gai?

Wentworth felt something soft crawl along his finger, inside the paper, and a moment later a bee crept out, remained motionless an instant, and then flew up. The detective-sergeant tried to follow the bee's eccentric circles and oscillations. Each time, as the bee swung above the newspaper concealing the honey in the box, it seemed to sway to one side, so that the honey was at the edge of its circle instead of the center, as if the bee were throwing a loop about the sweet to make positive of its exact location. Then, in a straight line, it darted northeast.

Wentworth's eyes instantly sought the clock on the old cathedral. Four minutes to twelve. He stood there quietly, reading his newspaper, as if waiting until twelve to go for his lunch.

A moment before the clock boomed the hour, a bee hovered over Wentworth's head, and, after one swoop, again crawled to the concealed box in the newspaper. Wentworth could hear its excited humming and buzzing as it tried to enter the box, but he did not open the slide, lest another bee escape. Instead, he again glanced at the clock; one minute to twelve!

The bee had been gone three minutes. The bee expert said that a minute and a half was consumed by a bee delivering the pollen at the hive. That meant the bee had spent less than a minute going to… where?… and less than a minute returning. A bee could fly a mile in five minutes. Therefore the place where it went could be no more than a block or two away… in a northeasterly direction!

The captive bees, laden with honey, buzzed in the little box as Wentworth marched along his beat, as if he had decided to make one more round, and, as he often did, go to his lunch at one instead of twelve.

Wentworth paused the second time before the basket shop belonging to a member of the Wang family, where no questions would be asked, and repeated his performance. Again he timed the greedy bee, which, like its fellow, had difficulty in obtaining food in the city where it had been brought. Again he checked the direction of flight. Twice more he did this, until he had but one bee left.

Then he walked calmly along the street where the lines had crossed; where the bees seemed to be going. Even allowing a half minute leeway, it seemed probable to the detective that the location of the hive must be in the middle of the block somewhere, and as he reached it he let the last bee escape.

Again the bee circled, but this time darted straight up. Wentworth looked with an air of disinterest, and saw that the windows of the third story were boarded up. As if, according to Chinese custom, someone had died and the body had not yet been shipped to China. No unusual occurrence—except because of the flight of the bee! And as his eyes lowered, and he shoved his newspaper into his hip pocket again, he caught an opened wicket in a basement door across the street... 'binders, watching! Kong Gai's men.

As if he had not seen them, Wentworth crossed the street, entered a drug shop, and, by pointing, was sold a packet of cigarettes. He put these in his pocket, and then strode leisurely up the street. When he turned the corner, he pulled out his watch—in case he was being spied upon—and then walked slowly up the long hill, out of the district, as if now going for food.

HE WAITED UNTIL he was two blocks from the district, and then entered the first apartment house.

"A telephone, quick," he told the switchboard operator in the lobby. "No, not one here. In an apartment. And if anybody comes in, or you see anyone looking in, you haven't seen a cop come in Get that!"

The operator took Wentworth to a ground-floor apartment, and the sergeant called Headquarters immediately.

He was given Dunand at once.

"It's Number Ninety-one Ninety-two Fish Alley, sir," said Wentworth eagerly. "No mistake about it. Three boarded-up windows, third story. Which makes the bee expert correct. He said the bees wouldn't be active, nor sting, if they were kept in any cold dark basement...."

"We're ready," snapped Dunand.

"Tell 'em to go along Stockton Street, chief. To Sacramento. Down two blocks. Left turn to Fish Alley. The seventh house. That's the one. Middle of block, right hand side. I'll swing on when they turn off Stockton."

"Better get goin'," ordered the gray haired captain. "I'm givin' th' order to start, boy!"

6

—

KONG GAI LAUGHS

THE BLUE-CLAD PATROLMAN making his regular beat
on Nob Hill saw the hurrying figure of a fellow officer, and
ran to meet him; when he saw who it was he said:

"What's up, sergeant?"

"Plenty," said Jimmy swiftly. "When you hear a racket—
you'll hear it—come along and see!"

With that he hastened back toward Chinatown. At the
corner of Stockton and Sacramento, near the mouth of the
tunnel where he had once found a murdered flower girl
killed by Kong Gai, he paused, and then turned northward,
walking slowly along the pavement, stopping to play with
a Chinese urchin in pink jacket and red pantaloons; he did
this until he heard a sudden roar, coming from the tunnel.

A moment later hook-and-ladder Number Fifteen
roared out of the tunnel, siren wailing and engine humming
a high tune. Behind it Wentworth saw a red-and-gold hose
wagon, with men in fireman's blue hanging to the sides....

Chinatown gaped, wondering where the Fire God
was striking. As the hook-and-ladder slowed, and swung
around the corner, barely missing the lamp-post on the
sidewalk, Wentworth leaped to the side.

Nobody would think anything of that. It was a policeman's duty to get to a fire as rapidly as possible.

Wentworth heard someone next to him shout, "Nice goin', sarge!"

The deep voice was that of Officer Reilly, holder of the department's record for marksmanship, and no fireman at all. Only the driver, and the rear wheel-man, were from the fire department. Every other person in slicker, or in blue uniform, was a member of the riot squad....

Down one street! Left turn! The scream and squeal of brakes and tires, and a sudden noiseless operation that shot the first length of mechanically operated ladder into the air, in front of the windows of the house Wentworth had told about.

A spying 'binder popped his head out from the basement across the street. Officer Reilly waited until he saw the flash of metal, and the raising gun, before he drew trigger. The sound of explosion was covered by the roar of the hose wagon's engine as it drew up beside the hook-and-ladder.

Men were already running up the ladder. The first two were axe-armed, and the raising ladder took them to one of the windows. As an axe crashed against the barrier, Wentworth, followed by other men, swung to the building-side of the ladder, and continued frantically up to the roof.

Wentworth's head cleared the coping first, and almost the same instant his gun roared. He saw a 'binder leap high in the air; saw others turn and level drawn weapons, and then the riot squadman behind him had shoved the nose of the deadly chopper across the coping, and the rat-tat-tat of the little gun sprayed death over the Chinese.

Wentworth knew there was not a moment to be lost.

While some of the *bo' how doy* were still trying to get a bullet into the slim target afforded by one eye and a bit of forehead of the man operating the chopper, Wentworth pulled himself to the roof. He felt the sting of hot metal in his shoulder, and the impact half swung him about.

Nothing better could have happened. Had he continued straight forward, he would have been riddled with billets.

Jimmy Wentworth, the smiling young detective-sergeant of the Chinatown squad, had gone berserk. Here was a chance to get his hands on Kong Gai! He made one leap, notwithstanding the pain in his shoulder, and fell through what had been a skylight, but had been changed to a row of light slats, to give the bees air at times. The stairway to the roof was ten feet further along the roof. For a fraction of time something seemed to stay Wentworth's fall—a black curtain of heavy silk, which had been used to cover the opening most of the time—and during it he managed to squirm about....

The silk ripped, and Wentworth fell, landing on hands and knees. His gun was up at the very time of impact, up, and blazing at a black-clad figure.

A shrill, sweet voice screamed, *"Hola!* Get him, snake-brothers! It is the white fool himself! Get him for Kong Gai!"

WENTWORTH'S HEART STOPPED as his eyes and gun flashed up. He expected to die now, but if only he could get one shot at the King Cobra, and end his reign of terror! Then, so swift that it bit into Kong Gai's last words, he heard the tapping sound of the chopper at work, searching out corners of the room in a vain effort to get the Venomous One.

Jimmy's head began to work sanely again. He yelled, "Look out! The kids are somewhere here—"

"They're behind you, sarge," shouted the machine gun officer. "All's O.K.," and he alertly kept the muzzle of the chopper moving, ready to fire.

Despite this assurance, Wentworth waited. Would Kong Gai, from some clever point of concealment, kill him now? It could easily be done....

The sweet voice droned on, "Your eyes, oh white fool, I will tear out with my fingers! Your mouth I shall sew together, so you cannot destroy my sleep with your screams when we cut your body apart, inch by inch, and put little serpents to feed on you while you are still alive! The day will come soon! I could kill you now, but that is not my way of killing!"

A storm of bullets from the chopper ended the terrible promise. Then all was silent, save the hammering of axes and the stamping of feet.

For the three closed windows had not shown the room in which the kidnapped white children had been found, and when the officers smashed inside they found only a place of awful worship, with a great naked headless idol surrounded with crushed white flowers and many impaled dead bees, killed as sacrifices after they had served Kong Gai's horrible torture of Whitcomb.

And a row of the little insects which, maddened, had stung Whitcomb to his curious death, was found about a sheet of paper before the idol. On the paper was a statement of the account of one Sam Gee Quong, who had lost several thousands of dollars in the stock market. And it was easy to guess that Quong was only another name for Kong

Gai, and why the Venomous One had picked Whitcomb to kill, and his children to be held for ransom....

Jimmy Wentworth's shrewd deductions had been close enough, and had led the riot squad to the building itself, if not to the inner room. The other room must have been the chamber in which the bees had been kept, and a search at once found a small, makeshift hive, with a volume of instructions on bee-keeping beside it. The constant burning of incense in the other room made it impossible to keep the bees there, save when it was intended to let them sting someone... Whitcomb.

Kong Gai had lost the children, and seven hatchetmen to boot. Four more were caught alive, but wounded. The remainder of the Brotherhood had escaped along some secret passage.

Captain Dunand felt that only Wentworth's mad promptness in leaping to the roof in face of the 'binders' bullets had prevented the Cobra Men from rushing off with the children. Apparently it had been Kong Gai's command that the children be carried to the roof, and to some secret hiding place. That would be Kong Gai's way, too—not taking any chance that the police might follow the children along his own secret tunnel deep into the dark places of Chinatown. He cared for his hide, did Kong Gai, and took no chances.

"If we'd nabbed Kong Gai, this would have been perfect," commented the gray haired captain, as he surveyed the strange, terrible headless idol, supposed by the Chinese to protect those who kidnap children, and before which the Snake Brotherhood had bowed low.

"He was here," said Wentworth quietly.

"See him?"

"No. Heard him."

Captain Dunand said thoughtfully, "Say things, did he?"

"Some day," Jimmy answered, "we're coming face to face. Then… we'll see."

Kong Gai's horrible laugh shrilled in the room.

"We'll see!" screamed Kong Gai in English. "Yes! We'll see!"

Try as they might, the riot squad could not find from what vantage point the fiendish Kong Gai had spoken. Once more the Evil One laughed, and then the room of the Headless Idol, with its crushed white blossoms and dead bees and streaming incense bowls, was as silent as death.

WHITE AND YELLOW

In That Wholesale Slaughter of One White Man and Eleven Chinese, Jimmy Wentworth Sensed the Treachery of the Evil Kong Gai

1

GONGS AND FIRECRACKERS

CHINATOWN WAS AT peace. The hour of the Approaching Year was coming closer with every movement of the hands of the clock on the old cathedral. Long strings of scarlet firecrackers hung from balconies; china lilies bloomed in blue Canton porcelains in every window. The great oiled paper lanterns, yellow and green, waited for the evening to be lighted.

Soon there would be a great eating of *tche hou'n*—fine fat food additionally greased by perfumed sesame oil. Suckling pigs, stuffed with the dried black meat of Peking ducks, were roasting in the kitchens of the wealthier Chinese. Strange soups, concocted of sugared seaweed and pea tendrils and fish, simmered in the cooking pots of the poor. Squat bottles of rice brandy, all without the stamp of the customs officials, would soon be opened, and the liquid set to warm in the ovens.

Jimmy Wentworth, leaning against the side of the cathedral, marking the southerly boundary of San Francisco's Chinatown, looked down the street with a smile on his lips. All peaceful. All quiet. Children munching coconut candy. Fathers and grandfathers, their debts for the old year paid, talking in high good humor as they thought of the feast which would follow the fast of the day.

Not even Kong Gai, the Evil One, would dare anything in Chinatown on this eve of the Approaching Year. The most peaceful Chinese would have torn him to shreds. The only untoward thing which might happen would be some suicide; some poor devil of an Oriental who must save his face through death, being unable to meet his obligations.

In some high room a flower girl was singing nasally to the accompaniment of *san-hien*. Wentworth could imagine the girl in her finest silken trousers and jacket as she practiced a song for the evening. He wondered if she had "found her luck"; if the china lily bulbs she had planted in rock and water had bloomed for her during the day. He hoped that they had. Never had he seen such a profusion of the white and yellow blossoms of Heavenly Delight, not

Someone shouted: "A knife in him, brother of the snake!"

even in China itself, where the young detective-sergeant in charge of the Chinatown detail had been born.

The clock struck the hour. Instantly firecrackers began to sputter as the fuses were lit, and then the *crack-crack-crack* resounded all over the Asiatic district. The old clock's mellow tone was almost obliterated in the terrific din. Wentworth glanced up at the sign beneath it:

> Son, Observe the Time
> And Flee from Evil.

"Not today," Jimmy Wentworth thought. "The worst thing I've got to do is to eat a million course dinner tonight,

A half dozen slinking figures came forward like evil ghosts

and remember to do it wrong, so the Chinese don't realize how much I know about their customs."

At the time of the Newest year even the blue-coated officers of the law were not permitted to go hungry in Chinatown. Wentworth was to attend a dinner given by some of the richest merchants.

The firecrackers sputtered, hissed, crackled, and then, above the increasing racket, Wentworth heard the death shriek of an Asiatic, and saw the Chinese throng become a solid black mass, a block away. Eyes on the milling horde, Wentworth walked swiftly down the street. He did not break into a run, being certain of what he would find— some debtor who had made the only payment possible to save his face. It would be messy, as proven by the scream. A knife drawn from belly to chest.

Although he was watching the mass of Chinese, he saw a man hurrying up the street, toward him. This was not right. Every Chinese should have tried to get as near the dying man as possible, to see if, in his last breath, he acknowledged the debt as honest. Otherwise, the Chinese who should have received payment must present an equal sum, times five, to the temple or his tong. Irrespective of the justice of debts, they must be paid in Chinatown. With gold, or with life.

As the detective, in his guise of beat patrolman, strode along, he saw a form slip into a doorway. He was after the man like a shot, and found a wiry Japanese trying to conceal himself in shadow.

"Where're you going?" Wentworth demanded.

The Nipponese tried to appear as if he had merely

stopped to tie a shoestring. He sucked in his breath politely as he said:

"I go home, please."

"Why'd you duck out of sight when you saw me?"

"Duck?" giggled the brown man. "Duck is bird. I not un'stand." He was standing straight now, as he added, "I go home?"

Above the continuous crackling of the firecrackers Wentworth heard a familiar voice, crying in English:

"Officer!"

Dropping his hand to the Japanese's shoulder, Wentworth turned. He saw Wang Chen-po, his friend, racing toward him, obviously excited.

"I go now?" the Nipponese repeated.

Wentworth retained his grasp.

Wang Chen-po was out of breath.

"Thought you'd be—by the—cathedral," the young Chinese gasped. "Old Wang Hi'tze—our family—he's been—shot. And"—his voice suddenly very cold—"you've got the murderer!"

Other Chinese were following Wang Chen-po's course up the street, and their loud, vengeful shouts, involving torture and death, made Wentworth go for his gun. He said grimly:

"Keep 'em off, Wang."

"I'll try," Wang Chen-po growled.

Wentworth asked his captive:

"Why'd you shoot the Chinaman?"

"I shoot nobody," the Jap cringed. "I see dead man, yess. I not like. I say, 'No place Japanese boy here.' I hurry away, yess."

The light was none too good in the doorway. The wiry body beneath Wentworth's left hand seemed to be standing perfectly still, and yet with the quickness of light, while hundreds of enraged Chinese stormed up the street, the Jap's hands went to the detective's wrist.

Jimmy felt terrific pain as the Nipponese wrenched at him with expert grip. Even in this agony which numbed his left arm, Wentworth swung, and brought the butt of his gun down on the hard round head of the Jap.

Whether his wrist was broken he did not know. Straddling the fallen form of the Japanese, he snapped:

"When you've told 'em not to try anything, Chen-po, sneak away and call the wagon. Then come back."

And he had thought there was peace in Chinatown!

MURDEROUS CRIES ROCKED up and down the street; black-clad Chinese hemmed the youthful sergeant of detectives against the wall of the doorway. Wentworth kept his gun pointed at the throng.

Above the vengeful voices, above the banging of New Year gongs and the sound of firecrackers, young Wang Chen-po cried:

"The white man has caught him. Justice will be done. Today is the Fortunate Year. We must not kill others—"

An old grandfather shrilled:

"I will tear his eyes out with my nails!"

"He will mount the Thirteen Steps of the hanging machine," Chen-po shouted. "It is the greatest disgrace."

"Who is he?" a portly merchant bellowed.

"He is not of our country," Chen-po said in shrill Cantonese.

"A brown one?"

"A brown one," agreed the young Chinese.

Wentworth saw the gleam of knives now. He knew well enough the antagonism between the two races, flaming to fire now because of events on the far side of the Pacific. Just why Wang Hi'tze, rich and influential member of the family of Wang, had been murdered, even if the Jap had done it, was, at this time, of little real importance. Wentworth knew the humor of the crowd. The main thing necessary was to get the unconscious brown man safely inside the Hall of Justice, and worry about the rest after this was accomplished.

So Wentworth shouted, careful to speak in English instead of the Chinese he spoke so well:

"Who saw this man kill old Wang?"

Jimmy knew the Chinese as well as their language. He was not at all surprised when dozens of them perjured themselves without hesitation.

"I saw it!"

"And I!"

"With a gun he killed Wang Hi'tze. Nine bullets are in the dead heart."

"He used a knife! I saw the blade in his hand!"

Wentworth pointed to an old man holding to the hand of a child.

"How about you?" he called loudly. "You, old man! You with the red paper bundle under your arm. Where were you? Did you see this murder?"

The grandson whispered hastily in the ancient's ear, translating the detective-sergeant's question. The grandfather nodded vigorously, and cried out in Cantonese:

"I? *Hai-ya!* Did I see it? Assuredly I saw it! I will swear to that, by the sacred bones of the Dragon!"

A Chinese grunted. Another muttered a word. His companion, nodding also, began to chuckle. Then someone laughed, and almost at once laughter rippled through the entire gathering.

The old man was stone-blind, as Jimmy knew perfectly well.

"On your way, Chen-po," Wentworth snapped now.

He had correctly gauged the temper of the crowd. They were now willing to leave the matter in the hands of the police. Several young Chinese even went so far as to carry the body of their dead countryman up where Wentworth stood.

When the wagon from the Hall of Justice roared up Sacramento Street and swung, with tires and siren screaming, into the packed street, Jimmy Wentworth was again leaning against a brick wall, waiting peacefully. At his feet was a dead body. Propped against the wall was the now-conscious Japanese, securely handcuffed. Wang Chen-po, returned, was calmly reciting the first of the Thousand Words of Perfume, as is proper on the eve of the Approaching Year.

"And it is for this ye send in a riot call?" demanded Sergeant Mulcahy. "Did th' firecrackers scare ye, Jimmy?"

Chen-po decided that explanation was necessary.

"One wrong word, and we Chinese would have taken Wentworth's prisoner and cut him up into bits," he said. "Too small for a meal for a sparrow."

"So he talked 'em out of it?" chuckled big Mulcahy. " 'Tis Irish ye should have been, Jimmy Wentworth. Irish for talk, and Irish for luck! Here ye are, with th' body and th' murderer both together, and th' business all settled."

"I wonder," said Jimmy Wentworth.

Wang Chen-po bowed to his friend:

"The banquet is at seven," he said, ignoring Wentworth's words. "Until then, may the wisdom of the dragon assist you in determining what caused the death of the honorable Wang Hi'tze."

2

THE SLAIN AVIATOR

WENTWORTH REPORTED DIRECTLY to Captain Dunand. He explained briefly what had happened, saying that the report of the gun must have been covered by the banging of the firecrackers. No gun had been found on the Japanese, who said that his name was Matsu Miyamoto, and that he knew nothing whatever of the killing of the Chinese.

"He was beating it from the scene," the gray-haired captain of detectives said, "and that's suspicious. We'll see what we can learn from him again, later, and in the meantime check up on him. His story may be straight."

"I think he did it, chief, but that's not enough. Wang Hi'tze wasn't killed for tong vengeance," Wentworth said. "The Wangs are at peace. Therefore, why was he killed? He's a rich man. Or was. He is very patriotic. Which makes me wonder if—"

Laughing, Dunand said:

"Are you bringin' the war across the Pacific, Jimmy? I don't say I'm disagreeing. I'm just glad that for once you haven't got a crime to pin on your friend Kong Gai... damn him."

"I can't see where he fits into the picture," Wentworth admitted.

Dunand shrugged.

"It's the wrong way to feel," he said soberly, "but I can't help thinking how much simpler it is when a Chinaman's killed. The newspapers don't care, much. They call it a tong murder, and let it go at that. And—"

The telephone rang. Dunand answered it, listened and said, "I'll be down and look at the body myself."

For a long minute he stared out of the window. Then he looked at the top of his desk. Finally he glanced at his sergeant of detectives.

"Floater," he said shortly.

Jimmy Wentworth said, "Yes, sir. Er… Chinese?"

"No. White man. Flower in his buttonhole."

"Suicide?"

"Murder," grunted Dunand. "The flower was a china lily, sergeant."

"I'll go down and look with you," Wentworth suggested. "Although the flower doesn't mean anything to me. They're in lots of gardens now."

"Simpson recognized the man," Dunand said slowly. "From pictures in the paper. It's Harrington, Jimmy. The aviator fellow. Who was going to Shanghai to organize a flight for th' Chinese. It's a mighty lucky break for the department that you caught your Jap, boy. We're sittin' pretty now. But we've got to be mighty careful! This'll be a complicated affair. Perhaps an international case. Let's be mighty careful."

Together, captain and sergeant walked down the corridor, and took the elevator to the basement. The department surgeon, several detectives and officers were waiting in the icy cold white-tiled morgue.

Dunand looked only once at the still, dead face.

"Accidental, suicidal, or homicidal?" he asked of Dr. Nye.

"Possibly any of the three, captain. I wouldn't care to make a positive statement until an autopsy is performed."

The captain of detectives turned to one of the patrolmen.

"You found the body, Simpson. Where?"

"A longshoreman saw it jammed in the piles of pier 77, sir."

"You were on your beat?"

"I was, sir."

"And saw nothing suspicious?"

"No, captain."

"Umm. Well, he's dead. We know that much. And I agree it looks like Harrington, the aviator. Papers on him?"

Detective Winters nodded.

"Positive identification, captain. Papers, wallet with cards. Body wasn't robbed. Seventy-odd dollars in cash, fountain pen, keys, wrist-watch—"

"And china lily," said Jimmy Wentworth.

"In his buttonhole," agreed Winters. "What does that mean, sergeant?"

Wentworth said, "It's a new one on me, if it means anything at all. Harrington may have been in Chinatown, of course, and put the flower in his buttonhole. Everyone in Chinatown knew that money had been collected to send a 'foreign legion' to Shanghai. Aviators. White men, mostly."

"And," went on Dunand, "a Chinaman was murdered a little while ago by a Japanese. Get this straight, men! No talkin' to the papers about that!"

While the officers had been talking, Dr. Nye had been busy. He cleared his throat now, and began to speak:

"Gentlemen," he said, "it is now my opinion that the man Harrington was murdered. In view of—"

Dunand stared at him, and then biting off caustic words, said: "Go on, doctor. I'm listening."

"THE QUESTION AROSE," said Dr. Nye, "as to whether the man was dead or alive before the body was submerged in the water. The external appearances were of no assistance, since no marks of violence were found on the body. There was no froth at the nostrils, indicative of previous death, however. Nevertheless, captain, I am willing to state that Harrington came to his death by… er… to put it in plain English, he was choked to death! If the body had been in the water a little longer, the purplish marks on his neck—see them—would have disappeared, and a post mortem would have merely confused us. As it is, he was murdered."

"Sure he was murdered," blurted Dunand.

Another detective walked into the chill room.

"I've been checkin' on Harrington," said Detective Haight. "He's ex-Army. Good record. Fine fellow. No bad habits, except a little gamblin' once in a while. So I called this place and that, and it seems that he was in a crap game at the Silver Dollar. That's the place we've been trying to nail for sellin' hop and coke, captain, on Wentworth's tip. The owner of the dive said—"

Haight paused, and looked almost apologetically at the still face of the dead man. Then he continued slowly, "The owner of the Silver Dollar said that Harrington damn' near lost his shirt last night, sir. Said the fellow was taken to the cleaners for… thousands."

Dunand snapped, "Meaning that he may've lost what wasn't his, and then jumped into the bay?"

"That's the implication."

Wentworth asked, "Do you trust the Silver Dollar man, Haight?"

"No, sergeant. Not an inch. I'd like to see him doing a ten to life rap. I've gone to him for information before, and this is the first time he was ever willing—anxious, even— to give it."

"Let's get our facts together," the gray-haired captain of detectives said soberly. "A Chinaman is killed up on Dupont. Sergeant Wentworth catches a Japanese trying to sneak away. That's one crime. A white man, an aviator intending to sail for Shanghai, is found by Simpson jammed in the piles of the pier. Doc says he was strangled before he was thrown in the water. That's the second crime.

"Now, if we're intended to believe that Japanese killed Harrington, as they appear to have killed Jimmy's old Chinese, why all the effort to make it appear suicide? Come on, somebody! Let's have a solution!"

All eyes shifted to the lean figure of the young sergeant of detectives.

Jimmy Wentworth said slowly:

"It would seem that the Japanese were attempting to cover up on killing the aviator, captain. Catching the Jap in Chinatown gave us our lead. That's the way it looks, isn't it?"

"In which case," said Dunand, agreeing, "somebody got to the Silver Dollar owner, and made it worth his while to lie, eh? Otherwise he wouldn't admit any gambling going on in his joint."

"He's a snake," grunted Haight.

Jimmy Wentworth's forehead wrinkled at the word, the deadly symbol of Kong Gai. Nevertheless he saw no possible connection between Chinatown's Evil One and this crime, except the remote fact that the owner of the Silver Dollar was suspected of selling drugs—an industry controlled by Kong Gai.

"I'll see what I can find out," Wentworth said at last. "I'm going to an Approaching Year banquet tonight. Maybe I can pick up something. Chinatown'll be talking about the death of Wang Hi'tze. I'll keep my ears open."

"Meaning that you aren't satisfied with your own solution?" Dunand rumbled.

Jimmy Wentworth said:

"Look here, chief! Would you put a china lily flower in your buttonhole?"

"Not me! I can't stand the odor of the things."

"Neither can many white men, sir. So I'll see if I can learn where Harrington was given the flower. Probably it won't do us any good. Probably somebody in Chinatown—someone who made arrangements for the Shanghai expedition—just handed it to him for luck. But it won't hurt to learn, will it?"

"I'll send some of the boys up on the Fillmore beat, sergeant, into the Japanese colony. They may be able to help. Now, the lot of you here forget what's been said, d'ye hear? I'll communicate with the Federal authorities and see what they've got to say. I don't like this mess!"

After the morgue was emptied of officers, Wentworth spoke to the surgeon.

"One thing, doctor," he asked. "The body hadn't been in the water very long, had it?"

"A very short time, sergeant. You can see the clothing. Still gray. Salt water turns fabrics blue. That's why"—grinning—"the newspapers always have floaters wearing 'blue serge suits.' I've often laughed at it."

"Show me the finger marks on the man's neck, please."

WENTWORTH LOOKED AT the small purplish places carefully. He said then:

"A man of Harrington's powerful build couldn't be killed by one man squeezing his neck, doctor."

Dr. Nye blinked.

"No," he admitted. "However, there are no other marks of violence, sergeant. No bruises anywhere. A chemical analysis of the clothing might show unusual dirt in the weave of the fabric, ground in when the man was held against the earth."

"Not much proof," Jimmy said, thinking aloud. "Please show me Harrington's clothing."

"The officers examined it closely, Sergeant Wentworth."

"Let me look."

In the office off of the morgue were the various articles taken from the murdered man. Even the bruised, broken petals of the china lily. Immersed as the flower had been, the Oriental, pungent odor, offensive to many Americans, was still present. In spite of the smiles of the surgeon, Wentworth asked for tongs, and carefully picked apart every petal, peering at the center of the blossom, and then shredding it also. He found nothing at all.

"Think it was poisoned?" Dr. Nye chuckled. "You've handled some strange cases in the past, haven't you?"

Jimmy Wentworth put down the final bit of blossom.

"Just looking," he said.

Thinking of Wentworth's reputation, the surgeon said suddenly, "If you wish, sergeant, we can do a complete autopsy."

Jimmy Wentworth was holding a thin, taut, stiff bit of material in his hand, that he had plucked from the sleeve of the dead man's coat.

"Not necessary," he said quietly. "D'you know what this is?"

The surgeon took the quarter-inch thread from Wentworth's fingers. He twisted it this way and that, and then laughed.

"Jute, isn't it?"

Wentworth nodded.

"I hope it's indicative of the sort of material the department will get around the neck of the murderer of this man," Nye said heartily. "Jute! Well, well! Must have been on the pier somewhere, eh? Part of a shipment of raw jute from India, maybe intended for San Quentin's jute mill. Where the convicts make sacks. Curious! A strange coincidence. Or does it mean something, sergeant? Was… hmm… let me think… was this crime committed by a convict? I have it! He had a sack stolen from San Quentin, and threw it over the head of Harrington! I can visualize exactly what happened—"

"Sounds fine," Jimmy Wentworth said, halting the impossible theory of the would-be detective. "Only, doctor, this isn't Indian jute at all. In the first place, jute from

Calcutta would have been ruined by moisture. That's why
it can only be made into cheap sacks and burlap and poor
grade twine. This is Chinese jute. See how stiff and yellow it
is. I've seen enough of it to recognize this. Never heard of it
being imported into the States. No demand. But in China
it is used to make exceptionally fine rope. It has a name,
doctor," Wentworth concluded grimly. "Assassin-rope.
Murderers use it to bind their victims."

"You think a Chinaman killed the white man?"

Wentworth, in place of reply, said:

"Have someone look closely, and see if he can find more
of the Chinese yellow jute. Then you can determine just
how and where Harrington was bound, by the rubbed-
off particles of jute. I didn't think a fellow of the aviator's
courage would go down without a battle, and he didn't."

"We'll do that at once. Shall I inform Captain Dunand
of this discovery, or will you?"

"You tell him," said Jimmy Wentworth. "I've got to hurry
off and eat a million course dinner with the Chinese. A
number-one first-chop banquet. Birds' nest soup and all.
You tell the captain. And you can tell him, also," Wentworth added, "that way down deep under this crime we
may find a snake."

"A snake, sergeant?"

"His name is Kong Gai," said Jimmy Wentworth.

3

THE FEAST OF FOUR FAMILIES

WANG CHEN-PO AND his father, Wang Yü, dressed in their finest silks, were waiting when Wentworth arrived. In a corner of the family room incense fumed. Precious old silks hung on the wall, taken from iron-bound camphorwood chests for the festival. In one corner a single china lily bulb sent up its white and yellow blossoms.

Old Wang sat on his teakwood stool, his eyes closed in proper meditation. Young Wang grinned as Wentworth, in new uniform and with shining star, closed the door. Instantly Jimmy's manner changed. On the street he had been the Chinese district policeman, coming in uniform, as was expected, to a banquet to which American peace officers are invited. But here he was suddenly neither patrolman nor sergeant of detectives, but a young man in the presence of a wise and honorable elder.

"*Cho san sin sang hola,*" Wentworth said, bowing deeply. "And may your lucky star auspiciously shine, oh honorable Wang Yü."

Old Wang opened his eyes, and then blinked. "Your star," he smiled, "shines brightly today, my son. I thank you for your wishes." It would have been improper for an old man to felicitate a younger."

"He means," laughed Wang Chen-po, "that you dazzle the eye, James."

No mention of the killing of Wang Hi'tze, the head of the family. No sign of sorrow. That, also, would have been improper.

"Are we ready to leave, and enjoy the food brought from the Heavenly Kingdom?" suggested old Wang.

Wentworth knew that there was one chance in a million to startle an answer from the astute old Chinese, and yet it was worth a trial.

"We are ready to walk behind your august person," said Jimmy. "But why was the man who was to have fought for the Chinese army killed?"

Wang Yü blinked once. With his son's aid he came off the stool. Then he fixed his bright eyes on Wentworth, saying, "If you were not my son, and respectful in most things, I would rap you with my fan."

"Didn't work, did it?" Wang Chen-po said in English.

His father promptly brought the hard edge of the fan against Chen-po's cheek. When you speak in white-man language, I know it is something I should not hear," he said crisply. "I think you were laughing at your brother, and just for that I will tell him what he wishes to know!

"So the white man who flies is dead? Such is the way of the world. Why did he die? Twenty thousand good gold dollars is the reason, my son. That is the amount Wang Hi'tze gave him, to buy this and that. Wang Hi'tze is dead. The white man is dead. So. Let us go and banquet, my sons."

"On the white man's coat," Wentworth began, "was a china lily blossom, oh honorable father—"

"I am very hungry," said Wang Yü.

"On the white man's coat," repeated the sergeant of detectives, "were bits of assassin's rope, where he was bound."

"And thirsty," said Wang Yü.

The old Chinese walked clear to the door, and then said:

"And also old and impolite, my son. An improper question does not demand an improper answer. For once I will depart from custom, and tell you this: I am glad that the white man was murdered, and not a thief. That was the word already in Chinatown. He fought? Yes? I knew he was brave. It is a puzzle, my son, but do not let it interfere with the good food you will soon eat!"

"And don't forget to eat like a white man," suggested Wang Chen-po. "Or everyone'll be wise to you!"

All of which did Jimmy Wentworth no good at all. Did the Japanese kill Wang Hi'tze? Because the Chinese was financing the Shanghai-bound aviators? Were they responsible also for Harrington's death? Or were the two murders unconnected? And what earthly reason had he for trying to hook up Kong Gai with the crime, or crimes, except for the presence of the bits of Chinese jute, and the fact that the owner of the Silver Dollar was supposed to be in the drug ring?

In silence the trio walked along the lantern-lit street. Head high, as if the family of Wang had suffered no sorrow and loss through the death of their leader, old Wang Yü shuffled along with a smile on his thin lips. Wentworth and Chen-po followed, the dutiful three paces in the rear.

Chinatown's shops and bazaars were all closed. Moreover, for the first time in a year Jimmy Wentworth saw no lurking black-clad figures; no hatchetmen, nor 'binders, nor vicious *bo' how doy*—any one of whom would have gladly killed the white aviator for the mere joy of killing. If a 'binder had strangled Harrington, it would have been done by an expert twisting of the jute assassins' rope, not with fingers. That was more a Japanese method of killing. And Wentworth had already learned that there were no sharp indentations near the purplish fingermarks on the dead man's throat, as there would have been had a long-nailed Chinese done the strangling.

Again the indication was that the crime must have been committed by the same persons who had planned the death of Wang Hi'tze.

Peace was in Chinatown, although guns rumbled across the sea. Lilies bloomed. Incense swirled high. Debts had been paid. There was peace, but there were two dead men. Why?

JIMMY WENTWORTH WAS forced to stop thinking as Wang Yü entered the brilliantly lighted doorway of a brick-faced building, the meeting-place of the Four Families. Here the men of the clan gathered; the men of Wang, Ying, Yee and G'oung. Wentworth recalled Chen-po's sensible warning—that the sergeant of detectives must remember to eat and drink in white-man fashion, lest the Chinese wonder at his knowledge. No handling of chopsticks. No noisy inhalation of wine. No proper sipping of jasmine tea. Nor must he hearken to any Chinese words. The Chinese must consider him only as the district patrolman.

In the great central room of the Four Families tong, hung with silken banners, were long tables spread with

Nanking blue linen. Priceless rice bowls of rare Canton were before each blue plate. The chop-sticks were of carved ivory. Several white men were already seated at the tables, scattered among the Chinese. There was the head of a bank. The attorney for the Four Families. A friendly South American consul. Several immigration officials. These, like Wentworth, were honored guests.

A Chinese orchestra; two-stringed lute, *san-hien,* flute and round drum, set up a terrible din. Wentworth, alone of the white men present, recognized the famous Song of the Ascending Dragon. To the others it was merely an ear-splitting racket.

At the head of the central table, where Wang Hi'tze should have presided, was a red-painted hand carved teakwood coffin, lined with crimson silk. In it, within the week, the body of the murdered man would be shipped for burial in the Celestial Kingdom. The gruesome object was not at all incongruous to the Chinese.

One table only was hardly filled at all. Three old Chinese sat there. An Old One from the Ying, Yee and G'oung families. Wang Yü shuffled over to join them. But this still left about ten seats unfilled.

Chen-po and Wentworth sat side by side. *Kan fi,* pure white rice, was heaped in bowls before them. Wentworth immediately reached with a china spoon for some of the food, but Chen-po gently restrained his hand, saying in English:

"Not yet, please. It is not the time."

Knowing this well, Wentworth said: "Why not? I'm hungry."

"We are not all here," Chen-po explained with a straight face. "See that empty table, sergeant?"

A Chinese mumbled to his tablemate:

"These white men are without manners. They know nothing. The man of keeping-law is so ignorant that he will probably go ahead questioning Wang Chen-po, and the son of Wang Yü, being courteous, must answer him."

"Which was just what Wentworth wanted to do, and what he did safely now.

"Somebody late?" he asked.

Wang Chen-po kept his eyes on his plate, and said, as if reluctantly:

"Yes, sergeant." Under his breath he added, "officer, I mean. It's O.K. Just looks like flattery, Jim."

Nodding slightly, Jimmy went on:

"Important fellows, are they?"

Chen-po sang out in nasal Cantonese.

"All men are important, oh man without understanding," and, knowing Wentworth understood, said in English, "Not important at all, officer."

An old Chinese on Chen-po's left grunted:

"Well done, son of Wang Yü. But he will ask more questions. It is the way of the white men. You will see."

Wentworth did exactly that.

"Then why wait for 'em, Chen-po?"

"Hai-ya!" snorted the old Chinese. "Tell him any lie which comes into your head, son of Wang Yü. Or the truth. It makes no difference, and may stop these improper questions."

Bowing agreement, Wang Chen-po said sedately:

"Some of our younger men return to China, officer. All

of this day they have been at their devotions, praying and making vows. They are late, but they will soon arrive, and then the banquet will begin. Be patient."

Jimmy Wentworth sat silently for a full minute and then said quietly:

"And if they don't come?"

His Chinese friend was startled, and fought to keep from showing it.

"What then?" Wentworth insisted.

"Even now," Chen-po said slowly, "they are probably leaving the sacred room of the lilies."

Jimmy Wentworth ran his finger around the empty bowl. Here was a ceremony he did not know. Of course he understood that before acts of violence, or patriotism possibly resulting in death, it was necessary for men to contemplate some beautiful object—an idol, a flower, a finely-made mirror, anything—to divorce their minds of all evil. But there was a "room of lilies"?

"Never fear," muttered a Chinese to Chen-po; "he will ask about even our innermost customs. Do not tell him that our ten young men go with the white man-who-flies-in-air, son of Wang. Do not tell him that all ten have been trained, so pitifully little, to fly also. Lie now. Whatever comes into your head. Nevertheless"—to a companion, softly—"it is strange that the young men have not arrived after their ceremony of purification in the room of lilies. I, for one, do not like it."

Neither did Wentworth.

HE SAID LOUDLY:

"Say, Chen-po, I got to telephone my chief. I forgot all about it. Where's there a telephone, anyhow?"

"When once a man sits at the banquet of the Approaching Year," grumbled a Chinese across the table, understanding the loudly spoken, simple words, "he remains in his place until the last bowl is drunk."

"Nevertheless," said another, addressing Chen-po, "it is wise to remain at peace with the white men. Son of Wang, it will be permitted for you to take him where he wishes to go."

A chorus of grunts agreed.

"I will show you the way," Wang Chen-po stated coldly.

In the hallway, alone with his friend, Wentworth said swiftly:

"I don't like it one bit, Chen-po. Where's this room of the lilies? I want a look-see."

"No man," said young Wang, "is allowed to enter the room unless the devotees have completed their devotions. You ought to know that, James. Oh, well, have your own way. I'll show you where it is. Not many, even in the Four Families, know the location. Ready?"

They were on the street before Wentworth said, "I don't like it."

"Neither does anyone else," retorted Chen-po. "But custom is custom. Why, we'd all die before we violated the room of lilies. The Old Men are worried, but you know it's improper to show it, just as my father can't show sorrow because Wang Hi'tze is dead. You—don't fool me, Jimmy—you think something's happened to the young men? You suspect the Japanese?"

"I wish I knew what to suspect," Wentworth said honestly, as they hurried along. "Harrington had a china lily blossom in his buttonhole, you know—"

"Sure. Some of the young men probably gave it to him for luck."

"Was he at the room of lilies?"

"Hanged if I know, Jimmy. Might have been. It's up this street, then right turn on the alley. Fourth house. Second floor. Room in the rear. You go through one room, and another door's behind a long silken hanging. No window. Just a skylight. That's kept open so the men can look up at the Vault of Heaven as they pray. Then—"

"I'm going on alone," Wentworth said. "You, Chen-po, go to the priests' house just below the cathedral. Tell Father Vincente I asked you to use the phone. Call Dunand. I want men at each end of the alley. He'll know how many. They are to arrest whoever they see. Make that plain, Chen-po! Anyone they see!"

Chen-po demurred uneasily.

"If there's a rumpus, Jimmy, the Old Men will raise the devil with me."

"If there's a mess," said Wentworth, "you'll be glad you violated every proper custom, old man!"

Chen-po put a hand on Wentworth's uniform.

"The young men are apt to kill you if you go into the room of lilies. They're armed. Let me go with you. Sometimes they work themselves up into a fervor, Jimmy. I ought to be there."

"I'm only taking a long chance that anything's wrong," Wentworth said. "But Wang Hi'tze was shot, Harrington was strangled, and the young men are mixed up in the same venture. It's my job to be suspicious. And I'm going to do my job. Please, Chen-po; get going!"

"And have you knifed by a fervent patriot, all worked

up by contemplation of the sacred lilies and the blue Vault of Heaven."

"We'll see," said the sergeant of detectives. "Anyhow, do as I said. And in a hurry. I'm going to have a look-see at this room of lilies, and you can't talk me out of it."

4

THE ROOM OF DEATH

LIKE THE PRINCIPAL streets of Chinatown, the cross
street was deserted also. The smaller shops, catering only to
Chinese, were closed and shuttered. Inside, women awaited
the return of their masters, after the heads of the household had eaten and celebrated their fill. All was silent, dark.

Wentworth marched along, as if on patrol, until he came
to the alley. Then he immediately slipped into a doorway,
taking note of the position of the fourth house. That was
the place Chen-po had told him. Fourth house, second
floor, room in the rear, entered through another room in
front of it. No window, but a skylight.

In the room ten young brave Chinese, who had spent
the day in contemplation, and in arousing one another to
the deeds they must do when they crossed the ocean and
would fight for their country.

Had the Japanese learned of this meeting-place? Had
the brown men arrived already, and, possibly through the
skylight, potted the Chinese? It was the only thing to
suppose. If this were the case, Harrington's murder was
for the same reason, as everyone believed at Headquarters.

Wentworth, waiting in the doorway to give Chen-po
a chance to telephone, knew how slim his own doubtful

case was—a case depending upon bits of Chinese jute and the owner of the Silver Dollar dive. There was a man they must take down to Headquarters and question. Perhaps uselessly. The Silver Dollar proprietor would fear Kong Gai more than the police.

Wentworth thought, "Why can't I accept the obvious solution of these crimes? Am I going daffy about Kong Gai? Even the Wangs didn't mention him. I've got to keep a clear head. Just because I've found Kong Gai in almost every Chinatown crime is no reason why he's in this! Why, Harrington might have gambled away his twenty thousand, and the tongs had him murdered! Hi'tze might have been murdered for any one of a hundred reasons. Another tong might have finished him. No, that's out. Not on New Year's Eve. It's a mess. Just the same, I'm going to look inside this room in a minute."

From doorway to cellar, from cellar to behind low steps, and then to another doorway, Wentworth worked along the street. Fourth house. The next one. Black doorway. Was the door barred? Chen-po hadn't said so. Was it watched? Had the Four Families set 'binder guards? Or did they feel secure, believing no one knew the location of the room of the lilies? Did—here was the one chance!—did anyone else watch the doorway to the fourth house?

In the black, empty street, Wentworth lay down and wriggled ahead like a snake. Once a button scraped on cement, and he lay very still, hand ready to go to his gun. All was silent as the grave.

Swiftly he leaped to his feet, and was inside the fourth house. The door had swung open on well-oiled hinges, noiselessly. Wentworth shut it carefully behind him in the dark, and then drew his gun.

If the Chinese inside the room of the lilies ran amuck, he must depend on his uniform to save him.

His groping hands found the banister, and he made his slow, cautious way to the second floor. More than once he wished for his electric torch, or even a match. The stairs creaked and groaned, and Wentworth wondered that no one opened a door to see what was taking place.

The house was as quiet as death.

Patiently the sergeant of detectives slid along beside the wall until he reached the very end of the hallway. His fingers found a doorknob, and he turned it. The room inside was empty of everything save one teakwood stand, on which a tiny lamp burned with sickly yellow flame. The room was close, suffocatingly close. It, like the room he expected to find behind it, was lighted only by a skylight above, which was a few inches open.

Jimmy Wentworth saw the silken hanging, and pushed it aside. He tried the knob; it turned, but the door did not open. He put his shoulder against it, increasing the pressure.

Baffled, he did the only possible thing: called out in Chinese:

"Oh, young men! The banquet of the Approaching Year is waiting for you! I will make many devotions tomorrow for summoning you, but the Old Men demand your presence. Open the door."

Silence.

Was the door of steel? If so, Wentworth could never break through, and the one plan he intended would be impossible, if anything were wrong in the room. It was entirely possible that the men inside, earlier, had departed for the Four Families tong chambers. Well, he had come this far; he might as well find out.

Wentworth slid his gun into its holster, backed away a half-pace, and then smashed elbow and shoulder at the door. A panel splintered and gave; Wentworth hammered through it. Automatically he did as he was trained; ran his hand down toward the inner knob.

The key was still in the lock!

In an instant Wentworth turned it, and opened the door.

For almost a full minute he stared inside, unable to determine anything in the dark chamber, unable to recognize anything save the overpowering odor of china lilies. The scent half dizzied him, seemed to burn through his eyes and into his brain.

Before the minute was over Wentworth went to the far door, and opened it also; a gusty breath of air from the black house almost blew out the feebly flickering rape seed oil lantern. Wentworth picked it up, protecting it with his other hand, and then again looked into the last room.

He stood as still as the ten bodies he now saw on the floor.

Ten dead Chinese! The young men of the Four Families huddled on the floor as if asleep. On a stand was a lamp, burned out. Ranged around the room were ten enormous pots, blue Canton ware, filled with drooping china lilies, their white and yellow petals nodding as if they, too, were slowly dying.

WENTWORTH PUT DOWN the lamp on the floor beside one of the Chinese. The man was dead. Wentworth knew that before he lifted a lax hand, the muscles not yet stiffened. There was even a faint warmth in the body.

Again the sense of nausea, not as strong as before, made Wentworth's head swim and his eyes burn. It was rather pleasant. Like being overpowered with delicious perfume, once you forgot the curious, Asiatic odor of the lilies.

Wentworth immediately looked for signs of food, which might have been poisoned. He found nothing at all. Had they partaken of poisonous liquor, or tea, before they had entered this chamber of death? Yet how peaceful each face was! A man poisoned did not look like this.

Each man in the room lay peacefully on the matting floor, as if he had gone to sleep—to death!—while at his contemplation of the china lilies, and the Vault of Heaven above....

And then Jimmy Wentworth looked up. There was the skylight. Was it so dusty that you couldn't see the sky? That would be wrong. Surely the Chinese were supposed to have a glimpse of the heavens, even if the presaged clouds had covered the sky at times. Slowly, high in the heavens, he made out the glitter of a distant star. As he stared, the bit of scintillating light almost hypnotized him; he was no longer cognizant of the intervening panes of glass.

Chen-po said that the only air came through the skylight. It was closed. Wentworth muttered: "Flowers're taken out of sick rooms in hospitals. What'd china lilies do, in a sealed room with ten men and a lamp? Make a man sick? I wish my own head'd quit spinnin'. Makes me drowsy. Hard to think."

His drooping eyes snapped open wide. "That's what killed 'em! What a fool I am. Either they forgot to open the skylight, or somebody closed it on 'em, and they died in their sleep without knowin' what happened. Killed by white and yellow flowers. Killed by accident, or… by design?"

Wentworth was almost willing, despite his excitement, to sit down. He knew how disastrous this would be, should the door close on him. But the odorous lilies continued to breathe out their Oriental perfume in the room of death, just as they must have done during the day; they sapped the vitality of the powerful young white man until he at last managed to force himself to leave the room and close the door behind him.

It was several minutes before Wentworth could think clearly. Then he wasted no more time. He reentered the deadly room, picked up the body of one of the Chinese, and, with it in his arms, strode shakily along the hall, keeping contact with the wall with an elbow.

His mind was made up now. Chen-po wouldn't fail him. At either end of the alley would be men from Headquarters. Good. Now he would learn whether the ten young Chinese had been murdered, or had merely died through curious accident. His head was still a little confused. He no longer wondered who had killed the Chinese, if this was the case. He did not think of the Japanese at all, nor of war across the Pacific, nor anything except the deadly Kong Gai, the Venomous One of Chinatown… who was the sort of fiend with a warped brain that would think of using white and yellow blossoms to commit murder.

If the china lilies were really deadly Wentworth did not know. There was only the testimony of his own senses. Yet ten men had died in the room of lilies, and died with smiles on their faces. Was it accidental, or another link in the chain, of which Wang Hi'tze and Harrington were other parts? Were the Japanese the forgers of the chain of death, or was it Kong Gai himself?

In another minute Wentworth felt he would know.

5

BROTHERS OF THE SNAKE

JIMMY WENTWORTH, PROPPING the slowly stiffening body of the dead young Chinese warrior against the wall, opened the front door an inch. First he breathed deep of the fresh night air, until his head completely cleared. Then he peered out.

The street was black as ever; black and silent.

Were Headquarters men at either end of the alley? If not, if Chen-po had failed in his telephoning, Wentworth might soon be in a difficult position. If they were, and his planning had been ridiculous and over cautious, he would soon be well laughed at. This bothered him as little as the possible absence of assistance.

He slipped the hand holding his gun under the Chinese's own right armpit, and used his left hand to further support the dead body. With the muzzle of the gun he pried the door open a full foot, and crouched in the protection of the Asiatic's form.

Wentworth began to cry out in nasal, whining Cantonese:

"Hai-ee! Air! I must have air! I am sick, very sick!"

A swift beam of light from an electric torch flitted to the doorway, illuminating the Chinese who seemed to be standing there. Then it winked out, leaving everything blacker than before.

Wentworth moaned loudly:

"Come, oh Four Families men! Here is life! Air! I… I will live!" Then, screaming piercingly, the Chinatown detective sergeant made the body of the Chinese tremble violently. "I die," he shrieked. "Air! Air! I die!"

Wentworth hoped this would not bring the Headquarters men. He had asked that they go after anyone they saw—men running in the alley. If only they would wait now!

He let the body of the Chinese fall in the doorway realistically, and darted back into the hall, leaving the door open.

Across the dark street, emerging from a cellarway, were black-clad figures. Not one or two, but a full half dozen. Slinking silken dressed 'binders, *bo' how doy,* all slipping toward the prone figure of the dead Chinese like evil ghosts. No curious honest Chinese, these!

The stabbing finger of light flicked out again, lighting on the crumpled body. Someone said, "A knife into him, brothers of the snake, and then we will go up and finish the others. Kong Gai was wise to have us watch, even if it was supposed the lilies would kill the fools after we closed the window of the ceiling while they prayed—"

Then feet were pounding down the alley. An American voice roared:

"Don't move, or we'll shoot!"

Only once the startled hatchetmen looked—up the alley, and down. Blue-coated figures, guns out, raced from both directions. Escape into their lair across the street was not possible. With one accord they rushed to the stairs of the house of death.

Wentworth's gun roared. A hatchetman dropped, screaming. Two others fell over him. A second time Jimmy fired, as the three remaining 'binders tried to leap past their companions, and then the Headquarters men had all six Chinese captured and disarmed.

"We saw the flashlight," said Haight of the riot squad. "Then it was easy. Th' yellin' put us on our toes, but we waited to see somebody, like your Chink friend insisted. What is it, Jimmy? Tong outbreak? The chief's waitin' for a report."

Wentworth said:

"Can't tell yet. You fellows wait here. Somebody'd better get the wagon for these 'binders. And I've got nine more Chinese upstairs. Dead."

"What? Did you get 'em?"

"Somebody else did," Jimmy said. "I'll be back in a few minutes. Can I borrow a flash?"

Wentworth hurried up to the room of death. He placed several of the teakwood stands together, and then carefully mounted to the skylight, smashing the glass. He managed to get his head and shoulders through the aperture, wondering if he would draw fire from anywhere, or if all the hatchetmen of Kong Gai assigned to this task had been watching across the street.

There was no shot. Wentworth was able to examine the dusty remains of the skylight sufficiently to find the marks of hands, of fingers. Good prints. Enough to hang the Chinese who had made them, provided they were the men captured by Headquarters. Jimmy took no chance that the skylight might be removed before the photographers could come. Instead of waiting, he took with him several of the larger pieces of glass, all well marked.

FINALLY THE HEADQUARTERS men marched their captives to the taxis waiting three blocks distant, just outside of Chinatown. The dead wagon was ordered. And at last Wentworth was back in Captain Dunand's office.

"Fingerprint 'em," the gray-haired captain of detectives grunted, after hearing his sergeant's story. "Maybe we can't hang 'em, but we'll try. And at th'worst we'll deport the lot!"

"First, let's search them," Wentworth suggested.

Even the wounded *bo' how doy* was handcuffed, after being given first aid. Detectives went about their task efficiently. From each neck a token-bag was removed. Every silken bag contained the likeness of a king cobra. Best of all, one of the Chinese had a short rope wound about his middle. A rope of Chinese jute. Yellow. Not whitish-gray Indian jute. Stiff jute. An assassin's rope.

Dr. Nye stammered:

"We found more pieces of that stuff, sergeant! That's the rope with which Harrington was bound!"

"What works one way might work another," Jimmy Wentworth said. "Think there's a chance of the stiff, bristly jute having removed any bits of fabric from Harrington's clothing?"

The Headquarters doctor said:

"A microscope will show! If not, a test for color will. We'll analyze!"

"Print 'em," growled Dunand, glaring at these 'binders who had killed a courageous white man about to go to defend their own country.

Wentworth's quick eyes told him something.

"Look at the hands of the wounded hatchetman, chief," he said softly. "No long nails! All the others have 'em, of course. He's the biggest and strongest of the lot. Powerful hands. He's the one who strangled Harrington after his mates bound the white man!"

Sure enough, the wounded 'binder had fingernails cut very short.

"I looked for indentations—cuts—on Harrington's neck," Wentworth told the captain. "Found none. That put me off. Made me suppose it really was a Japanese crime. 'Binders are proud of their long nails—"

Dunand muttered, "How about the Japanese that killed Wang Hi'tze, Jimmy?"

"Do any good to question him, sir?"

"Can't do it. He's a hophead, Jimmy. Bad one."

Jimmy Wentworth relaxed. The last link in the chain forged at last!

"If you'll keep the stuff away from him for a bit, chief, and then let him talk, with plenty of proper witnesses, he'll tell you that Kong Gai told him 'No more hop' unless he killed Wang Hi'tze. That's guessing. But you'll find out it's true."

"But why the murdering at all, sergeant?"

Every officer and detective in the room leaned forward.

"The best I can do," said Jimmy Wentworth, "is to tell you what little I know. Harrington was carrying a large sum of money. It happened to be twenty thousand dollars, but it might have been more. That was kept secret. Kong Gai has the money now, chief. He had plenty of time to plan the crimes. Everything pointed to murder done by Japanese, to prevent the aviator and his Chinese assistants from going to Shanghai. It's the sort of affair Kong Gai would figure up. He'd enjoy watching us run rings around ourselves, while he sat back and laughed! I think the money was at the bottom of the business, although Kong Gai loves to stir up trouble—to kill for the sake of killing. If—"

Dr. Nye came bustling over, his face shining.

"I've found it!" he cried. "Blyth doesn't mention it. Neither do some of the other authorities. But look here, in this book, captain! Read it! 'Narcissus poisoning!' No, not there, please. That's narcissin. Different poison altogether. See what it says? 'The perfume from a certain type of narcissus blossom, namely, the china lily, has been known to produce death when breathed for a considerable time in a closed room. No trace of the poison can be discovered after death.' And that's how the ten young Chinamen were killed!"

"That's how," said Wentworth.

"You knew it, Jimmy?" demanded Dunand.

"No, chief. I only knew when I went into the room I became sick. Doctor, does it tell how the poison works?"

"Why, yes, a little. 'The sensation of narcissus poisoning is said to be very pleasant in the early stages, and completely narcotizes the victim. It is never recognized as deadly until action on the part of the victim is too late.'"

"I missed the pleasant part," Wentworth said. "But the poor devils in the room of the lilies died smiling… now, I'll be off, chief. Got to take my chair at the Four Families banquet."

"Be a sad affair now, eh?"

WENTWORTH SAID, "IT would be a whole lot worse if we didn't have this prime collection of 'binders here, chief."

"They'll swing," said Dunand. "Thanks to you, sergeant."

Jimmy Wentworth wanted to hurry. A police car drove him to the door of the Four Families tong, and he went hastily inside. Wang Chen-po had returned. High, laughing Chinese voices, warmed with wine, fought with the shriek and clatter of the orchestra The air was heavy with cigarette smoke and the aroma of magnificently cooked food. The gay family banners flaunted themselves as before.

The chairs of the ten men were removed; in their places were ten gorgeously ornamented coffins. No food was placed on the plates intended for the young Chinese, nor on Wang Hi'tze's, but before each a taper burned with white and yellow flame. One china lily blossom, white and yellow also, lay in front of the candle.

Eyes may have flicked toward the young sergeant of detectives as he sat down, but no other sign of his presence was made, except when old Wang Yü said cheerfully, "Our guest must eat rapidly, for he is doubtless hungry. Since he departed on duty, he can be forgiven any discourteous intent."

Wentworth said loudly to Wang Chen-po:

"I'm certainly hungry."

"Don't be a fool," growled his friend. "Tell me, quickly: what happened, Jimmy? Anything?"

"How'd you know the ten are dead?"

"A Four Families hatchetman told us there were shots, Jim. Tell me!"

"Killed by Kong Gai. All of 'em. Kong Gai finished Wang Hi'tze. And Harrington."

"And?"

"We didn't come anywhere near Kong Gai. But we've got the others."

"You aren't fooling, Jimmy?"

"If we can't hang 'em, they'll be deported."

Wang Chen-po said only:

"Ah!" and then stood up. He walked quickly to the table where old Wang Yü sat between a rich Chinese merchant and the head of an American bank; then, dutifully, he bowed three times, and requested permission to speak.

"If your words are not important," snapped old Wang Yü, "I will beat you with my slipper when we return to our miserable house. What is it you would say?"

Every ear in the room—every Oriental ear—was listening.

"Those who killed the honorable and learned Wang Hi'tze have been caught, my father," said Chen-po.

"Is it so? And is that all you have to tell me?"

"Those who killed the ten young and brave men of the Four Families are also captured, honorable Elder Wang."

The room was as quiet now as the deadly chamber of lilies had been.

"That," said Wang Yü, "is swift vengeance for our tong. I bend my head before the justice of the gods. Who, oh son of mine, has captured these two-legged beasts of horror?"

"A white man, Elder Wang."

Voices buzzed once as the Chinese were unable to restrain their excitement, and then a glare from old Wang brought silence.

"So," he decided. "We are revenged. But, I ask"—he raised his cracked old voice—"is it proper that a man other than of the families of Wang, Ying, Yee, and G'oung bring our enemies to justice? I am of the opinion that it is not. Therefore, until that man, white or yellow, be a member of the Four Families tong, my head is bowed in shame. How much longer must it remain so?"

Wentworth realized that great praise was being given him by the distressed, unhappy tong, and then as the true meaning of Wang Yü's words became clear, his face became very pale. What an honor! Did Wang Yü really mean it? Would the other Chinese agree?

Three of the influential men of the tong, wordlessly, left their places, and shuffled to the image of Kuan Yin glittering in a corner. From the hands of the goddess they took a silken robe, into which pearls had been woven, and brought it to where Wentworth sat.

In Chinese one of the men said, as he slipped the beautiful strands over Wentworth's head, "Welcome, O newest brother of the Four Families! Your blood is ours. Our lives are yours. You are white, but now you are our brother nevertheless."

Applause rippled through the members of the tong.

Wentworth, very pleased and excited, knowing as he did that no other white man had ever been made a member of a Chinese tong, stammered—forgetfully—in pure Mandarin:

"*Ya' s'a'am.* Such a great honor for this miserable person—"

"*Hai-ee!*" shrilled a Chinese. "The gods speak through his lips! For he is speaking in our language, and he does not know a word of it!"

THE CRIMSON COFFIN

*While Monstrous Idols and the Cobra
Killers Watch, Kong Gai Concocts a Terrible
Trap for the "White Fool," Wentworth*

1

THE CAVERN OF THE SNAKE

THERE WAS NO sound in the underground chamber save the steady crackle of fire, although a full hundred yellow men were in the vaulted room far beneath the teeming streets of San Francisco's Chinatown. Black clad hatchetmen and highbinders fed the flames under a gigantic melting pot, six feet across, five feet deep, suspended by heavy chains from the great beams overhead. The thick gray smoke curled slowly to the ceiling, and, finding the vent, crawled out and up, higher and higher, to come out at last through a chimney above a Chinese restaurant—where smoke might rise at any hour without causing suspicion.

Until the flames sprang up brightly, it had been impossible to determine who and what was in this room deep below the city. Slowly, now, the fire began to make a muttering sound, and, as oil-soaked wood and prepared charcoal were added, the noise deepened, to a steady roar, like an approaching typhoon on the Yellow Sea. The contents of the melting pot began to liquefy, to change color, and gradually became a blood-red lake of metal as the heat increased.

It was possible at last for the Chinese to see the room clearly. Many of them had been here before, but the newer *bo' how doy*, imported killers smuggled across the Mexican border, had never seen this secret cavern. Ranged about the enormous room were strange, terrible idols, the gods of Abominations, the demons of Evil, the devils of the Lowest Hidden Hell. Monsters, these were; headless idols, painted figures of wood, some with seven arms, some with the bodies of women and the heads of animals, others, naked except for the forehead jewel of Sin, brandished weapons.

At one end of the chamber, where only one 'binder lurked, feeding a silver lamp which burned with a steady yellow flame, were two images more terrible than any of the other sculptured foulnesses. These were naked also.

At first glance the figure on the left seemed a Kuan Yin, a goddess of mercy, until the demoniac face was seen, until the objects in the female demon's hands were observed. In every one of the nine hands was a skull, small, but human. Skulls of babies, stolen and killed by these vengeful, terrible Asiatics in the performance of their horrible rites conducted in this very chamber."

If the carved figure of the female Object of Terror was horrible, that of the companion god to the right of a thin, gauzy crimson curtain was even more fear-inspiring. It was a god with broad face and heavy eyes, thick lips and double chin, betraying his Hindoo origin. His shaven pate was deeply wrinkled. The eyes were half closed. Across the monstrous belly were strings of precious stones, looped this way and that; the fiery red of rubies flashed defiance to deep blue sapphires; the soft hue of great round pearls changed to an ugly green because of the presence of harsh emeralds.

They dragged the old merchant to the melting pot

The hands of this god were pressed close to his breast, and he held close to his skin something green and black and gold—green with precious jades, black with teakwood, yellow with soft fine gold—something which seemed to wriggle and writhe in the uncanny light....

The terrible symbol of the Brotherhood of the Snake! The king cobra, emblem of Kong Gai!

Here was the secret place where the Cobra Men met, for which the police had searched long. A meeting place guarded by twenty ferocious 'binders, by steel doors, by passages which could be collapsed, by tunnels fifty feet below the surface. Here the venomous Kong Gai, director of all evil things, gave his orders, interviewed his slaves and hatchetmen, and tortured his victims. None of the victims ever lived to tell of this place, for all of them were dead.

No white man except the youthful sergeant of detectives in charge of the Chinatown detail, Jimmy Wentworth, born and raised in China by an *amah* who had herself once been the wife of a notorious Number One 'binder, could have explained all of the terrible things in this terrible room.

He would have known that the bright, lovely headdress hanging on a wall was not a bridal crown at all, but an implement of torture, to be placed on the head of some unfaithful Flower Girl. He would have known that inside the crown of silk and jewels was a poison which would slowly burn through skin, and bring agony of death to the frightened brain beneath. A secret poison, brewed from strange herbs found only in the far bleak Tibetan hills. He would have known this for instead of the Six Gems of Good Fortune on the head-dress, there were only five. The Jewel of Constancy was missing. By such small matters did Detective Sergeant Wentworth run to earth the awful crimes directed by Kong Gai.

He could have told the purpose of almost every deadly object in the room, the reason for the odd-shaped bottles, the types of murders to be committed by the differently shaped knives, some of which had bone handles, some lacquered wood, some metal. And he could have instantly explained—with a cold heart, had he been there as prisoner—the purpose of the enormous melting pot, in which the liquefied metal was now bright like the red of a sunset.

EVERY EYE IN the room watched the fire, since the elevated, chain-held pot was too high to look inside. Every hatchetman and spy and brewer of drugs and seller of opium knew that first the metal must turn to gold hue, and then the gold must whiten until it almost blinded a man to see it, before the entertainment of the evening could begin.

As the hatchetmen continued to feed the raving flames, the room became hotter and hotter. Here and there an evil-faced 'binder opened the neck of his high-buttoned black silk jacket. Bottles of fiery *ng ki po* which had never paid any government tax circulated freely.

Excited by the presence of men, and warmed by the ever increasing heat, cobras in a wire mesh cage began to twist about. With outstretched hood a giant king cobra reared high, and each of the Snake Brotherhood muttered a prayer, not for long life and fortune, but that they might serve the Cobra and Kong Gai faithfully, and kill at least their two score of men before they themselves died and went to the After-world for the promised reward of opium and women.

Suddenly, apparently from behind the gauzy silken curtain, a high sweet voice cut through the rumble of flames:

"It grows warm, brothers!"

"It grows warm, O mighty and powerful Kong Gai," cried the hundred men of the Evil Brotherhood.

"Shall we be entertained while we wait?"

"We wish what Kong Gai wishes!"

The beautiful voice announced cheerfully, "Good, brothers. Let us be amused."

Almost at once the strings of a snake-bellied *san-h'in* were struck, and a wailing flute accompanied the jangling minor notes of the Chinese guitar.

All knew that the Evil One himself was behind the gauze curtain. None was able really to see the man who owned their lives. The little lamp burning between the two dread images was able to show a dark shape behind the crimson gauze, but nothing more. None of the hatchetmen could observe the features of their master.

Somewhere behind the silken hanging on the right—a heavy covering painted with the symbol of the snake—a drum began to roll, softly at first, but soon becoming louder than the sound of the ever-fed fire. Five times the drum gave its summons, and at the fifth beat the curtain on the right was drawn aside. Here several lamps glowed, and the hatchetmen and 'binders saw a Flower Girl standing. She swayed as if she were about to fall, and then advanced into the room with hesitating steps.

The men sat with tight lips. Never had they seen such a lovely woman. How good was Kong Gai, to give them this vision of beauty!

The Flower Girl's sad, frightened eyes stared straight forward; then, at a quick word from Kong Gai, her heels tapped sharply on the floor with a sort of savage energy, and she bent forward in a deep graceful bow. Quickly she started her curious dance, her white silk jacket and dead-white painted mask of a face like something strangely pure in this chamber of evil.

Her fan opened, and the wailing music ceased.

She began to talk in sing-song, sadly, tenderly. As she chanted her Chinese tuneless song, her thumbs turned inward and rising slowly to her forehead without touching it—the Oriental gesture of grief—she began to move very slowly toward the two terrible images, between which was the crimson curtain leading to Kong Gai. Her song was simple; she told the ancient Asiatic love story, of how a girl first saw many things—birds and animals and flowers and the blue sky—but when she finally met her lord, she became blind, and saw nothing save his honorable face.

Her voice trembled. Her eyes were tight shut. She

seemed to be groping forward in the pitiful fashion of the blind.

The flute uttered a piercing, long note.

THE MEN MURMURED words of praise, and then Kong Gai's lovely voice came to them again:

"Poorly done," said Kong Gai. "She is the least of my Flower Maidens."

The assemblage screamed instantly, "Poorly done!" in agreement. "An insult to our Great One!"

"And," went on the King Cobra, "it would not be wise to allow her to repeat what she has seen here, brothers." He was silent, and then said, "O Mu'y Yee, you have four killings to your credit. Will you make it five?"

Only once more did the Flower Girl sway. Before she could come erect, Mu'y Yee had thrust his heavy blade expertly between her shoulders, and the white clad figure slipped to the floor.

"I have killed five, thanks to the Powerful and Mighty Kong Gai," shouted the 'binder. "I am your slave, Kong Gai! For ever and ever, through the Nine Worlds of Torment, I am your servant!"

"Good," said the King Cobra suavely. "Now you have not only had entertainment, and seen the very least of my maidens, but you have added one to your reckoning of kill-ings. It was as a reward, Mu'y Yee, for having so expertly executed the blind nut vendor who said that I am a lesser person than the god of Hell. And now, Mu'y Yee, look in the great pot and tell me what you see."

As simply as that did Kong Gai dismiss the casual murder of the dancing girl. A pair of hatchetmen had already dragged the little dead body out of sight, and she was already forgotten. The Snake Brotherhood killed for the sake of killing. They were as murderous as their master, but less cunning. Kong Gai killed for the love of killing also, but generally he had a reason.

The Flower Girl had really been murdered because Kong Gai had seen her look through the silken hangings of her room high above Chinatown; look out into the street and put her hand to her breast when she saw a handsome young Chinese walking along.

Mu'y Yee pulled a teakwood stand near the fire and stood on it. Shielding his face from the heat, he glanced inside.

"The gold has turned to white, O Kong Gai," shouted the 'binder. "The inside of the pot appears like the silver face of the full moon."

"Then," said Kong Gai, from behind his masking crimson curtain, "first bring the crimson coffin, brothers, and when it is here bring the honored and respected merchant Teng Ma, and we will possibly have some better entertainment, which will bring fame to the Men of the Snake."

Wiping perspiration from their lean yellow faces, several of the hatchetmen hastened to obey the commands of their master. All sniffed blood and death, and sinister smiles played about the thin lips of the deadly killers of Kong Gai. What was about to happen to the merchant, Teng Ma, all were able to guess… but why the sacred crimson coffin? Was it a jest to make the dying hours of the merchant more horrible?

None save Kong Gai 'himself knew the reason for bringing the coffin. Not even Jimmy Wentworth, had he been there as victim, would have understood it, for all his knowledge of the savage ways of the Chinese killers.

2

THE MYSTERY OF THE PALE LILY

IT WAS EVER Kong Gai's way to play with a captive, to extract, for himself and his 'binders, the last fragment of enjoyment from a man's torture. And so, when the merchant Teng Ma had been brought to the terrible underground chamber, the leader of the Cobra Men said:

"It is an honor to have you here, Teng Ma. You look well. *K'u chuk, kau' si sap 'ng soi mo siu yat, yat!* Surely you are not a day over forty-five! Does he not look young, O brothers?"

"*K'u'i pu yeung san t'ai!*" howled a gleeful 'binder. "He takes good care of himself."

The old merchant, in his late sixties, bowed his head.

"It is the night of our family dinner, Kong Gai," he said wearily. "Tell me what I can do for you, and it will be done even before I sit at table."

"They wait for you?" asked Kong Gai from behind his curtain, as if he did not know it already.

"They wait for me," agreed Teng Ma sadly. "My sons and my sons' sons."

"It is good to have many male children. Then…"

Kong Gai did not finish, but Teng Ma knew what was meant. It was as if Kong Gai had said, "Then you will have many to worship your memory when you are dead."

The old merchant's eyes were glued to the waving crimson curtain. He had already seen the terrible caldron, and sweat was bursting from his forehead. But he managed to say quietly, "I have always been a faithful man, Kong Gai. Whatever you have asked, I have granted. What can I do now?"

The terrific heat of the room seemed to send Kong Gai's always high voice to an even higher pitch. He sang out, "He asks what he can do, brothers! It is not what he can do, but what he has done already!"

Teng Ma's old heart missed a beat, and cold began to creep up his thin legs, to unhinge the joints of his knees.

His voice cracked as he repeated miserably, "I have always done your wishes, O Kong Gai, because you hid my second grandson from the police when he sold—oh, sorrow to the honor of my family!—when he sold opium—"

Kong Gai shrilled, "Honor! *A-ee!* Is it a disgrace to sell the juice of the poppy? *I* sell it, Teng Ma! Am *I* a dishonorable man?"

"You are a great Person," said the bewildered, unhappy Chinese merchant. "What you do is different from what I, a miserable man, dare do. I meant no harm, Kong Gai, in what I said."

"I am very glad to hear it," said King Gai soothingly. "You are forgiven, Teng Ma."

"Then I can go?"

A 'binder laughed.

"Of course you can go," the King Cobra told him. "Just as soon as you tell me that you did not inform your oldest son that I am the one who stole the white woman two years ago."

"I did not tell him," said Teng Ma slowly.

"How unfortunate! When I asked your son, Teng Li, where he obtained the information he said, after proper hesitation, that it came from you. Now, since he had lied, I must punish him. You, naturally, may depart in peace."

Old Teng Ma's head drooped to his chest. The roar of the flames in his ears was nothing compared to the roar in his head. His old mind went back almost two years… the white woman who had visited his bazaar, looking for a white jade ring. A white girl with skin like the precious colorless gem; as smooth and lovely and pale. A girl with hair like the soft, pure gold of the ring in which the jade had been set.

Teng Ma remembered clearly what happened. While the girl—he learned later that her name was Mary Heath— was looking at Teng Ma's gems three men in black slipped into the shop. They said to Teng Ma, "Our Master has told us to tell you that he will now collect the debt you owe him for protecting your second grandson from the police," and went on to explain that Kong Gai had seen the Pale Lily and desired her, and that Teng Ma must show them a hiding place in the bazaar….

They had gagged the girl named Mary Heath then and there, and on the police records in the Hall of Justice was the simple statement:

Mary Heath, 22. Missing.

When Wentworth had been assigned to the Chinatown squad he was told nothing of the case, for the wily Kong Gai had led the police far from the lanterned streets and tiled roofs of the Asiatic district, and the case of Mary Heath was one of the unsolved, clewless mysteries....

Teng Ma remembered all this.

He said gravely, "Kong Gai, what you say is true. I am an old man. When I explained my life to my oldest son I told him of the woman. The Great Book says, 'To an Oldest Son everything must be told before death.' I told him. He will tell no one until he, too, is an old man. Your secret is safe with the family of Teng. No harm has been done. In your way of Honor, show mercy to an old man who wishes only to serve you."

KONG GAI SAID thoughtfully, "You see what you see, Teng Ma. What do you see?"

"I see flame and fire, Kong Gai."

The Venomous One showed his claws for the first time. "You know what it means?" he demanded.

Teng Ma bowed his head. "My crime is not sufficient to merit such punishment," he pleaded. "You would not destroy every inch of my body, so it can never be returned to the shadow of the Great Wall."

"What else do you see?"

Teng Ma stared about the terrible room, and at last his eyes lit; he had seen a great coffin. A marvelous coffin, such as only the Respected Dead can hope to obtain. A coffin of heavy teakwood, lacquered in crimson, the color of fire and blood. A coffin good enough for an emperor.

"You are good to an old man," said Teng Ma, since he knew now that he would never escape alive. "My family will gladly pay whatever the coffin is worth. And what was Teng Ma can be sent to China honorably. I am an old man, Kong Gai. If my death will please you, I am willing to die."

Kong Gai must have been smiling as he said, "Well, brothers, it pleases me that Teng Ma is happy, but I am wondering how he gained his reputation as a wise man! He thinks"—Kong Gai's voice changed, and now it rasped horribly—"he thinks we are going to waste a fine coffin on him! *Hai-ya!* Shall I tell him what we are going to do, brothers?"

"Tell him! Tell him!" the Snake Men urged, since they themselves did not know.

Teng Ma began to pray as Kong Gai spoke.

"It is a plan worthy of me," said the King Cobra. "Firstly, old man, we put you in the caldron, which has not had blood for a long time! Then no one will ever need worry about finding you! I only wish that you were the fool white policeman who has luckily been able to bother me a little." And how Kong Gai would have liked to hurl Wentworth into that pot of boiling metal! "Then, when you, and your son also, can never tell what you know, a letter goes to the family of the dead girl.

"It will say, 'We can tell you where your child is.' Just that; nothing more. We arrange to tell, and to receive payment. We say she is alive. We demand much gold. And finally we deliver her, or say where she can be found. She is dead. We say we feared to return her alive, lest she tell who killed her, who kept her as a Flower Girl. And then we lay the trail to the door of your oldest son, O Teng Ma, and we have it seem that he, and you, because of the shame on your head, have killed yourself; There will be a great wailing in the house of Teng!"

Teng Ma, knowing the worst, raised his head.

"You cannot make one dead for two years appear as if but recently killed," he said.

"I knew you heard too much," screamed Kong Gai. "So you know she died two years ago because she hated me? *Hai!* That is true, but such is my power that all will believe she died only today!"

The Snake Men began to whisper together. Their master was a veritable god of the Underworld, to preserve the dead.

Teng Ma wanted only to die as soon as possible. And so he shouted, "You lie, Kong Gai!"

"Show him," the voice behind the curtain ordered. "Bring lights! Open the coffin, brothers! *Hai-ee!* Not in the usual manner, brothers! Care, care! Open it as the white man opens a coffin, from the side! Do not ask me why, but do as I say… that is how to do it, brothers!"

Lamps cast a white glow. Hatchetmen slowly lifted the side of the great crimson coffin, and, dressed all in immaculate white, the assemblage saw the lovely girl inside. The 'binders gasped, for the beautiful body seemed alive.

"She has been dead for two years," announced Kong Gai from behind his crimson curtain. "If I wished," he added, as a new thought struck him, "I could bring her to life, such is my power. But that would not be my way, for then I would be delivering to her family what they would really be paying for. I will deliver her dead body, with a knife hole in it supposed to have been made by you and your son, Teng Ma, and disgrace will come to you, and gold to me! And"—more gleefully than ever—"since the trail leads to Chinatown, the young white fool will follow it…"

The Cobra Men began to whisper again. They had seen their numbers depleted by the "young white fool"—Jimmy

Wentworth—and were none too anxious to match wits with him again.

"Do not worry," roared Kong Gai, displeased. "I say he will follow it, but for a very short time, brothers! The crimson coffin itself is going to kill him, for it will do to him what will bring him to us, and then we will have a torture that will be a torture, for his body is strong and he will last a long time!

"Now we have talked enough! Have you prayed, Teng Ma, to the gods who will not help you?"

"I have prayed that the pigs will some day eat your body," retorted the valorous old merchant.

Kong Gai refused to become angry. His voice was very sweet as he said, "Let me see who shall have the honor… *ae-ee!* Yes! It shall go to L'uk Wong, Ko Mi Fi, and Gee Ling, who first seized the white girl in the bazaar of Teng Ma. Yes, the honor is theirs. Brothers, the great pot is waiting for the bones of Teng Ma! Do not disappoint the fiery liquid a moment more!"

THE THREE 'BINDERS leaped up, and, while others brought stands and stools and ranged them close to the melting pot, they dragged the old merchant forward. It took only an instant to lift his spare frame high. The lava of the caldron roared to receive him, and spattered flakes of flame to the ceiling as his body was dropped into the pot. A whirling fountain of many colors sprang high, bursting a little over the edge; it subsided quickly, with a terrible hissing noise, and then the only sounds in the chamber were the quick breathing of the Killers of the Snake and the steady muttering of the fire.

The wide eyes of the dead girl stared straight forward, clear, blue as the sky so far above this chamber of horror.

"Let the fire go out," ordered Kong Gai. "Have I given you enjoyment, brothers? Was it fun for you all?"

"Great is Kong Gai! And will we soon feed the young white fool of a policeman to the pot?"

"Inch by inch," screamed the King Cobra. "We will soon bring him where he will be ours, brothers, this man who dares set himself against me! We will lay a shrewd, clever trail, and he will follow it, and soon we will all be in this room again, and inch by inch we will torture the Man in Blue until he pleads for the death we will withhold as long as possible! He will come by himself, brothers, and deliver himself to our hands when he follows the trail to punish the people who caught and killed the white girl—"

"Will he not be satisfied to arrest some of the family of Teng?"

"Wait," laughed the King Cobra. "Soon you will see. He is a fool, but in the glare of the obvious he will not be blinded to what he thinks is the truth. I have planned carefully, brothers, to give us gold and vengeance. *Hai!* Let us do honor to our god before we depart!"

A flute began to wail, and the live king cobras in their cage began to rear up and weave back and forth. The lamp before the evil god near the crimson curtain was sprinkled with something which made it send up brilliant red sparks. One by one the Brothers of the Snake, with undulations of their hands like the action of the cobra, crept up to the god and bowed their heads to the floor.

When every head was low, the curtain parted a moment, and the face of Kong Gai was visible. But only the lovely sightless blue eyes of the dead girl was looking at the features of the Evil One.

3

THE HIDDEN, SECRET THINGS

JIMMY WENTWORTH KNEW that it must have been something out of the ordinary for his captain of detectives to have ordered him to wait at the call box until an automobile from Headquarters would arrive and take him back to the Hall of Justice. As the youthful sergeant of detectives in charge of the Chinatown detail waited, he did his best to figure out what it might be.

So far as he knew—and he knew a good deal—all was peaceful in the Asiatic district. The tongs were engaged in their own affairs. There had been no greater thievery than the stealing of a few li-chi nuts by Chinese urchins; there had been nothing nearer combat than the customary argument between old men as to which would live longer, and which had the greater number of grandchildren to worship their memories.

Nor could the driver of the police car enlighten him. All that Wentworth learned on the short ride was that Captain Dunand evidently was excited about something. Obviously it had something to do about Chinatown, for the gray-haired captain had sent down to the Chinatown squad room for a map.

Dunand enlightened him, swiftly, when Wentworth, in patrolman's blue, stepped inside the captain's office.

"How much do you know about the disappearance of Mary Heath?" Dunand snapped.

"It was before I was in the Department, sir," Wentworth told him. "There isn't anything in the records. I seem to remember a report that she was supposed to have gone downtown shopping for a present for someone and that was the last anybody ever heard—"

"Correct. A couple of reports also show that she was in some antique shop somewhere in the Mission. The owner of the place was picked up last year as a seller of drugs, but we didn't get a conviction. He closed up shop after that."

Wentworth's eyes brightened, although his lean, brown face remained expressionless.

"I said," Dunand growled, "that the fellow in the second hand shop was a dope peddler—"

"And you sent for me," Jimmy Wentworth grinned. "I've already put two and two together, sir. Now if you'll tell me why the trail leads to Chinatown, to Kong Gai, I'll go to work."

"It leads to Chinatown all right, but not to Kong Gai, Jimmy. Here. Read this!"

The note was short:

> We can give you information regarding the whereabouts of Mary Heath. Insert advertisement in either morning paper, saying LEAVING CITY TODAY and signing this AAA.

"Now take a look at this one, sent to Daniel Heath two days after he put the personal advertisement in the columns of the *Chronicle*."

Mary Heath is alive. If she were not sick we would not be willing to return her to you. However, she is no longer of any value. If you place a value on her, and that value is exactly $25,000, we will make arrangements. We warn you that she is not well, And we do not dare send her to a hospital. Insert advertisement in the newspaper, saying COME HOME and signing this MOTHER.

Jimmy Wentworth said quietly, "Of course the girl is dead, chief. You can see how that's being led up to. Now, where does the trail enter Chinatown, aside from the first feeble clue? Those notes weren't written by a Chinese, unless by a very educated one."

"Daniel Heath didn't come to us until he received the third note," said Dunand. "Not that either of the first two would have helped us much. Here's number three, and it ought to be of assistance."

Mary Heath died this morning. Go to the store in China-town operated by Teng Ma, and you will be told where she is buried. We still demand $25,000 for the return of her body. We do not expect payment until you have recovered your daughter. After that, we will tell you when and how to make payment. If it is not done, you yourself will disappear in the same manner as Mary. Come to the shop of Teng Ma ALONE and the information will be furnished you.

"Has Mr. Heath gone?" Wentworth demanded.

"He's waiting here," Dunand answered. "Do you advise him to go, lad?"

Wentworth said softly, "Why not? The only thing about

Teng Ma I've ever heard is that he had a grandson who was mixed up in selling hop. The old Chinese is probably acting as a go-between—for Kong Gai."

"Why Kong Gai?"

WENTWORTH SLID LOWER in his chair. He said, "Don't say anything of this to Mr. Heath, sir, but I've heard stories about a Pale Lily in Kong Gai's chambers. I didn't do anything about it, firstly, because a Pale Lily might be a half-caste, or a Flower Girl from one of the seaport towns in China, and secondly because I couldn't find Kong Gai's quarters even if I tried. The talk about the Pale Lily stopped just a week or so after I was assigned to Chinatown.

"Next, Teng Ma and his oldest son are supposed to have gone up-State on business, and that doesn't fool the rest of the Chinese. A man and his oldest son never go anywhere at the same time. Therefore, one or both are either being held by someone, or are dead.

"Thirdly, this thing doesn't smell right to me. Excepting, of course, that Chinese would pay any price to recover a missing body so it can be shipped to consecrated ground in China. But that's done only for men—"

"The Chinese know we white people think a great deal about our women—"

"True. It's funny, chief. With the girl dead, I don't see why I shouldn't stick my nose into the affair. Even if Mr. Heath doesn't recover the body, little is lost. I tell you I don't like it. What's behind it? Why return a dead body? Just for money? Too dangerous! Looks to me as if someone's so sure his tracks are covered that he's willing to accept twenty-five thousand as a gift. That's part of it, but what does the rest mean?"

"Well? Shoot, Jimmy!"

Wentworth said, "I wish I knew, sir. But—"

The telephone jangled; Dunand answered the summons, and then said, "Seattle police wire that two bodies are being shipped to China on an Empress boat, Jimmy, They want to know if we have criminal records on 'em. They say it's a clear case of an honor suicide, and that the dead men are Teng Ma and his son, Teng Something-or-other, and that a note was found on the old man saying that he regretted an evil deed. Two rings and a woman's wrist watch engraved on the inside with the single initial 'H' were found on the younger man…"

"Planted," said Wentworth grimly. "The more I hear, the less I like this, chief. Teng Ma and his son were murdered, I believe. But, again, why? Why in Seattle? Why not here? What took the two north, traveling together like that? It isn't proper Chinese custom! I've got to learn more, sir! Let's have Mr. Heath go to Teng's shop and see what happens—"

"And if something does happen—to him—then where are we?" Dunand frowned, and added, "Suppose Heath himself is held for ransom by this fiend?"

"He isn't going," Wentworth explained. "I'm going to send Cassion from my squad. He knows a few words of Chinese, and he's about Heath's probable age—around fifty. He'll be Heath. Then we'll see what he's told. There's something behind this I don't understand, and if you hadn't told me about the only clue leading to a second hand shop—far from Chinatown!—which was operated by a drug seller, who disappeared afterward, I wouldn't be excited about it. But drugs mean opium, and opium means

Kong Gai, and Kong Gai always works in horrible, devious ways. Have I your permission to send Detective Cassion to the shop, as if he were Daniel Heath?"

"Go ahead," Dunand grunted. "I can't make head nor tail of this, Jimmy!"

"Neither can I," said the Chinatown detective sergeant, "and that's why I'm hopeful that a clue can be picked up. In Chinese crime, sir, we always disregard the obvious, and look for the hidden, secret things."

"I wonder if Kong Gai realizes you think like a Chinaman, lad!"

Wentworth picked up the telephone, and told the desk sergeant, "Please send Detective Cassion to Captain Dunand's office." Then he said, "It goes deeper than that, chief. I try to think like a Chinese, but back of that I make white man deductions. I've just been lucky, sir."

Dunand smiled without humor.

"Find out whatever is back of this thing, Jimmy, and I won't call it luck!"

"I'll try," said Jimmy Wentworth. His swift, agile mind was darting this way and that, trying to piece together the curious, unexplainable parts of the strange puzzle. And he was convinced—as Kong Gai felt no "young fool of a policeman" would ever be convinced—that the obvious trail leading to the door of the Family of Teng was a false one, although as yet he had little reason except the clue of the opium-seller and the gossip about a Pale Lily, that at the end of the path it might be possible to discover the sinister, unknown figure of the terrible Kong Gai, the Vengeful One.

4

AT THE HOUR OF THE RAT

IN LESS THAN an hour Detective Cassion returned, after having first started in the direction of Heath's home, and then doubling back to the Hall of Justice below China-town. He made his report to Dunand and Wentworth:

"The shop was empty when I got there. I waited, and a Chinaman came out from a back room. He asked me what I wanted to buy, and I said something about not being sure if I was in the right place, but that my name was Daniel Heath....

"Then the Chinese stared at me, and said, 'How I know?' and I handed him the pocketbook Heath lent me. That satisfied him. He said, 'Tomorrow morning, early, you go cemetery for Chinese. You go Row Five, Lot Six. It marked in American numbers, like all cemetery—'"

"He said 'cemetery'?" asked Wentworth.

Nodding, Cassion said, "Yes, Sergeant. He spoke slowly, in pidgin English. I spoke to him very rapidly, and he had no trouble in following me. He probably could have spoken as well as any white man."

"Go ahead."

"Then he explained that during the night this grave

would be opened, and all I would need to do was to help myself.

"I am to bring a hearse, or police, or anything I want—"

"He said 'police,' did he?" Jimmy wanted to know.

"Said it a couple of times," the detective agreed. "He made the point that I need not be afraid, going to a lonely cemetery before six in the morning, and that I could have as much of a guard as I wanted."

Dunand pounded on the desk. "Wait until those ghouls open the grave, boys! We'll give 'em a surprise they won't forget!"

"The grave will be opened by digger-coolies," Wentworth said, "men who are half-witted. Nobody else would do it—not even a killer. It's Chinese custom. All the coolies would say is that somebody they wouldn't have sense enough to describe had paid them to open the grave at the Hour of the Rat, when the spirit of the dead is sleeping. That's out, sir. Now"—to Cassion—"how about paying the money?"

"I'm to be told that later, apparently. All the Chinese said was, 'We already tell about payment. You wait. We say when and where.'"

"That's when we grab somebody," Dunand snapped.

Wentworth wasn't sure their task would be so simple.

"If Kong Gai's back of this, chief, I wouldn't bank on that. There's ways and ways of paying ransom. But that all comes later. However, Cassion, still supposed to be Heath, and a hearse, and some of us from the department, will certainly go out to the cemetery—"

"Will Kong Gai trap you there, Jimmy?"

"With a dozen men from the riot squad along? Not

Kong Gai! He'll get me when I'm alone, and when it's safe. He'll get me in some terrible, strange way. If he only wanted to kill me, chief, he could do it any hour of the day. But he'd lose face if he did it that way. He's got to entice me with a deep, hidden plan… like… like this one," Jimmy Wentworth ended, grinning wryly.

"I DON'T LIKE it," Dunand growled. "You all alone in Chinatown, out of sight of the other patrolmen—"

"Sometimes I don't care for it myself, chief. When I see a couple of 'binders shuffle past, hands in their sleeves. But I tell myself that Kong Gai wants to kill me himself—"

"What's to prevent four or five hatchetmen from knocking you on the head, and taking you to Kong Gai?"

"They've learned that I walk down the middle of the sidewalk, sir. That I never run into a crowd, even when it looks like a free-for-all fight. That I do not stand in doorways. It'd take a fight to get me, and I might be killed then and there. That isn't what Kong Gai intends. To keep his standing with his 'binders, he must kill me himself. The 'binders mustn't do it; give them too much 'honor.' They could catch me for him, but not kill me. It's hard to explain, but that's the way it is. And I'll say this much right now; duty or no duty, if ransom is to be paid in some out-of-the-way place, by a single man, Jimmy Wentworth will be a long way off, unless he has a riot squad armed with choppers right beside him! That's what I think of Kong Gai and this scheme, sir, little as I understand it!"

"You've got to be careful, Jimmy. Our one chance to get Kong Gai is through you. With you gone, we wouldn't have a chance! If… you aren't listening to me! Wake up, lad! Or… what are you thinking?"

Wentworth shrugged.

"I was wondering why all the Pale Lily talk stopped so long ago, sir. If Kong Gai had a white girl in his chambers, he'd boast about it to his 'binders, and his 'binders would boast the honor of their chief—"

"Perhaps Kong Gai was afraid we'd pick up the trail of Mary Heath."

"No. The talk was there, when I was first in Chinatown. Then it stopped. That's worth thinking over. The first notes may have been a hoax, a come-on. Mary Heath may have been dead a long time, and the notes were intended to arouse Daniel Heath so he would do whatever they wanted, or... or...."

"Or what?"

"It's the sort of nasty thing Kong Gai would do," Wentworth snapped. "Let a man think his child was alive, knowing all the time that the girl was dead. Now, hang it, I'm no longer sure of anything—not even that Teng Ma was killed, or committed suicide, in Seattle! I'm doubtful about everything. There's a hidden motive behind this affair, and until that's found, I'm going to try and be careful."

"For once," Dunand told him. "And about time, too!"

In the very early hours of the morning two machines and a hearse drove between the gates of a small Chinese cemetery, thirty miles from San Francisco. In the first car was Heath, Dunand, Wentworth, and three officers armed with the deadly little choppers. In the machine behind the hearse were six more men from the riot squad, who had their orders to shoot at any disturbance, and were prepared to do it, although Wentworth did not really believe any ambushing was intended.

Nor was a single soul except one Chinese digger-coolie squatting over tea and pickled fish seen in the graveyard. Questioned, the coolie pointed to a tongueless mouth; Wentworth pulled down the man's blue shirt, revealing the mark of a brand. The digger-coolie had lost his tongue for perjury, and lost what store of wits he once possessed when the punishment was administered.

Wentworth held up five fingers, and the coolie showed the way to Row Five. To find the opened grave was easy then, from the heap of fresh dirt.

Daniel Heath's face was as gray as the cold slabs of marble now. With officers close to him he walked to the excavation, and, looking down, saw what all saw—a huge, magnificent crimson coffin, carved and lacquered. "Steady," Dunand said gently. To the undertaker's men, "We'll swing the coffin up, eh?" and it was done efficiently, swiftly.

The wretched father stood staring at the gorgeous red coffin.

"Gentlemen—may I—may I see—my child?"

One of the undertaker's assistants breathed a professional objection.

"I can't wait," the father choked. "My girl...."

Captain Dunand suggested, "We'd better wait until we are back at Headquarters, Mr. Heath, but—Sergeant Wentworth, will you open the—the coffin—carefully, please?"

An undertaker's man, seeing the detective sergeant walk to the head of the coffin, said softly, "The catches are on the side, Sergeant—"

Wentworth stopped in his tracks.

"That's strange," he said, half to himself. "It isn't the

way Chinese Coffins open." In a louder voice he went on, "There are fastenings on top also. That's where they ought to be."

WITHOUT HESITATION WENTWORTH stooped, and all heard the clear little clicks as the sergeant of detectives released the catches. An instant later Wentworth pushed up the cover of the handsome crimson coffin, and then the unhappy father was on his knees beside his child.

He choked out words, "My girl… Look!… that knife… they said she was ill… see how wonderful she looks… and only a day ago she must have been alive.…"

The undertaker's first assistant said softly, "Now, Mr. Heath, let us close the coffin, sir. We'll take your daughter to—"

"The Hall of Justice," said Jimmy Wentworth.

Every eye went to the youthful Chinatown detective sergeant.

"Your daughter, sir, has not been alive for almost two years," Wentworth explained quietly. "She has—"

"Nonsense," the assistant protested. "You can see for yourself, Sergeant, that the fingernails and hair hasn't grown, and the condition of the—"

"I don't care about that," Wentworth broke in. "The Year of the Yellow Dragon was two years ago, and if you'll look closely you'll see that the little semicircle on the base of each fingernail has been painted yellow, and—"

"What d'ye mean?" Dunand demanded.

"And if—if anybody—any Chinese—had Miss Heath alive this year, the base of the nails would be blue, since this is the Year of the High Heaven, and you can argue a year and not convince me that Mary Heath has been alive for two years!"

"If I only could believe that," Daniel Heath muttered. "Ten times rather dead than…."

"You can take my word for it," Wentworth assured him. "And before long, if there is anything in American science, as against diabolical Chinese methods, we'll prove it to you, sir!"

Heath agreed to have the body taken to the Hall of Justice, although the undertaker's men were entirely unconvinced. Wentworth's assurance had converted the miserable father of the beautiful dead girl.

As the coffin was placed in the hearse, Captain Dunand said, "You made him feel better, anyhow, lad, with your nonsense, and no harm's done—"

"I meant it, chief."

"What? Mean to tell me a body could've been buried two years and look like what we saw? No mold? No hair growth? Your Kong Gai isn't a god, Jimmy."

"No, chief. He's human. He slips up on small things sometimes. He knows a great many of our customs, just as we know his. He knows we open a coffin on the side. He knows that you would order whoever was in charge of the case to do the opening, and that I would be the person. So we're going to have a mighty good look-see at this crimson coffin when we get back to Headquarters!" Wentworth's voice dropped. "The further we go, the more every symbol, every clue, spells out the name of the Evil One, Kong Gai."

5

WHITE SCIENCE AND
YELLOW MAGIC

IN THE WHITE-TILED laboratory at Headquarters, Wentworth and Dunand waited until Dr. Morrison was ready to talk. He had rapidly gone through a single test, without having done more than taken a single look at the body. First the medical man had made a swift examination in the presence of a coroner's deputy, and then he put the selected parts on a piece of platinum foil, heating it rapidly. A black residue remained.

"Antimony," said Dr. Marsh softly. "It had to be either antimony or arsenic, and it was the former. Antimony, gentlemen, when administered as a poison, in a single large dose, is deadly, of course, and, in addition, it acts as a preservative. This case is not at all unusual. In 1902 the body of a woman named Bessie Taylor was exhumed after two years of interment. She was certified to have died from natural causes. Unless antimony poisoning is suspected, that always happens. The body appeared to have been that of a woman who had died only a few hours before!

"There is another case, that of Mary Isabella Spinks. Every autopsy surgeon and police doctor knows of these cases. The woman died in 1897, and was buried in a public grave, together with seven other coffins. A year later the body was exhumed, and not only was there no evidence of disintegration, but neither the hair nor nails had grown. A remarkable drug, this antimony, gentlemen."

"And in the normal procedure," Dunand growled, "this would not have been learned. If Sergeant Wentworth had not insisted, the body would have been turned over to the undertaker—"

"Who would have merely replaced it in a different coffin, and thought nothing more about it," agreed Dr. Morrison. As he spoke, he continued with his experiment, using a blackish powder. He tried it in test tubes filled with various salts, watching the results closely. He passed a gas from a retort over the powder, and when no precipitate was formed he looked up, keenly interested. "This isn't one of the common forms of antimony," he remarked. "Not the usual combination. Possibly it may be one of the rare Asiatic forms of the mineral, of which I'm not familiar—"

"Probably it is," Wentworth agreed. "Then what?"

Dr. Morrison said, "Little is known about them. Antimony occurs in free metallic form sometimes. There are many combinations. Some are extremely rare, and are used in the Orient for poisons. There is even one, I believe, which need not be swallowed, but, like a snake virus, acts through the skin. Shall I look it up for you, Sergeant?"

"While you're doing it, we'll open the coffin."

With a pair of pliers, Wentworth unfastened the side catches one by one. When all were loose, he gripped the middle catch with the pliers, and slowly pulled up the heavy crimson lid. It rose easily, and bits of dirt from the grave fell to the floor.

Not until the coffin lid was open did Wentworth bend down. Within the first lid was a second, of thinner, lighter wood. When the end had been opened, the inside of the coffin had been revealed, but this time there was a lid, which had two holes on the edge, by means of which it must be raised. Two holes, into which the index fingers of both hands should be thrust. Like raising a trapdoor.

"Pull it up," Dunand ordered.

"In a minute," Jimmy Wentworth said. Instead of putting his fingers into the hole, the youthful Chinatown sergeant thrust the handle of the thin pliers down, and with it raised the lid. Then he looked closely.

"What's wrong?" demanded Dunand. "Find anything?"

"Look for yourself, sir," Wentworth urged.

"I don't see a thing…wait a minute…hmm…looks like something sharp inside…."

Wentworth went to a laboratory table and returned with a heavy sharp surgeon's saw. With it he began to cut through the wood about the holes, carefully. When he had bitten out the piece of red lacquered wood, he took a keen knife and slowly split the material down the middle. At first the strong, close-grained wood resisted, and suddenly it almost seemed to drop away from the knife.

Inside the wood of the inner lid was a small rubber sac, with a tube leading out to the hole. On the edge of the hole was a tiny needle point of steel, and when Wentworth pressed it with the edge of his knife, pressure was exerted on the rubber sac, and a yellowish-green liquid spurted out. DUNAND'S HONEST FACE was gray with understanding of what would have happened had Wentworth thrust his fingers into the twin holes.

"The devil," said the captain of detectives. "The yellow devil! And that's cobra poison, of course."

"I don't think so," Jimmy Wentworth told him. "What sense would there be in Kong Gai's killing me outright like that? He can do it any time he wants. We'll have this stuff analyzed and see what it is, and what it does—"

"What made you suspect the coffin, boy?"

"Because it had the side fastenings. That proved to me that it was a trick coffin, and I took no chances. And the inner lid is all wrong, according to Chinese reading. The inside lid would prevent the spirit of the dead from getting out of the coffin. Here's Dr. Morrison—I wonder what he'll say to it."

The Headquarters scientist scraped some of the spilled yellow liquid from the wood; he said, "It's probably the same stuff I was thinking about," he said. "A rare antimony salt, or metal, or non-metal, or whatever you want to call it. Found only in the Chinese plains, and not very often found there, either. However, I'll make you feel better, Sergeant; it really isn't a deadly poison—"

"What does it do?"

"Well, about three or four or five hours after it gets into the blood stream, by means of a scratch, you become rather faint and dizzy; you do not lose consciousness, or anything like that, but, curiously, you continue to do whatever you started out to do—"

"Like walking my beat, if I were doing that?"

"Exactly, Sergeant! You'd just plod along your regular course, but you wouldn't really know what you were doing...."

"Where're you going?" Dunand broke in, as Jimmy

Wentworth reached under his uniform coat and moved his automatic an inch or two forward, even while he was walking toward the door.

"I'm going to walk my beat," Wentworth said quietly. "Doctor, do I show signs of dizziness, and how do I do it?"

"Theoretically, you should rather let your head droop a little, Sergeant. Do not raise and lower your feet rapidly, but go a little more slowly. That's all. The action of the drug keeps you going, just as if you weren't drugged at all. But… well, you just wouldn't know what you were doing. It's a fiendish drug. The only one I ever read about like it."

"I'll see you when I come off duty, Captain," Wentworth said. "Or, with luck, perhaps a little sooner. I'm late as it is. I've got to get on my beat—"

"We'll have men ready to help," Dunand said slowly, understanding just about what his sergeant intended.

"No sense in that, sir. Kong Gai will be so sure of everything—he's planned it so carefully and well—that I think you can send for the newspaper boys in about another hour. That's when the drug ought to begin working, if I'd been poisoned. We should have a good story for them—the solution of the Mary Heath case!"

"You watch your step, Jimmy," Captain Dunand insisted. "Don't take chances."

"I'm not the cock-sure one, chief. Kong Gai is. That's where we're going to get results!"

AS JIMMY WENTWORTH started his slow march through the streets of Chinatown he was not nearly as positive as he had led Dunand to believe. Yet he wanted to meet each effort of Kong Gai to trap him alone, by himself, knowing that each time the Evil One failed, his terrible hold on Chinatown was made less firm.

He paused in the morning shadows cast by the old cathedral, and, glancing up, again read the familiar gilded sign on the bell tower:

> Son, Observe the Time,
> And Flee from Evil.

It was a thing he felt he would never do—flee from evil. He had to meet evil face to face, head on; he asked only that, if he must go down before the influence of Kong Gai, he could do it with gun out and blazing.

Along Dupont to Jackson. Up Jackson. Back. Through the teeming alleys, crowded with children, merchants, purchasers, with a sprinkling of lean-faced 'binders lurking in dark doorways. An hour passed. Another half hour. Wentworth had been marching along at his usual brisk pace, in the middle of the sidewalks, eyes alert always. He knew that he was being watched, being followed, and he knew that Chinatown knew it also. Respectable merchants stared at him briefly, but, not daring to enrage the Venomous One, head of the Cobra Clan, said nothing. Yet Wentworth saw.

Gradually his steps became slower, as if he were tired. Then, once, he almost stumbled as he walked.

He felt the ceaseless cat-step behind him quicken.

The sergeant of detectives stopped on the next corner, and almost began to climb the hill which led deep into Chinatown. Out of the corner of his eye he saw a thin 'binder slip out of sight down a cellar. Then, as if only momentarily confused, he swung back along a main street, along his customary beat. His steps were slower than before, and he no longer marched along the middle of the pavement. Again and again he weaved near the line of shops and buildings and cellarways, but never did it when close to any entrance. Only when a blank wall was at his side did he sway inward.

Wentworth was ready. Every muscle was tense, every nerve in his lean body waited to give him the command for action, although his arms hung limply at his sides.

He actually saw three dark-clad figures slip out ahead of him, and stand squarely in his path without raising his hanging head, without seeming to understand what was in the way....

And then, as the three 'binders darted forward, Wentworth's gun was out.

He knew the sort of men with whom he was confronted. He fired coldly, as he would have fired at the cobras in Kong Gai's underground chamber. Not to kill, but to disable. Three times he fired, the third time when a hatchetman was so near that the long nails of the Chinese tore at Wentworth's cheek as the 'binder attempted to seize the supposedly drugged policeman and drag him to the doorway.

Then the pursuing spy, made brave with opium, had his knife out. It was in the air while Wentworth was whirling about, sensing the attack because of the shift in the eyes of the stolid, silent onlookers; it was in the air, and, as Wentworth was about to press trigger, a high, thin, sweet voice cried out:

"Do not strike, O Mu'y Yee! Save him for me, O brother!"

THE KNIFE-ARM SEEMED turned to stone in the air.

Wentworth, never taking his eyes from the figure of the 'binder, shouted in Chinese: "Come and fight like a man, Kong Gai!"

"So you speak our language!" screamed the furious King Cobra.

"Come and fight like a man," repeated Wentworth grimly.

"I am no man, so I do not fight like one! Wait, O fool-who-is-not-a-fool, and I will tear out your tongue and feed it to my snakes!"

Holding his gun on the 'binder, Wentworth tried to see where the voice of Kong Gai came from, and then the Evil One screamed, this time in Mandarin Chinese instead of Cantonese, "Run, Mu'y Yee! Run, brother!"

Wentworth's gun roared, and Mu'y Yee fell writhing to the pavement.

"Now what, O Kong Gai?" Wentworth shouted.

Only the echo of his words came back to him. For a moment he stood there, gun in hand, waiting. He was as cold as ice. What happened made no difference. Everything save this close contact with Kong Gai was forgotten.

A strange figure! The detective, in his blue patrolman's uniform, standing above the stricken bodies of the ferocious hatchetmen who had intended to take him to torture.

Then Jimmy Wentworth, gun shifted to his left hand, went to the wounded Chinese. He kicked one assassin's knife out of reach, and then rapidly tore open the black silk coats, reaching inside for the silken bag in which all hatchetmen carry their treasures. Even at that moment Wentworth found out enough to know that three of the men had actually been involved in the kidnapping of Mary Heath.

He found in each bag a single lock of lovely hair.

Chinatown was silent as death now.

The honest merchants knew that the Man in Blue had again thwarted some awful scheme of Kong Gai, and that the Evil One would never rest until he was revenged. In what way white science had foiled yellow magic none knew.

In a clear voice Wentworth said, addressing an old man who stood in the doorway of his shop:

"Telephone police. Say four hurt. You can do?"

The Chinese ignored the fact that Wentworth had earlier spoken in Chinese, as he said laconically, "Can do."

While Jimmy Wentworth waited, gun still out, for the arrival of Headquarters men and ambulances, he wondered where Kong Gai could be.

Deep under Chinatown was Kong Gai. Alone in his chamber of terror he was bowed before the ugly, naked image near the crimson curtain, praying terrible prayers, asking that the live body of the white policeman be granted him, that it might be offered in torture to the gods of hell.

And when Kong Gai finally struck a little bell, which would tell the gods and demons of the Underworld that his prayers were on the way, the great bell of the old church struck the hour, and young Jimmy Wentworth, standing in the silent street with gun in hand, again glanced up at the words on the tower:

> Son, Observe the Time,
> And Flee from Evil.

THE HOOD OF KONG GAI

*Jimmy Wentworth Finds the Lair of the
King Cobra—Comes Face to Face with
the Fiend, His Enemy, Kong Gai!*

1

THE DEATH OF LUI SEE YET

AS JIMMY WENTWORTH swung off the front dummy of the California Street cable car, the great bell of the old cathedral on the edge of San Francisco's Chinatown announced the hour with slow brazen strokes. Eight in the morning, and already uncomfortably warm.

Chinatown's shop doors were wide open. Children in blue and red and saffron clothes sucked little bitter oranges in the purple shadows. A few Chinese matrons hurried to finish their daily food buying before any white tourists were staring at them. Coolies were beginning to carry slimy tubs of edible snails back into dark basements. Old men in black silk, seated on tall teakwood stools, fanned themselves instead of clicking up the previous day's profits on their bright beads. Their sons prepared without haste for the coming day's business.

It looked like the start of another long, tedious morning to the sergeant of detectives, who patrolled Chinatown in the uniform of a police officer. A day with nothing happening.

And Jimmy Wentworth supposed it would be just as well. He had been told last night by Captain Dunand that the Chief himself had asked for a complete summary

"There is a pan of water with the sacred snakes," said Kong Gai

of all crimes committed in the Oriental quarter, which usually meant that a shake-up was being considered. If one came, Wentworth was positive he would be involved, and it would probably be only a question of time before he was sent out to the suburbs. The newspapers would magnify every street brawl to a tong war, and headline him out of Chinatown.

All of which would please Kong Gai, leader of the band of villainous Chinese, the Brothers of the Snake. Their dreaded symbol was a hooded cobra, ready to strike; Kong Gai was the King Cobra.

Kong Gai! Head of the opium traffic. He had his body coiled about Chinatown. His hatchetmen and highbinders were feared by all honest merchants, who paid them tribute.

Wondering whether he was actually going to be called on the carpet after the Chief had gone over the Chinatown records, Wentworth began his steady march through the district. He was halfway down the second block when

"...When you thirst, push back the glass and drink with the cobras!"

he saw a Chinese come to the open doors of the Peacock Bazaar, owned by Lui See Yet, one of the richest and most respected merchants. Slowly the Oriental closed one of the double doors. Before he could close the other half, Wentworth was there.

"Pretty hot," Jimmy said in English. "Going to keep the heat out by shutting the doors?"

Lui Y'uong, son of Lui See Yet, bowed gravely. He said, in perfect English, "A warm day, yes, Officer."

Wentworth smiled. "I never saw a merchant himself close a door. Aren't there any clerks inside?"

"The clerks receive the day off, Officer. You see...."

His blank, fathomless eyes met those of the detective; Lui Y'uong said suddenly, drawing in his breath, "I believe you know why *I* am shutting the doors!"

"Because it's a warm morning?"

"You know better," the Chinese said slowly. "You are

not the simple man we have credited you with being! You know, because of what I am doing, that the honorable head of this household, my father, Lui See Yet, has departed for the Uppermost Region of the Sky."

Jimmy said softly, "I'm sorry. Everybody liked your father."

"Had it not been for that, he would be alive today!"

"Why is that?" Wentworth asked gently.

"Yesterday was our clan celebration. We had a great banquet. Many presents were sent us. Among them, packages of food my father liked so well. Black squid. Fat pigs. Dried duck from Peking. And, O sadness! O sorrow! a few of those little black mussels he alone loved."

"The newspapers have been telling that mussels are poisonous in July. Who sent them?"

Lui Y'uong shrugged. "Who can tell, now? And we must say nothing about it, lest the person who gave them, in kindness, blame himself for causing my father's departure." He shifted to singsong Cantonese, "How painfully he died! His chest tightened like steel. The air could not reach his lungs. We sent for a white doctor, but nothing could be done." In English again, warily, "You must excuse me, Officer. Much remains to be done."

"If you want, I'll have a street cleared for the funeral procession this afternoon. And try to get you a permit to use firecrackers."

"Thank you," said the bereaved son gravely. "The funeral *is* to be this afternoon; you knew that, didn't you?"

"Your father had no enemies, Lui Y'uong? No one could have sent him the mussels to hurt him?"

"He had no enemies. None."

Wentworth spoke very softly, "Then he paid tribute?"

The Chinese said urgently, "I have very much to do, Officer. You must excuse me, really."

He was turning to close the second half of the door when Wentworth reminded him of something, "On the day of death, Lui Y'uong, a man speaks only truth, for the gates of heaven are open, and the gods can hear."

Lui Y'uong paused. He said, almost under his breath, "My father was friendly to the police, as guardians of the law. Where tribute had to be paid, he paid it cheerfully, glad that it was no more. Is that an answer for you, Officer?"

"I'm sorry to have troubled you," Wentworth said.

Lui Y'uong bowed deeply. In louder tone, he said, "If you can see to it that Clay Street is ready for the procession at the hour of four, Officer, we will be very glad,"

WITH THAT HE slipped inside, and Wentworth heard the bolt drop into place. The detective did not realize why Lui Y'uong had raised his voice until he, also, turned to continue along his beat. Then he saw that two black clad Chinese, 'binders, were shuffling side by side along the pavement.

It might be accident. It might only mean that Kong Gai was shadowing him. But in Chinatown nothing happened by accident. And Kong Gai's spies were in many windows, watching, reporting what went on in the district.

The presence of the evil-visaged hatchetmen set his nerves on edge. But he told himself that Kong Gai would never descend to an ordinary knifing or shooting. That was not the way of the Evil One.

Jimmy Wentworth, as he strode along his beat, outwardly at ease, wished that he could lay a successful trap for Kong

Gai. It had been tried before, but the King Cobra refused to be enticed inside. What deviltry the venomous Chinese was about Wentworth could not even guess. It seemed obvious that Kong Gai was in no way involved in the death of old Lui See Yet. What had Kong Gai to gain? Nothing. Lui See Yet paid his tribute, willingly. Was this just some of Kong Gai's fiendishness? The detective doubted this. Kong Gai always had a reason for acting. And there was no reason at all to suspect the Venomous Person in this case.

And no reason for Jimmy Wentworth to do anything except pace his hot beat, and wait… wait… wait….

Wait, while Headquarters were getting ready to demand action! What action could he give them? What could he do that he wasn't already doing?

"They'll get me," Jimmy thought.

Then, finally, for sheer lack of anything to do, and to hear if Captain Dunand had anything to say about the rumored investigation, he called Headquarters. He had his excuse ready when he was connected with the grayhaired captain of detectives:

"Lui See Yet, the head of the Peacock clan, died late last night, sir," Jimmy reported. "Apparently mussel poisoning—"

"Apparently baloney," exploded Dunand. "You'll have to do better than that tonight, Sergeant! You're comin' up before the Commission, Jimmy, and you'll need your wits, lad! And so will I! Mussel poisoning! Nonsense. Why, I saw the chemist's report, and the mussels're O.K."

"But the doctor on the case said—"

"I don't care what he said, Jimmy! That M.D. himself sent a sample of the mussels for examination. He wanted to be positive that his signing of the death certificate was proper. The mussels are not poisonous, but the M.D. insists absolutely that the symptoms and death were those of mussel poisoning. That it's… wait until I get the report… mytilotoxin…"

"Then I'd better—"

"You'd better watch your step for the rest of the day! We've got an investigation comin' up tonight! This's no time to be digging up another unexplainable murder in Chinatown, lad. But"—Wentworth could hear his captain banging on the desk with a big fist—" you get to work on the case, if there's anything you can do."

Jimmy said grimly, "Yes, sir. Of course. Usually I can figure out a reason for Kong Gai's killings, but this is one I don't understand at all."

"Don't worry about that! Just bring in Kong Gai!"

"Shall I bring along a bowl of the west wind with him?" Jimmy Wentworth laughed shortly, bitterly. "Or do you want a couple of rays of sunlight, sir?"

Dunand's voice came raspingly over the wire: "I realize all that, Sergeant. But I'm afraid that this time it's apt to be Kong Gai's head… or yours." Almost instantly the gray-haired veteran added, "I know what you're up against, son. Only the Commission doesn't. I know you aren't making excuses. But somewhere in Chinatown is Kong Gai… and *you've got to get him!*"

Wentworth's "Yes, sir," meant only that he had heard the order, and not that he thought it possible to execute.

"And," warned Dunand, "pray for peace in Chinatown today!"

"We'll have that," the youthful sergeant of detectives

promised. "Lui See Yet's funeral is this afternoon. You can count on Chinatown's being as quiet as a graveyard. Nothing is more sacred to the Chinese than a funeral procession, sir."

2

THE CHALLENGE

BY NOON NOTHING more criminal had taken place than
an argument between two porter coolies over which should
pay for a pipe of tobacco, but all ended peacefully. Wentworth watched them step into a doorway, where the pipe
vendor prepared a pipeful of silky tobacco, out of which
each would get about one full puff.

When the old bell of the cathedral struck twelve, Wentworth was deep in the heart of Chinatown, just opposite
the bowl shop of his friends the Wangs. So far as he knew,
his shadowing had ceased. If he were correct, the 'binders
who had been on his trail had given up their task after he
had twice passed the Peacock Bazaar, owned by the dead
Lui See Yet; passed it without attempting to go inside.

Wentworth had thought considerably about the case,
without seeing where the police could be involved. Also,
since he was young, and human, he had wondered what
would happen when he was called before the Commission.
Captain Dunand would stand back of him squarely. How
much did the Commission know about Kong Gai, if they
knew anything at all? Each individual crime in Chinatown
had resulted in arrests and convictions; if Wentworth had
been unable to get the Evil One himself, who was respon-

sible for the murders and robberies, he had at least caught the lesser criminals. That ought to count in his favor, unless someone, not knowing what he was up against, became stubborn and demanded a change.

A young clerk was sitting behind the counter in the Wangs' shop, and Wentworth said:

"I like mebbe-so see Mr. Wang. Can do?"

The clerk, who knew that his masters and the blue-coated detective always spoke together in scholarly Chinese, bowed gravely, and scuttled off to the rear of the shop. Wentworth could hear him crying out nasally that the white policeman was here, probably demanding a squeeze on the month's business. From the living quarters upstairs a deeper voice answered, suggesting that the officer be told to come upstairs.

Wentworth dutifully followed the clerk all the way to the end of the lower floor, and then up a rickety back stairway. At the top the door stood open, and, inside, in a lovely room of teakwood and silk hangings and thick, soft Chinese rugs, the two Wangs, father and son, were at their mid-day meal.

While Jimmy bowed to the old man, and Wang Yü acknowledged the greeting in Chinese, young Wang Chen-po said in English:

"Don't the department pay you enough to buy lunch, James? Are you beginning to bum meals from your friends?"

"I do not understand such talk," old Wang Yü broke in severely, although his keen eyes twinkled. "In America, friends abuse one another. It seems that if you like a person, you say miserable things to him—"

"And it seems to me," broke in the son, "that for a man

who insists he knows no English except 'one dollah' and 'velly cheap, lady,' you do pretty well, honorable father."

Old Wang appealed to Wentworth. "There is no courtesy in this son of mine," he said in his own language. "I sent him to your schools, where he learned nothing of importance. *Kam chi' li tak ngo ch'ü sak fan ma*... will you dine with us this noon? Good!" Wang glanced once at his son, and then clapped his hands. "We have a guest," he called loudly.

Here was an honor Wentworth had never been granted before. It meant that the women of the household were to serve him, as if he were as much a child of Wang Yü as his real son. In no other way could the old man have shown his trust and confidence. And affection.

Wentworth sat with lowered head while a lovely young Chinese woman brought hot water, tea-bowl, rice and shredded chicken. New chop-sticks were placed between bowl and pewter pot, and as the young detective picked them up he muttered the customary prayer to the gods of food.

Not until the wife of Wang Chen-po had shuffled softly out of the room, leaving a faint odor of some strange Oriental perfume behind her, did Wentworth begin to eat. No word was spoken until he had finished, but when Wang Chen-po lit a cigarette for him, old Wang said gravely:

"For what you have done in Chinatown, my son, I have always wished to thank you. Your name is already written on the roll of our tong. Tonight we will write it on the family shrine. *Hai-ya!* I had one son; now I have two!"

"THAT'S JUST WHAT I expected," Wang Chen-po grinned. "You come along and do me out of my inheritance! A swell friend you are, James!" He began to laugh. "Next thing, my honorable father will look for a wife for you! A very old one, who has plenty of money left by her first husband—"

"I think," old Wang Yü announced slyly, "that our James has already taken care of that part of his life."

Jimmy thought of Lucille Carrington; a year ago he had rescued her from a den of Kong Gai's, where the Venomous Person had used her as his mouthpiece.

Still smiling, he said quietly, "Lui See Yet has gone to his fathers, O Wang Yü—"

"A son," snapped the old Chinese, "does not address his father by name, O uneducated and illiterate child!"

Jimmy began again, this time gravely, "Lui See Yet is dead, honorable father. Is there a reason why he should have died, Wise Man?"

"Lui See Yet died because he was a slave to his belly. He ate of the little black mussels, and they poisoned him."

"So it has been said," Wentworth agreed. "But is there any other reason why he is dead?"

Old Wang glanced shrewdly at his newly adopted son. "No," he said at last. "He was in all things—save his love of good food—a virtuous man. His son, Lui Y'uong, is also honorable. Surely you suspect nothing?"

"Only that two of Kong Gai's hatchetmen watched me while I spoke with Lui Y'uong as he closed the shop—"

"They are everywhere."

"And that while the doctor swears that Lui See Yet died from eating mussels, a sample of the shellfish seems to show that they aren't poisonous."

Wang Chen-po said earnestly, "Don't ask for an autopsy,

Jimmy! The Lui family are very religious, and very rich. The body of Lui See Yet is sealed in a teakwood coffin right now. You'll have the whole Six Companies on your neck, demanding your head on a platter, if you try to open that coffin!"

"I know," Jimmy Wentworth agreed. "I'm not going to call for an investigation. You see, Chen-po"—bitterly—"I'm going on the carpet tonight anyhow, and my chief wants everything quiet here today."

Old Wang Yü, who "no talkee Ingris," had been listening soberly. Now he reached to a teakwood stand, opened the door, and took out a very modern telephone. He called his number placidly, and after a moment said, in Cantonese:

"Ho-la! Six Companies? *Ni kam yat!* I will speak with the honorable president. This is Wang Yü...."

"Wing Ma?" the old man demanded. *"Ho-la!* How is the affair concerning your son and the daughter of the Yee family?" The old man listened, and then shook his head. "It must wait," he said firmly. "There must be no trouble in Chinatown. I do not care if the Yee family have insulted you twenty times, old goat! If there is fighting, it will go badly for my son—"

Wing Ma's shrill voice was audible to Wentworth. "And what has your son got to do with a daughter of the Yee household? Has he not one wife already?"

"I have now two sons," said old Wang proudly. "Wang Chen-po, and Wang Wen Wor', who you know only as a policeman. If there is fighting, my new son must bear the brunt of it. And I ask you, scraggly beard, what will happen if the blue coat is removed, and another put here in his place?"

"The Men of the Law would not be so foolish," Wing Ma squeaked. "Is it contemplated?"

"It is!"

"The Six Companies will protest! He has kept the peace well. And because of his swift vengeance on crime, the Mysterious One is actually fearful! Without the white man, who can say what will happen here?"

"Good," said Wang Yü. "Until I speak with you, let there be no fighting, even if the family of Yee has insulted your tong."

"I congratulate you on your new son," the other old man shouted. "If he knew some of the stories I could tell about his father, when you and I were younger men, he would revere you less—"

Wang Yü hung up the telephone swiftly. He said to Wentworth. "That tea is cold, my son. I will order more hot water—"

While Wentworth was refusing, Wang Chen-po said softly, "What were you telling me about calling a friend names, my father? It seems that Wing Ma is not only a goat, but that his beard is falling out."

The old man held up his hand. He said coldly, "You will say an extra prayer at the shrine tonight, Chen-po." For a moment he was silent, and then he began to chuckle. "*Hai-ya!* Old Wing Ma! There was a flower girl in Peking, and both Wing Ma and myself…"

The old man's sharp eyes caught a fluttering in the curtain concealing the women's quarters.

"The story will keep," he said, still smiling. "In the meantime, you have nothing to fear in Chinatown, my son. All will be quiet."

A CLERK KNOCKED softly at the door. When the boy entered, he handed Wang Yü a folded piece of paper, on which was Wentworth's name. Wang Yü held the paper in his hand until the clerk explained that two men, Chinese, had brought it to the shop; held it in his hand until the clerk left the threshold and closed the door. Then, in complete silence, he handed the unexpected message to the young sergeant of detectives.

Wentworth stared at the printed letters which made up his name. He opened the paper very slowly.

It read:

> Would you like to see Kong Gai? I shall be within the rice shop on Waverley Place at two o'clock this afternoon. Men will be with me, but you will be safe if you come alone. Even if escorted by other police, you will all be safe, unless you attack. I offer you this opportunity so that we may combat on equal terms. You are known to me. My appearance is unknown to you. Kong Gai desires no advantage when we meet.

At the bottom of the challenge was the long, slim, olive-colored body of a huge king cobra, with yellow head and the terrible, curiously staring eyes of orange. An artist must have painted the reproduction of the most venomous of snakes—the only snake which will pursue men to kill them.

Wentworth handed the challenge to Wang Yü. The old man read the English words without difficulty, and then said, "And you will go to the rice shop, my son?"

Jimmy said slowly, "No, honorable father. I will not go."

"There is fear in your heart?"

"Yes," Jimmy admitted.

"But," said the ancient, "that is not the reason you refuse to accept this challenge?"

"The rice shop is too far away from middle of China-town," Wentworth said softly. "If Kong Gai had named a different meeting place, I might have been tempted. Especially now, when if I could get him—or even make a good try at it—I'd be able to explain that to my superiors. But the rice shop's a good half mile from—from where the funeral procession will march, at just about two o'clock. Two in the afternoon! That's the hour when the Gates of Heaven are open, and the gods can look down, to see if Lui Y'uong is acting in a filial manner toward his father. Something's behind this dying of Lui See Yet, but I'll be hanged if I can see what it is. No, I won't be at the rice shop!"

"I am glad that my son is not fool," said Wang Yü. He spoke a short word with Chen-po, who immediately went to the window, and carefully pulled back the inner curtain. Then he dropped to his knees, and moved enough of the outer hanging so he could peer out.

At once Wang Yü shrilled, "What do I care about messages? What affair is it of mine? Go to this rice shop if you wish! But leave me in peace. I know nothing at all!"

Wentworth was amazed at the angry quality in the penetrating old voice. But he was not surprised when, after drawing the heavy inner curtain again, Chen-po said, "As you supposed, my father, there were heads listening across the street. They withdrew from the window when you finished speaking. What you said was overheard, and will be duly reported."

"Good," said old Wang seriously. "Now, I have not only

freed this household from suspicion, but have also given the Evil One the idea that you will be at the rice shop. There is only one thing I ask, my son."

Jimmy bowed, waiting.

"In the presence of the unknown; be careful! Be brave, but not foolish. And I will be praying for you."

3

THE FUNERAL PROCESSION

AT THE CALL box at the southerly end of his beat Wentworth made his arrangements with Headquarters. At two o'clock exactly, two riot cars from the Hall of Justice were to approach the rice shop on Waverley Place, one from each end of the street. If *bo' how doy* in black were about, these 'binders were to be picked up and taken back to the station. If, however, all seemed placid, and the challenge was either a hoax or a plot to trap only Wentworth himself, the riot cars were to drive on, slowly, toward Headquarters again. Once they were back on Kearny Street, and out of Chinatown, both were to go at top speed, but without using sirens, until they were at either end of Clay Street, where the funeral procession would march.

Then they were to repeat the process. By this time it would be about eight or ten minutes after two, and the procession would be in full swing. If Wentworth *had* gone to the rice shop, it would take him almost fifteen minutes to get back to Clay Street.

Captain Dunand was won over to the idea with difficulty.

Here was exactly the thing he didn't want—excitement in Chinatown. Did Jimmy think there was really something up? If so, he was for any plan, no matter what the result. But if Wentworth were on a wild goose chase, that was very different.

"The funeral starts at two," Wentworth protested. "Kong Gai wants me to have a look-see at him—yes, he does—at the same time, at a place as far from Clay Street as will still be in Chinatown—"

"Coincidence!"

"You'll admit that we're puzzled about Lui See Yet's death, without enough to demand an autopsy which would raise the devil in Chinatown. Next, I've been shadowed today, or was, until the 'binders were satisfied I wasn't going back into the Peacock Bazaar. I don't want to get you in wrong, sir, but I'll be the goat anyhow, and—"

"Who'll be a goat?" Dunand blazed. "There're no goats in this department! We all stand together. I only wanted to make sure that you weren't just kickin' up a rumpus to make it look like we're on the job. If you're suspicious of a single damn' thing, you can have your riot cars. The Commission can say what it pleases. All I say is… good luck to you!"

At one o'clock, or a few minutes after, Wentworth boarded a cable car as if Headquarters-bound. This was perfectly in accord with what Kong Gai would expect. Wentworth would have reported the challenge, and his superiors would order him to come and give a detailed explanation.

When the sergeant of detectives stepped off the car at Kearny, and started toward the Hall of Justice, a black clad Chinese loitering at the corner turned and padded up the steep hill. But if the spy had waited, he would have seen that Wentworth walked only two blocks along the street, and then vanished suddenly.

The sergeant of detectives hurried down a side street until he reached the next artery, and there halted the first passing automobile.

"Sorry to bother you, sir," he said, "but I've got to ask you to drive me up town." He gave the address, and, getting in beside the driver, took off cap and uniform coat. "If you're busy," he added, "stop the first time you see a cab."

"No trouble, officer," the man smiled. "I'll bet you're glad to get out of that hot coat this afternoon. Just coming off your beat, eh?"

"That's it," Jimmy agreed.

They drove in silence for a half dozen blocks, and then the man said, "Well, it may be hot on a beat, but it looks like it'll be hotter for some of the big shots in the detective bureau, according to the afternoon paper."

Wentworth asked, "How is that, sir?"

"They say that the Chinatown squad is pretty rotten. Hand in glove with the opium racket, you know. Hear anything about it?"

"No, sir. Not a word. All news to me."

"Going to be a big clean up. They say that the head of the squad's a rich man. Made it all by giving the Chinks protection. I understand he's been caught red-handed."

"What was his name, sir?"

The man slowed his car before the address Wentworth had given him. "Darned if I remember," he said. "Come to think of it, I don't think it was given." The car stopped, and the man said, "If I ever get a tag, Officer, I'm coming to you to fix it. Who'll I ask for?"

"Wentworth," Jimmy said, grinning. "In charge of the Chinatown squad, sir."

With that he jumped from the car, and raced into the building.

Not ten minutes later, in street clothes, and with a soft hat low over his eyes, Wentworth reappeared. He had still plenty of time, and so walked briskly several blocks to a car, transferring from it to another. In his dark gray suit he looked like any well dressed young man; he seemed, however, slighter than in uniform. Since Chinatown knew him only as the beat patrolman, he made no effort at any additional disguise. The noise of the funeral would attract every curious white man in the district. One more would be unnoticed.

Jimmy began to walk the last couple of blocks to Chinatown. He passed Officer Mulvaney, who glanced at him once without recognition. Keeping a close tab on the time, he reached the line of division between the Oriental district and the Nob Hill apartment houses at a few minutes to two. By two, just as the first flute began to wail the Lament for the Dead, he turned into Clay Street.

WHILE ALL EYES were on the strange gathering which began to emerge from a house—the meeting place of the Lui family—Wentworth quietly stepped into a dark doorway, and flattened himself into the shadows there.

The flute wailed a second time, and the discordant sound started the rolling of skin drums. Cymbals clashed suddenly, wildly, and the chant for the dead shrilled into the street.

Many soberly clad Chinese came from the Lui house. These stood about, leaving the doorway free. A moment later three priests, in yellow and black robes, with shaven heads bare, came into the street, followed by temple boys swinging incense burners. After these came the paid mourners, each carrying a pole, to which seemed attached something like yellowish cloth.

When all were in the street, a Chinese stepped up to the end of the twenty-foot long bundle of cloth, and applied an air pump to it; the cloth filled until it assumed the shape of a dragon—the dragon which would convey the spirit of Lui See Yet into the highest heaven. Soon the mourners were holding the dragon up on their poles.

Next men bearing trays of food appeared, that Lui See Yet's spirit might not be hungry on its final journey.

At the very end the heavy coffin was carried from the house—a great coffin beautifully lacquered and carved. In it was the body of the dead Chinese, which was to be shipped to China.

There were a full two hundred people crowding together. The priest gave a command. The coffin was lifted high on men's shoulders. The dragon began to weave and move as the mourners carried it slowly forward, walking this way and that. Cymbals clashed in weird cadence. The priests began to cry out, demanding that all unfriendly spirits be warned away by the great and terrible dragon which was protecting the soul of Lui See Yet.

None of the immediate family of the dead man were to be seen. These were all at the family shrine, saying farewell to Lui See Yet, who was now leaving them.

Wentworth watched the performance with little inter-est. He had seen a good many similar affairs, both here and in China. So he tried to keep his eyes everywhere but on the procession.

Although he wondered if the men of Kong Gai were robbing the deserted Peacock Bazaar, or other Lui family shops, this did not seem probable. Not big enough loot for Kong Gai.

The men carrying the great coffin seemed to be having a difficult time of it. Not fifty feet from where Wentworth was standing, one of the men at the front faltered, disordering the whole procession....

And then hell broke loose!

While the bearers of the air-filled dragon ripped their poles—heavy staves of teak—from the body of the yellow apparition, and began to strike about them at the lesser members of the Lui family, Chinese poured out of a near building, knives out and flashing.

For a moment Wentworth gasped. He had never seen anything like this in all his experience in China! Black clad men, with long yellow hoods over their heads! Straight up to the coffin they raced in a solid mass, cutting and slashing at anyone or anything in their way. Fully fifty of the yellow hoods, which entirely covered each face, were in the street. Hooded men! The hatchetmen of Kong Gai!

Wentworth's gun was out, but he hesitated. That he was one against fifty did not cause him to falter. He wanted to discover what this unheard-of attack on a funeral procession really meant. Intimidation? Was Kong Gai showing that he was more powerful than the gods who were watching at this sacred hour? Or... what?

Then the young sergeant of detectives saw the last thing he could have possibly expected. Yellow hoods swarmed about the coffin. On brawny shoulders it was raised again, with a guard of the dreaded Yellow Hoods surrounding it. Here and there loyal members of the Lui family tried to break through the cordon and get to the coffin, only to be beaten back.

One young Lui managed to squirm his way on hands and knees close to the legs of the coffin bearers; a cobra man swung his knife at him, scratching the lacquer of the great coffin in the backward swing.

Wentworth, glancing at his watch, held his fire. Two minutes after two… no, seven minutes after two. His heart was hammering swiftly. Would the riot cars come in time?

THE NOISE WAS deafening now, with the enraged shouts of respectable Chinese drowning the hisses of the Brothers of the Snake. While the hooded men continued making off with the coffin, a couple of Lui hatchetmen appeared, and about them gathered the entire clan. Voices screamed advice. An attack was being planned, and Wentworth decided to wait another minute; then, if the riot cars did not arrive, he was going to join in with the Lui tongmen in a desperate attempt to stop whatever the Yellow Hoods meant to do with the coffin and to rip off as many of the concealing hoods as possible, to identify the Asiatics….

Into a side street the coffin was being carried, with Lui relatives being held off by 'binders of Kong Gai.

Out of the corner of his eye Wentworth had a glimpse of Officer Mulvaney running down the hill. If the Yellow Hoods saw the officer, they would shoot him down instantly. Wentworth dared wait no longer. He fired once, high, and then began to fight his way through the press of Chinese and whites. Some of the tourists thought it all a part of the performance, until they saw knifed men writhing on the cobbles of the street.

The Chinese did not let him pass easily; to them he was merely a white man, and not a policeman, but Wentworth managed to get through the gesticulating group composed of the Lui family. Then he again saw the coffin. The Yellow Hoods were carrying it into a doorway... it was out of sight....

He heard the high pitched screech of a siren, followed almost instantly by the scream of brakes.

Wentworth leaped into the dark doorway, gun ready, only to sprawl headlong over the gorgeously lacquered coffin. The impact almost knocked him out.

Hands dragged him to his feet, Rainey, of the riot squad, was demanding what was to be done.

Blinking, Jimmy said, "No sense going after them. They're gone. Anyhow, the Luis still have their coffin."

"All this yelpin' for one coffin?"

"Looks like it. I suppose the Brotherhood heard your sirens, fellows, and didn't dare keep on going with the coffin. They probably thought I was in the riot car, and you were right behind me...."

Ten men of the riot squad stood around. Four of them held the deadly little choppers, fingers on triggers.

A Lui shrieked, "O white men, do not touch the sacred coffin!"

Wentworth said, "Hands off, men. We'll stick around until the procession is over, so the coffin isn't actually stolen."

As if he were overheard, someone laughed, sweetly, terribly. The laugh of Kong Gai! The sound made Wentworth grip his gun until his palm ached, but he saw no sign of a yellow hood.

Men of the Lui family had lifted the coffin to their shoulders. The priests prayed loudly, calling down curses on the fiends who had dared attempt to stop the business of the gods.

Jimmy Wentworth, eyes wide and half puzzled, slowly walked all the way around the magnificent coffin.

Then, back at the doorway, he spoke to his men: "The procession'll go down Clay to the China Mail dock. When it crosses Kearny, I'm going to arrest the whole outfit. Parading without a permit. Coffin and all, we take 'em to Headquarters." And Wentworth added aloud what he was thinking: "I want a look at that coffin!"

A voice shrieked, "Men of the Cobra! Attack!"

A knife clattered to the cobbles. Yellow hoods appeared from nowhere. Guns were shoved between the bars of high windows.

"Keep around the coffin," Wentworth ordered grimly. "Shoot their legs out from under them, fellows!"

Quietly, efficiently, the riot squad obeyed. The vicious little choppers kept the streets behind them empty. Bullets drove the snipers to cover.

Officer O'Toole, hit in the forearm, swore softly, and shifted his gun to the left hand.

The sprayed lead kept the men with the yellow hoods at a safe distance until the cars were reached. Then, without apology, and under cover of the four machine guns, the riot squad hoisted the coffin to the rear seat of the second open car, placing it crosswise.

Wentworth leaped to the running board. The driver let

the car slide down the hill, slipping it into gear. One more burst was fired, and then the second car, piled high with officers, covered the retreat of the first.

In Wentworth's ears rang the enraged screams of the men of the Lui family as they promised vengeance on the white men who had desecrated further the coffin of the venerated Lui See Yet. But high above the shouts Wentworth thought he heard the fearful shrieks of one Chinese, shrill, high-pitched, and yet somehow terribly sweet and beautiful. The voice of Kong Gai, the Evil One.

4

INSIDE THE COFFIN

JIMMY WENTWORTH FACED the five members of the Police Commission without flinching. The president, Daniel Jerome, was speaking:

"And now, Sergeant, you have aggravated the condition in Chinatown a thousandfold. I'm not up on Oriental customs, but even I know that the Chinese don't want any interference with their religion. All I can say is that it looks to me as if you wanted to start a riot in order to put it down. Is that the fact?"

"My report has been handed in already, sir," Wentworth said.

"I'm not interested in the report, Sergeant! I can draw my own conclusions."

Jimmy Wentworth said only, "Yes, sir."

"Let's get down to cases," the commissioner went on. "You were put in Chinatown to keep peace. You've made a few arrests, I'll admit, but—"

"There isn't a case on which the sergeant hasn't brought in his men," broke in Dunand. The gray-haired captain of detectives would never stand by silently when one of his detectives was under fire. "Not another section in the department can say as much!"

Jerome shrugged. "Possibly," he said. "I'll admit that the Six Companies seem to want Wentworth retained. Wentworth has probably gone to them, and asked that they write us a formal letter. That is all unimportant! Here are the facts. There is a traffic in opium going on in Chinatown, and I have information that Wentworth has been profiting by it. What have you to say to that, Sergeant?"

"May I ask where you obtained the information, sir?"

"That's no answer!"

Wentworth said quietly, "Anonymous letters aren't to be believed, sir. I've made Chinatown pretty hot for a certain Chinese. He'd like to get me out of the district—"

"Any crook wants the police out of the way."

"Admitted, sir. He could kill me almost any time he wished. But that would cause him to lose face. He's got to do it in a battle of wits, you see. Just putting a knife in me would make his men feel that he couldn't outwit me—"

"What's that got to do with opium, with the Master Mind of Chinatown?"

"It's the same person, sir. He's back of every crime in the district, and a good many outside it. I think he himself wrote you that letter denouncing me—"

"I do not put too much importance on the letter," Jerome snapped. "What I am saying, Sergeant, is this: for a year and a half you have been searching for this mysterious Chinese. Have you ever seen him?"

"Had a glimpse at him once, sir. In a tunnel under California Street. When the bank was robbed, and—"

"Did you have your gun with you, Sergeant?"

"I'd fallen on it, sir, in the dark. I tried to pot him, but—"

Jerome wagged his head. "You could have smashed him

over the head with the butt, if you wanted him very badly, Wentworth."

Jimmy thought of the 'binder on each side of the brightly clad form of Kong Gai. He would have been cut down before he could have reached the King Cobra. So he said nothing.

"And how do you explain your bank balance at the Peking-American Bank, Sergeant?"

"I have no account at that bank at all, sir."

"This pass book"—holding it out—"shows a credit of ten thousand dollars in your name, Sergeant. What have you to say to that?"

Captain Dunand began to breathe hard, but managed to remain silent while Jimmy answered seriously, "I've never put a cent in the Peking-American Bank."

"One of the clerks has sworn that you deposited the ten thousand last week, Wentworth. In large bills."

Heart cold, Wentworth said, "Then the clerk is affiliated with Kong Gai."

"We're getting nowhere, Jerome," another commissioner spoke up. "All of us are agreed that the deposit might be a plant, and we're not entirely convinced that the sergeant is guilty. So let's put our proposition up to him, eh?"

"I just wanted to show Wentworth that we have a few facts under consideration," Jerome agreed, nodding. "Now, the situation stands this way, Sergeant. It seems apparent that there is actually someone behind every Chinatown crime, and that while you have made a number of arrests, this mysterious person has never been brought to justice. So we'll put it this way: either this Kong Gai is apprehended at once, or you will be asked for your resignation from the force. Nor will we promise what our action will be regarding the money you've accepted—"

Dunand said fiercely, "If you'll just take the time to examine the sergeant's report, Commissioner, you'll find out that he couldn't have taken a bribe from the Chinese!"

The commissioner glanced down at the sheets on his desk, which had been brought him as the meeting began. Suddenly his gaze became excited as his eyes found figures on the report, and he began to read in earnest, silently at first, and then, as he came to the meat of the affair on Clay Street, he voiced what he saw:

"... 'and the contents of said coffin, duly unsealed in the presence of Deputy Coroner Williams, Deputy Health Officer Sanborn, an authorized representative of the Six Companies, and G.W. Bradbury, attorney for Lui Y'uong, were found to be as follows....'

"And look at this list, gentlemen," stuttered Jerome. "Good heavens! Who would have guessed anything like this!"

The commissioners bent over the desk. Wentworth and Captain Dunand exchanged glances, but neither said a single word. This was certainly enough to excite even a police commission. Here was what was on the report, carefully itemized:

$250,000 in gold coin

$170,000 in currency

Taels 26,477 in gold bars

£14,520 in sovereigns

$2,000 in silver dollars

$2,000 in Philippine pesos

249 unset diamonds, assorted rings, necklaces, jades, brace-
lets, et cetera, many identified as stolen, exact valuation
being determined, approximately
$400,000 minimum.

"Over a million dollars," Commissioner Janes said
slowly. He turned to face Dunand. "What does it mean?"
he demanded sharply.

"Ask the Sergeant!"

Jimmy Wentworth explained. "The coffin was Kong
Gai's treasure chest, gentlemen. He was preparing to ship
it to China in the only absolutely safe way he could figure
out. Lui See Yet's coffin was to have been shipped out of
the country; it would have been put on the boat without
further inspection. All that Kong Gai needed to do was
have a coffin exactly like Lui See Yet's, and then pull the
seal from the original coffin and replace it on the one he
had made—"

"How would this Kong Gai know what the coffin was
like?" Jerome queried.

"A spy in the Lui household, perhaps. It is my opinion
that Kong Gai had his coffin made, an exact copy of the
other one, and then when he was ready poisoned Lui See
Yet—"

Jerome's brows drew together. "You mean to tell me that
this Kong Gai would kill a man for no reason at all?"

"Yes, sir." Wentworth went on, "I can't prove that Lui
See Yet was murdered unless we find the body, but I've
learned that mussel poisoning has the same symptoms as
those produced by curare, the South American arrow-poi-

son. Kong Gai wanted Lui See Yet to die as if from natural causes—"

"How did you decide to bring the coffin here?" questioned Dr. Jenkins, another commissioner. "I don't understand that."

Wentworth smiled briefly.

"In the argument in Chinatown, when the coffins were changed, one of Kong Gai's 'binders drove his knife accidentally against Lui See Yet's own coffin, and scratched the lacquer. What made me suspicious was that Kong Gai had plenty of time to get away with the coffin, instead of leaving it in a doorway. When I had a good look at the second coffin, there wasn't any scratch, although everything else seemed just the same. You can't ever remove a scratch in lacq. So... well, we brought this coffin to Headquarters, and the report tells what we found."

"Kong Gai's whole collection of loot," Captain Dunand growled.

Nodding, Wentworth said, "Not only that, but his gains from smuggling Chinese across, from his narcotics trade, from selling slave girls—"

"You believe that this mysterious Chinaman intended returning to the Orient, Sergeant?" asked Jerome.

"It would seem so, sir."

"Now, of course, he won't go?"

"I'm afraid not."

Commissioner Jerome patted his finger tips together. "And if he leaves the country, of course if he were paying anyone for protection, those payments would automatically cease, wouldn't they?"

Although his face was white, Jimmy Wentworth said

soberly, "Perhaps Kong Gai's last act here—the false bank account—was to try and discredit me, sir. He would enjoy doing that. To the Chinese mind, disgracing an enemy—breaking him—is as bad as death."

Dunand could remain silent no longer. "Commissioner," he said, "is it reasonable that a crook would continue payin' an officer who took away his loot?"

Jerome held up his hand.

"I'm not making accusations," he said quietly. "I am merely considering every possibility, Captain. This is a curious affair. It appears, on the surface, as if Sergeant Wentworth had done a remarkable bit of work. I trust this is so. However, my experience with the Chinese leads me to feel that they are docile, and willing to do anything to placate the authorities. This Kong Gai may not be so desperate as we believe. Wentworth might be able to convince him—I speak frankly, gentlemen—that he carried out the attack only because of orders, and then Kong Gai's payments would continue...."

"I cannot understand," burst out the commissioner, "why this Chinese has not been arrested! The circumstances must be considered suspicious, Sergeant. I wish to be fair. So I voice the feelings of the commission when I say... place this Chinaman under arrest immediately!"

Wentworth stood very straight.

"I'll try, sir," he said.

"You've got to do better than try I Get your man, Sergeant, or...."

Jimmy knew exactly.

Commissioner Jenkins said. "We've never questioned your bravery, Sergeant. I suggest that you go straight to the haunt of this Kong Gai, with as many of your squad as you feel necessary, and drag him out."

"I've been trying to find where he lives for over a year, sir."

"Go to an opium joint, get an employee there, and at the point of the gun make him take you to the place!"

"There are too many go-betweens, sir."

Jerome broke in, "Then go up step by step, man after man. The trail must eventually lead to your Chinaman."

"Chinese will die before they'll help us find their dreaded King Cobra."

"I don't like these objections, Sergeant! This is a simple order. You are detailed to go back to Chinatown, at once, and begin the search for Kong Gai. Is that clear?"

Wentworth reached for his hat.

"Yes, Commissioner," he said.

Dunand, his old face suddenly seeming more lined than before, said, "Tell him what you told me, Jimmy."

Wentworth shook his head.

"Then I'll tell him," snapped the gray-haired captain. "Wentworth is to be killed the moment he steps across the line into Chinatown. Already Kong Gai has sent out the word. A friend of the sergeant's, named Wang Chen-po, telephoned and told us. If you send him to Chinatown, you send him to death!"

Jerome, puzzled, trying to be fair, and yet do his duty, leaned back in his chair. He was suspicious, but he knew that his captain would never lie. "Is there any way you can prove that?" he asked finally.

"If you'll look out of the window, sir, you'll see two hatchetmen across the street. Then, look closely, two windows to the right of the corner. See the place with the sign Dr. Lee Sing? I've had an eye on the doctor for a long time. You'll notice that both are open—the first time they've been raised, to my knowledge. The windows cover the door of the Hall of Justice; cover me, if I walk out. Kong Gai is not going to wait for me to come to Chinatown. He's reached the end of his rope, now that we've taken away his treasure, and he'll shoot to kill when I step outside—"

"Then let's get him up in the doctor's office!"

"He won't be there," Wentworth explained. "Hatchetmen do his killings for him. The King Cobra takes no personal chances—"

"We'll arrest his paid killers anyhow—"

Wentworth lowered his voice. "I've a plan, sir," he pleaded. "Won't you let me try it?" For several minutes he spoke softly, earnestly, with Captain Dunand shaking his head in complete disapproval. Wentworth ended with, "It might work, sir. I'd like to try it. For if there's one single way to get Kong Gai, this is the one. I'd like your permission."

Jerome glanced at his fellow commissioners, who were nodding agreement.

"Convince me that there are highbinders in the doctor's office, waiting to kill you, and I'm willing," he said at last. "We'll send a squad over there—"

"Don't do that, sir! I want Kong Gai to think that the department feels he's done for. Here's a better way; I'll put on a bullet-proof vest, if you like, and step outside. I'll duck back at the first shot, unless they get me in the head. But Chinese always shoot for the heart...."

"I don't like it," blurted Dunand. "Not any of it!"

Nevertheless, a few minutes later, with expert marksmen

from the department covering the killers who were waiting for Wentworth, the youthful sergeant of detectives stepped out of the door of Headquarters. He was on the last step when three gun muzzles were thrust out of the windows.

Before the first trigger could be pulled, a storm of bullets poured from the Hall of Justice, and Wentworth dashed back into the building.

Jerome had insisted on the counter attack; while a dozen officers now raced across the street, through the excited crowd which was already gathering, and up to the Chinese doctor's office, he said to Wentworth in the lower hall:

"You get your chance, Sergeant. However, even if you have always acted in good faith, and to the best of your ability, Kong Gai is too dangerous and desperate to be allowed at large. If you are unable to capture him, you can see that we must assign someone to Chinatown who can."

"Yes, sir."

"Coming close, this time, will not be enough," Jerome continued. "Making arrests of highbinders is hardly sufficient. We must get at the head of this terrible organization. You've got to bring in Kong Gai... or...."

Or be transferred to the residential district. Jimmy knew what the commissioner's "or" meant! Be removed from Chinatown. Branded as a failure.

"I understand, sir," Wentworth said quietly.

5

BEFORE THE MONSTER
OF CHINATOWN

ON A GRAY foggy morning, two weeks later, eighteen men were herded through Two Post at San Quentin, the state prison across the bay from San Francisco. Two by two they shuffled through the lower gate, cuffed together. Deputies escorted them, together with one guard from Folsom Prison, who was bringing down a convict in blue-gray for parole.

A miserable, hopeless crew. Forger handcuffed to robber, thief to second degree murderer. Only one wore a coat; the rest were in shirt sleeves. All, except the man in blue, puffed furiously on the last tailor made cigarette they would enjoy for many years. One or two tried to laugh and joke. The others walked with hanging heads. Prison!

Soon, after being photographed, finger-printed, measured, bathed, they would be like the lean, yellow-faced Folsom convict—broken by the justice they had attempted to flout. Why, the fellow was so weary he could hardly lift one leg after the other.

The first degree robber handcuffed to the man in convict blue, on his way to start a five to life sentence, said:

"How much longer you got, bud?"

Dull eyes looked up from under the long-peaked cap; the man said, "Bein' paroled." In a monotonous husky voice.

"How long you do?"

"Six and six."

The robber knew about sentences; he said, "They give you ten flat, hunh? An' you're gettin' time off for good b'havior."

"I'm sick," said the Folsom convict.

He looked it. His yellowed face was almost emaciated. Lacklustre eyes stared out almost unseeingly at the building housing the Captain of the Guard's office, at the double gates to the right of it, through which all prisoners pass. His knees trembled as he walked, his hands hung at his sides.

Even his cuffed partner forgot his own plight as he said, "Say, cheer up, punk. I'm goin' in; you're on th' way out. Say, how come you got all them roses in your cheeks? They bean you to death, hunh?"

"Three times a day," the man in gray-blue muttered.

A prison guard at the Captain's office growled, "Inside!" and the convicted men filed into the office, and, a moment later, out again, on their way through the double gates....

Only the man in gray-blue remained. To him the Captain of the Guard spoke shortly: "Jennings!"

The lean man said wearily, "Yes, Captain."

"Number-Forty-nine four hundred and eleven?"

"Yes, Captain."

The prison official glanced at the parole sheet before him. "Change inside," he said. "There's nine dollars on the books for you. Transportation to Stockton also. And a friend waitin' to see you. Now get into other clothes."

Three or four minutes later, the man who had been Number 49,411, two-time loser from Folsom, reappeared. He was in shiny blue serge, with a shabby cap pressed down over his eyes. The formality of transferring money to his credit, and the amount of transportation, was quickly over with.

Then the Captain said, "Jennings, it's none of my business, but if you're convicted again, it'll be three times and out for you. Life in Folsom! Got that, boy? You're young." The brawny captain came beside him, and discovered to his surprise that when the convict stood erect he was as tall as the six-foot official. "Let me give you one word of advice," the good-hearted old prison man grunted. "I say this, Jennings; stay off the junk! You're down on the records as a D.U. Leave th' hop alone! Th' Warden'd tell you all this, but he's away."

The convict lowered his head without speaking.

Feeling positive that this convict would tread the bitter path leading him back to prison for the remainder of his life, the old captain said cheerfully, "Now report to th' Parole Office at th' Ferry Building, Jennings. That's the man who's waiting to see you… Get going, boy."

The man called Jennings tried to throw his shoulders back as he walked slowly out of the office.

A thick-set man, well dressed, smoking a cigar, greeted him now. "Hello, Slim," he said. "I'm Charley King."

The dull eyes raised.

"Don't know you," the man said slowly.

"Sure not, Slim." As they walked side by side down the

narrow pavement toward the lower gate, the man went on, "Th' old Stockton gang's busted up, Slim. Joe Willis's in Leavenworth. Chuck Bradley—th' bulls got him. Enos Farrell got married. Billy th' Dope went off his nut—"

"I got a job comin' up," said Slim Jennings.

"I know, Slim. Sure. How long you goin' t' last in a steam laundry? Not"—hastily—"not that you don't look good, fella! You look grand!"

"Yeah," muttered the released man. "I feel grand. Look at my hand shake!"

"You want I should fix you up, Slim?"

The paroled convict began to shake from head to foot. "Yeah," he whispered.

"Soon's you go to th' Parole Office, you come with me, Slim, an' I'll fix you up!"

"I'm too sick f'r a shot," Slim whimpered. "But a pipe… just one pipe…."

"We'll give you all you want, Slim! With a Chinee girl to cook it f'r you!"

"Yeah," said the convict-clad man.

WHILE THE CONVICT went to the Parole Office, his new-found companion slipped off to telephone. What he said when he was given his number was this: "Tell Number One it's O.K. Slim's shot to hell. He'd strangle his mother for a couple of pipes. Huh? He's bein' paroled now. Sure. I'll bring him straight up. What? That's right. If he gets caught, it's three times an' out f'r him, an' he ain't got sense enough t' know his right name. Sure. Right away. I'll come with him."

Up in the Parole Office, behind locked doors, George Black was talking to his convict:

"Sergeant," he was saying, "it's been managed perfectly. Slim Jennings was due to be released any time. He's being held in solitary; only the Warden and one guard knows he's still there. I'll say this, Sergeant, you certainly look like a sick man! How'd you do it?"

Jimmy Wentworth said quietly, "No food to speak of. Heaven only knows what drugs I was given. The funny voice comes from an injection they gave me—done on purpose. Think I'll get by?"

"I wouldn't have known you," admitted Black. "If I hadn't been let into the plan, I'd have bawled hell out of you, thinking you were Slim himself. You've got as nearly perfect a disguise as possible, Sergeant, because it's all real." Grinning, the parole officer added, "I see in the paper that you caught a four pound trout up in the mountains, on your vacation."

"Don't talk about food," Jimmy Wentworth said, grinning feebly. "I'd give a leg for a cup of coffee and a couple of eggs. I certainly feel rotten, but—"

"Every decent man wishes you luck," said Black. "Anything more I can do for you, Sergeant? You've been here just about the right length of time."

"Give me a final word of advice as I go out, in case my good friend Charley King is waiting in the outer office."

So, as the door opened, Charley King, sitting in a chair and puffing valorously at a big cigar in the presence of these men he hated, heard: "And get this into your head, Slim; we're all for you unless you slip. Watch your step, Jennings!"

Silently "Jennings"—Sergeant James Wentworth—shuffled out of the room. In the hall King whispered, "They won't just watch you slip, Slim. They'll push you. Frame you. That right?"

"Yeah," said Jennings "I feel sick, Charley."

"Sure, Slim! We'll fix all that up pretty soon. First, I want you t' meet a friend of mine, Slim. He's a Chink, but a right guy. He'll fix you up, Slim."

"Yeah."

The officer at the foot of the stairway into Market Street saw the two men on their way to a taxi; he marched upstairs, his duty plainly before him. To a deputy parole officer he reported, "One of your released men got in a cab with Killer King. Want him picked up?"

"I'll ask the chief, Officer." The deputy telephoned the other room, and then said, "Let it go for a bit, Officer. The chief said he'd take care of it."

And so "Slim Jennings," two-time loser, thief, robber, murder suspect, and dope user, was released on parole— while the real Slim Jennings, still in Folsom, waited for the true parole which was to take him at last back to England, where, as a boy, he had started the career of crime of which he now repented bitterly.

"Slim Jennings" sat in a corner of the cab, smoking the cigarette which King had given him, and finding that it made him sicker than before.

What was he letting himself in for? Was he to be taken to the dens of Kong Gai, the Evil One?

So far everything had gone off perfectly. Wentworth had long known that the arm of Kong Gai extended to drag to the slimy body every released dope user from the penitentiary who could be added to the terrible Brotherhood of the Snake, the wearers of the Yellow Hood. He had decided to put this knowledge into helping him find the lair of the King Cobra.

He was entirely on his own. Unarmed. All that he had was his wits. Would it be enough? Was his disguise—the sallow face, the weary, unfamiliar eyes—sufficient to pass inspection?

Black, according to instructions, would report immediately that Wentworth was in the city, but Jimmy had issued instructions that no attempt must be made to shadow him, lest Kong Gai become suspicious, or feel that the police had any interest even in Slim Jennings.

The taxi slid to a stop; King paid the man in front of a waterfront gasoline station. At the rear of the place was a greasing rack; King called, "Say, you got my heap ready?"

Next, a slow ride along the waterfront. Chinatown was reached only after a full fifteen minutes of riding around, when King was positive—after much stopping and starting—that he was not followed at all. Finally, King stopped his car in front of a gaudy chop suey restaurant, and said to Wentworth, "Up we go, punk. Make it snappy."

As he followed King up the stairs, Wentworth realized that the presence of a big automobile in front of a chop suey place would never arouse anyone's suspicion; he wondered how many times King's car had been parked there while he had been marching his beat.

It was now almost noon; King led the way through the tables, and, when a Chinese waiter bobbed his head, said, "I go see Kee Lung Ko'u," and walked straight ahead. Through another door. Into an office, where the proprietor looked up without interest, and, rising, unlocked another door, leading into a black tunnel.

Then Wentworth had a chance to discover why he had never been able to find the lair of Kong Gai, the Venomous One. Great steel doors opened and shut. Lights flashed off and on. Again and again they came to deserted rooms, each seeming to be the end of the passageway, but each having a secret door, in floor or ceiling or wall, out of which led another tunnel.

HOW LONG THEY walked Jimmy did not know. He was growing very tired, being weakened from lack of food and the drugs the police physicians had given him. He said, "I'm all in, Charley...."

King was rapping on another door; it opened instead of being opened by the white man, and Wentworth was in a room with four Chinese. Highbinders. Men in black. All had been sipping tea and cracking watermelon seeds between their teeth while they played a game.

"I go see Number One Hood," King said.

The 'binders stared at Wentworth. Two of them he recognized; the other pair he did not remember. He forced himself to raise his eyes.

"Can do," said one of the hatchetmen finally, without suspicion.

With the Chinese leading them, they again went up and down, down and up. Once Wentworth felt very cold, and knew that they were below the surface of the earth. Doors. Tunnels. Rooms fitted out magnificently, as if each was the true den of the King Cobra.

A second time they reached a place where 'binders sprawled on soft couches. Powerful Chinese brandy stood in a square crystal bottle. Jade drinking cups, gold pipes, lay on a teakwood table.

King repeated his formula: "I go see Number One Hood."

A pock-marked *bo' how doy* shuffled over to Wentworth. With a long-nailed finger he tilted back the head of the young detective sergeant, staring into the dulled eyes, seeking, searching.

Wentworth, thanks to the drugs, was able to meet the gaze.

In English, the 'binder said calmly, "Good, Charley King. You wait here. I take this person to the Presence."

"But I was supposed to—"

"For what you have done," snapped the hatchetman, "you will be paid." He put a hand on Wentworth's arm. "Come," he said.

Charley King said, "You do what they tell you, Slim. You'll get your pipes."

"Yeah," said Detective Sergeant Wentworth, in the husky monotonous voice. "You bet, Charley. I… I'm pretty sick.…"

"We fix you," smiled the 'binder. "Many pipes, my friend, of the finest poppy. But first, you will have a little stimulant?"

He reached into a teak cabinet, and drew out a bottle, labeled in Chinese. Wentworth read, in the center of a floral circle: *"POISON."* His heart began to beat more rapidly, but again his eyes, so dull, did not betray him. When the hatchetman poured out a tiny cupful of colorless liquor, Wentworth took it with trembling hand—the hand of a man needing opium—and drained it at once.

"Now you will feel better," said the 'binder cheerfully. "Come!"

Wentworth thought, "That's an old trick. Every spy in China has it tried on him. If I can get by any other test as easy as this one...."

As he began again the endless march, during which he climbed ladders, crossed an open place between two buildings by means of a lowered platform, passed under raised steel doors, he worked on his story, to have everything correct. The details of Slim Jennings' life, crimes, experiences in and out of prison. He musn't slip anywhere. And, although his legs were unsteady, his head was clear as a bell... He was ready to do what he could.

One man against Kong Gai and his terrible Hooded Horde!

At last they began to climb, steadily. Up and up and up.

Now they reached a great room. A magnificent room, beautifully arrayed with carved stands and stools, hung with silk.

The 'binder went to the wall, and took down the least warlike object on it, a little print of the goddess of Mercy. Behind it—like the rest of the wall—was inlaid wood. The hatchetman counted bits of wood—up to seventeen. Then he pressed his thumb against the wall, and a great trapdoor opened slowly. A stairway rose, mechanically.

"Crawl down on your knees," hissed the 'binder. "Down, white man!"

Jimmy Wentworth slowly dropped to his knees, and began to creep down the carpeted stairs.

Not until he had reached the bottom did a sweet voice cry out, "Stand!" in Chinese.

Wentworth remained on hands and knees.

The hatchetman jerked him to his feet. "Here is the man,

O Benevolent and All-Powerful Great One," whispered the 'binder tremulously.

"Ah," sighed the King Cobra. "Remove his cap, Brother. Let us see if he appears worthy to wear the Hood of the Cobra Clan."

Wentworth's prison-made cap was torn from his head.

The young sergeant of detectives had at last come to the end of the trail. He was indeed in the presence of Kong Gai.

6

THE MOST AGONIZING DEATH

NOT A WORD was spoken. Wentworth, after the first moment, looked with natural curiosity about the strange, terrible room. No silken hangings here; no teakwood chairs, nor weapons, nor jade ornaments, nor jeweled opium pipes. The walls of the chamber were of plate glass, backed by steel. The ceiling was of glass also.

Clear across the room was a glass partition, and on the other side of this slept four giant cobras, at least fifteen feet long. Their horrible olive-colored bodies lay in glistening coils.

Watching "Slim Jennings," Kong Gai suddenly hissed. Not loudly. Four orange heads instantly rose from the coils of the bodies. Eight bright eyes fastened themselves intently on the face of Kong Gai.

The delicate, evil lips of the Evil One again made the hissing sound. Now the king cobras' heads came at least five feet from the floor of their glass cage. With a curious stare they all watched their master.

Suddenly, in perfect English, Kong Gai said sweetly, "The cobra—the king cobra—is the only snake which will attack without provocation, Mr. Jennings. He will pursue mankind, and kill him. Have you ever heard of the cobra, Mr. Jennings?"

"Yeah," muttered Jennings-Wentworth. "I seen one in th' pitchers. I—I'm kinda sick, mister."

Kong Gai smiled. "We will attend to your sickness shortly," he said. "Now, Mr. Slim Jennings, you say you are sick. How is it that you were paroled, a sick man?"

"I keeps m' head up in stir," Wentworth said. "Y' think I'm gonna lose parole by bein' sick, mister?"

"Very good," agreed Kong Gai. "Let me see; you were arrested in Stockton, and given a ten to life sentence, and paroled for your good behavior?"

"Yeah."

"Attempted murder?"

"Yeah."

"I see. You hit a certain gentleman over the head with a pick-handle, wasn't it?"

"Naw. A hammer. Y'see, mister, we was openin' up a shipment 'f coke, an' I sees him tryin' t' slip a couple packs in his pocket, an'—"

Kong Gai held up a thin hand. "Oh, yes, a hammer. I had forgotten." (And Jimmy was very glad that he had gone over every detail of the Jennings case!) "And the police said that you'd been jealous over some woman—"

"A dumb cluck on a newspaper said that," Jimmy Wentworth said. "Some day I'll see that guy, an'—"

"No violence, no violence," chided the King Cobra. "So you went to prison, and were deprived of the smoke of the poppy. All of which we will remedy, Jennings. In Folsom, you worked on the quarry?"

"Naw. Not husky enough. Veg't'ble garden."

Kong Gai thought that over, stroking his soft chin. His evil, yellowish eyes, so like the eyes of the cobras, which had again subsided into a mass of coils, darted this way and that.

He said thoughtfully, "So. Good. Very good, Jennings. Now, do not be alarmed. There is a formula to be followed." To his 'binder, "Brother, take off his coat. His shirt. His... no, that will be enough. What is in the pockets? Cigarettes. Matches. Hmm. And in the trousers? Just a few dollars, eh? Now, Brother, let us put Mr. Jennings through the formula."

Wentworth said, "Yeah. Hurry up, mister. I feel rotten."

Kong Gai was laughing, joyously, deliciously. From nowhere he had drawn a heavy automatic, and had levelled it at the white man.

"Do you, Sergeant?" he laughed. "That's too bad, isn't it?"

Wentworth's heart began to race, and then throbbed so that he thought it would burst.

"All I had hoped for was an opium smoking convict," Kong Gai said gleefully, "to be used, and thrown back into prison. And now I find the great Detective Sergeant Wentworth himself here! You are very welcome, Sergeant... even if your hands are not those of a man who has labored for three years and more in a prison vegetable garden!"

Wentworth made one last attempt.

"Hunh?" he said. He held out his hands—firm, brown hands, hard enough, but without the telltale callouses. "Wha's the matter with them hands, mister?"

"Nothing," said Kong Gai. "Nothing at all, Sergeant." He rubbed his own together with pleasure. "It is a splendid disguise. I congratulate you. I do indeed. Why, I was fooled myself! But now that I know who you are, I recognize you, in spite of your eyes and color and attitude. Do not fear, Sergeant; if you are not Wentworth, we'll soon discover that fact. I have finger-prints of you—which is more than you can say of Kong Gai! We will make positive before we… do anything to you!"

THE LITTLE CHINESE rose to every inch of his height.

His smiling face became more evil than before. *"Hai-ya!"* he shrilled in Cantonese. "O brother, this is our enemy! By my magic I have brought him here, that we may avenge ourselves on the damnable white man who took from us our gold and jewels, who has killed our brothers. The day of vengeance is come!"

Wentworth had no intention of admitting anything. Did Kong Gai really have his fingerprints? Just as well to find out.

"Y' c'n get my print at Folsom," Wentworth said. "Or Stockton, mister. What you tryin't' pin on me?"

For an instant Kong Gai was surprised.

Then he said, "Well done, Sergeant. But we really have a record of your prints. I'm not fooling you, I assure you."

"I'm all in, mister. Don't I get no pipe?"

Kong Gai shuffled in his beautiful silks until he was beside the younger man. Then, without warning, he spat in Wentworth's face.

The white man's fist drew back to strike; the alert 'binder grabbed his lean arm.

"I don't need a fingerprint," Kong Gai chuckled, "although I'll take it anyhow, Sergeant. You're no jail bird, hungry for hop! I've spat in the faces of a hundred white men, and they took it, Sergeant. Anything to get a pipe of opium. Anything for *yen hok*. At last I've got you, Sergeant, and I'm going to make the best of it."

Wentworth remained silent while several hastily summoned head highbinders did the fingerprinting, while a card index was brought, filled with cards. Kong Gai compared the records, and then said, "Please, Sergeant, don't insult my intelligence by trying to say that two men can have the same prints."

"Is there any way you can be insulted?" Jimmy asked, knowing that it was all useless. He had found the end of the trail, only to be outwitted by the devilish Chinese!

"None which will hasten the manner of your dying," smiled Kong Gai.

Involuntarily Wentworth's eyes sought the glass partition, behind which were the king cobras. Fold on fold of olive coils, with the venomous orange colored hooded heads almost hidden beneath the horrible bodies. Full fifteen feet long! A twisted mass of death.

"You have guessed correctly," the King Cobra himself said. "Observe, Sergeant, that there is a pan of water with the sacred snakes. You see it? Good. We are going to leave you in this room, which, as you have already observed, is absolutely empty. We will not bind you, Sergeant. So, today, or tomorrow, or next week, or whenever you begin to thirst, all you need to do in order to drink is to push back the glass, and... *drink with the cobras.*"

JIMMY WENTWORTH'S BLOOD ran cold.

"From time to time," Kong Gai continued happily, "we will look in and see how you progress, Sergeant. It will give my Brothers satisfaction when they see their hated enemy grovelling on his knees, with his tongue black and swollen. And at the end, you—will—push—aside—the glass! You will seek water, Wentworth, and the cobras will sink their fangs into your body. Then you will know the most agonizing death in the world.

"You came to find me—and here I am! Not even your superiors know where you are. Even if you were seen in the company of that man King, called the Killer, and if he is sought, let me assure you that he will never be found! He *was* a mercenary man."

From which Wentworth knew that the Killer had been murdered after he had served his purpose.

"And now," Kong Gai chuckled, "I will leave you to figure things out for yourself, O wisest and greatest of detectives. I will return tonight, and perhaps by that time you will already be thinking of water, cool, sweet water… Good-by, for the present, Sergeant."

Bowing ironically, Kong Gai mounted the stairway, keeping his gun trained on Wentworth. When he reached the room above, which must have been his secret lair, from which he could watch all over Chinatown in security, the staircase began to fold up and rise, to fit into the ceiling. The ingenious affair, when shut and in position, was invisible, and, like floor, wall, and ceiling itself, covered with thick glass.

Naked to the waist, Jimmy Wentworth stared slowly around the room. Not an object to be seen anywhere, except glass, cobras, and drinking pan. Nothing! On the glass partition was a small knob, by means of which a glass panel could be slid back. Wentworth's first wild notion was to wrench off this heavy section of glass, and, when Kong Gai returned, smash him down with it.…

But long before the terrible King Cobra returned, the cobras behind the partition would have stormed out, and fastened their deadly fangs in the white man's body. Wentworth knew well that the cobra alone will attack humans,even without provocation. And what had he to defend himself with?

His hands. At best, his shoes. And even if he managed to divert a blow from one cobra with a shoe, what could he do with the other three?

"He's got me," the young sergeant of detectives muttered.

Then, without reason at all, he walked slowly to the glass partition. Three of the hooded cobras slept; the fourth, as if on guard, raised an inquiring head. Long the burning eyes stared at the white man, and then slowly the head rose, and the hood expanded wide. Fascinated, Wentworth placed his hand against the glass, and, with a slow, writhing motion, less fast than that of a rattlesnake, the cobra swung forward, and then suddenly struck against the glass.

Wentworth saw drops of yellow venom where its fangs had tried to pierce the partition!

"What a way to die," Jimmy Wentworth groaned. "What a way to die!"

The brilliant eyes of the giant serpent bored into his very brain, and then a second time the infuriated cobra struck, this time sliding its awful head along the glass in its effort to get at the man outside.

A second cobra lifted its coils to look, and then, as if satisfied that all was well, dropped into a heap again.

Jimmy thought, "Wouldn't it be better to open the slide, and get it over with at once? Kong Gai can return and find me dead. No gloating for him that way."

But the young white man didn't want to die. To die fighting, that was one thing; to die in Kong Gai's lair, that was vastly different.

Yet what could he do about it?

His lips, like his face, were gray. Cold sweat began slowly to chill him as he stood there, unable to tear his eyes from the glittering orbs of the deadly cobra.

He had tried to do his duty. His reward was to be only an awful death of agony, either from thirst or from the fangs of the snakes.

How Kong Gai must be enjoying it all!

7

IN THE COBRA DEN

DOWN IN THE Hall of Justice Captain Dunand was uneasy. When the first report was handed him—that Wentworth had accompanied Killer King in a taxi, after leaving the parole office, Dunand sent out word to watch for the Killer—not to get him, but to keep him in sight if possible. However, by late afternoon no sign of the Killer had been found.

Wentworth had vanished, which was to be expected. Dunand had no real reason for anxiety. He realized what Wentworth was up against, but the details of the impersonation of Slim Jennings had been so carefully worked out that the gray-haired captain of detectives supposed his fears were ridiculous. Wentworth's disguise was the safest of all, since it was a real one, and not dependent upon dyes or anything else which could be detected. Even the husky voice, unlike the sergeant's real tones, was real.

At four in the afternoon Dunand called in Officer Crawford of the Chinatown detail. "You relieve O'Bannion," the captain said. "I've got no word for you at all, Crawford, except what we've already discussed. Keep your eyes open, and your ears. Wentworth's somewhere in Chinatown, and you may be the link which will result in success. The sergeant is to report to Headquarters, after he finds the way to Kong Gai's hiding place; if he spoke to you, he'd tip off the damnable fiend. But be on the look-out, Crawford."

"I will, Captain."

"It may take Wentworth several days to get back to us… No telling what he's doing. And I'll be better satisfied when this's all over," added Dunand, half to himself.

Had Jimmy Wentworth heard this, he himself would have agreed that he would be glad when it was all over. A fellow could only die once! And he had about made up his mind that the best way to die was before he pleaded for water, before Kong Gai and his villainous men were able to jeer and taunt. Better to die from the fangs of the snakes! Wentworth slowly made up his mind to another thing. Why not try to smash Kong Gai down with his bare hands, and let the King Cobra shoot him? At least this was a quick way to die, and he might get in one flashing blow before Kong Gai finished him.

He couldn't kill Kong Gai, of course. The Cobra Men would torture him anyhow; perhaps the Death of a Thousand Cuts, bleeding him white. But what difference did it make how a man died?

Kong Gai might even enter the room of the snakes alone, showing his men that he had no fear at all of the white man. Then, somehow, Wentworth might close with him….

A trapped man grasps at anything. Jimmy Wentworth played with the idea; it gave him something to think about.

Then he remembered exactly how Kong Gai had acted before—had stood a full dozen feet from him, gun always pointed at his heart. The King Cobra would never take a chance now! Before Wentworth could get at him, the gun would roar... but what of it? A clean way to die!

Kong Gai, truly Chinese, would have held to life as long as possible, and therefore would figure that Jimmy would do the same thing. He would be surprised into shooting to kill, rather than to maim, to stop the other, wounded.

Having argued this much out, Wentworth resumed his intent stare about the room. Not a thing to use as a weapon. Nothing!

In the room was one pan of water, the glass partition, and the cobras, with one of the olive bodies always on guard over the sleeping three. If he took the sliding door, the serpents would finish him before Kong Gai returned. That was out of the question. And what else was there in the room?

Although Jimmy Wentworth told himself that he was willing to die if he could get in one blow at Kong Gai, in his heart was still a shred of hope. A man wasn't dead until he was dead! Would this hope keep him alive until, exhausted, he begged for water? No! Never in the world!

SINCE IT WAS the one movable, available object in the room, Wentworth was unable to keep away from the sliding glass section of the partition. He did not know how long he had been in the room—it was well after seven o'clock—before a wild, impossible idea came to him.

It was so impossible, so really unworkable, that Wentworth actually shook his head. But it wouldn't vanish. The more he thought about it, the surer he became that he was going to try it!

And try he did.

He placed his right hand against the glass. The cobra

weaved slowly forward, and then struck. Wentworth, instead of removing his hand, kept it against the glass, sliding it along until it was directly over the line of the sliding panel. Then with his left hand he opened the panel almost a full inch. The cobra struck again at the opening.

Heart pounding, Wentworth opened the slide another inch, and a third. Again the vicious serpent struck, and was beaten back by the heavy glass. Its hood was extended fully, its rubylike eyes glowed with rage.

Another of the cobras lifted its head, and then dropped back into the heap of coils.

Quietly Wentworth moved the panel again, until it was five inches at the opening.

And again the cobra swayed forward, eyes on Wentworth's right hand, which was a foot behind the open space. Slowly the head lowered. Remembering the impacts of the glass, the cobra's head lowered more cautiously. The outstretched hood touched glass… the evil head began to slip through the opening.…

Wentworth jammed the slide shut, pinioning the head just behind the hood!

Both hands on the knob, the young sergeant of detectives almost severed the coil of the long olive body! The cobra writhed, twisted, olive coils hammering this way and that. The other cobras came out in a flash of color, smashing their bodies against the inch of opening which now held the dying coils of their mate.

Slowly the great body ceased its wild thrashing. And became still. Even more slowly the three cobras returned to their corner.…

With shaking hand, Wentworth grasped the lax hood

of the serpent, opened the slide, and pulled the long body
through and into the main part of the room.

One!

He was jubilant now. What real good the killing of the
cobras might do him in an attempt to escape he did not
think; without the waste of a second more than it took to
put the heavy coils in a corner of the room, he returned
to the glass partition, patting his hand against it again....

Two!

The third cobra was more wily. It took Wentworth
almost a half hour to get it to try for the opening, and to
crush the horrible fanged head between the glass.

And at any moment Kong Gai might return.

The fourth cobra, alone, refused to leave its wall near the
drinking pan. Not until Wentworth tried hissing, as Kong
Gai had done, was he able to coax the deadly snake toward
the opening. When it was trapped, it writhed furiously, and
almost escaped even the pinioning glass, but at last it, also,
relaxed—thrashed once more—and then the beady eyes
dimmed, and it was dead.

Four!

One cobra remained—the human snake, Kong Gai.

Jimmy's head was beginning to whirl. Half formed
plans! He must select the best of them, and probably none
would work. Would Kong Gai come accompanied by his
'binders? Or would he come alone, showing his contempt
of the white man? If the latter was the case, Wentworth
thought he had a bare chance....

He next went about a curious business. Three of the dead
cobras—whose coils, even in death, continued to writhe
and twist a little—he replaced in the glass cage. In coils, as

if they slept. The fourth he left in the corner of the room. Then he sat on the glass floor, in front of it, and waited.

No sound filtered into the glass chamber. Wentworth could not even hear the bell of the old cathedral. High above the serpent cage, protected by glass and steel, one light glowed; he had no way of telling the hour.

Midnight came and the dead hour of morning approached before Wentworth heard a little grating sound, and then the room was flooded with light. The stairway was unfolding.

Wentworth crouched in his corner.

Down the stairway, gun held carefully before him, slipped the silk-clad figure of the Evil One.

HE STOPPED AT the bottom of the stairway and said sweetly, "Good morning, Sergeant! Have you slept well?" As he spoke, his eyes, as bright as those of the cobras before death, swept about the room once, and were satisfied. His gun did not waver as he added, "I see you are not yet thirsty, Wentworth! But do not be impatient! All things will come in due time. *Hai-ya!* I tell that to my Brothers; they are anxious to see you die, but I tell them that they must be patient, if they wish to see a real performance! Well, you have matched wits with Kong Gai, and what has it brought you?"

"The department… know… where I am," Wentworth mumbled. "You let me go… I'll get a transfer…."

Kong Gai laughed.

"Breaking so soon, Sergeant? I am disappointed in you!"

Wentworth's right hand was tight about the tail of the great dead cobra.

"I have always been disappointed in white men," Kong

Gai continued contentedly. "Even Wentworth, in white women! I was even prepared for you to attack me, in which case I would have shot you through the legs, being a very good marksman! I thought you would fight against death, instead of sitting so foolishly in your corner..."

Suddenly the King Cobra shrieked.

Wentworth, with every ounce of strength in his lean, tired body, had swung up the long body of the dead cobra, and launched the olive coils squarely at the narrow chest of Kong Gai!

The Evil One fired almost instantly, proving his boast about marksmanship by shattering the dead head of the cobra.

But before he could shift aim, or pull trigger again, Wentworth was on him. For one instant the Chinese writhed under the second unexpected attack, and then, like the very snakes, the perfumed body in olive silk became limp.

Wentworth seized the fallen gun. With the man's own silken jacket he tied him, gagged him. Then he seized the unconscious body and, carrying it, scrambled up the stairs.

He was already positive that no one was in the upper room, or yellow heads would have come to the aperture at the pistol shot. His gun was ready, but the upper room was empty.

A voice cried, in excited, uneasy Mandarin Chinese:

"Is all well, O Great Master of the Snakes? I heard a shot—"

Wentworth, imitating the high-pitched voice of Kong Gai, called back—hoping that the heavy door would muffle the tones to fool the 'binder outside:

"All is well, Brother."

"Hai-ya! It is a great day for us, greatest of all Hooded Ones! Sleep well, O Master. We will awaken you at the hour of noon."

To this Wentworth made no reply, neither wanting to trust his voice, nor to risk an improper response.

Instead, without wasting time, he laid the gagged King Cobra on a couch and strode to the window. The city was still dark. Street lights mocked him, far below. He knew where he was. The building housing Kong Gai's lair was on a corner. No roofs were near it. Somewhere, Wentworth was sure, there was a secret exit, probably a narrow ladder-way down to another tunnel. Even if he could find the way to open the door to it, it would be useless to attempt escape in that way.

He looked down again. There was a drop of five floors. Below, over the sidewalk, was a canvas awning.

Wentworth thought, "Can I make it? It's the one way!"

He glanced at the bound figure of Kong Gai, and found that the blazing, evil eyes were fastened on his own.

Jimmy Wentworth's lips said words almost without his brain directing them:

"Just a little patience, Kong Gai," said Jimmy Wentworth, "and we'll crack your neck like the rest of the cobras'! You've reached the end of the rope, Kong Gai… or you will before very long!"

8

THE HOODED ONE

NO TIME TO waste. Swiftly, efficiently, Wentworth made a three-strand rope of the room's silken hangings and heavy silken cords.

The street lights were becoming pale, and the first gleam of the sun appeared over the shoulders of the eastward Oakland hills. Faintly Wentworth heard the *bong, bong* of the old cathedral's bell.

He remembered the sign he had so often seen under the clock there:

> Son, Observe the Time
> And Fly from Evil.

"I've got to wait," Wentworth decided. "I've got to wait a little."

He carefully tied Kong Gai to the end of the silken rope. Then, careful to make no noise, he moved a heavy teak-wood stool to the window, and braced it so it would hold weight, angling it against the bullnose window frame. To the stool he tied the other end of the rope.

The clock struck the half hour, and then Wentworth saw a slow-moving blue-clad form step from under the awning, and up to the stanchion of the street light. Saw a patrolman unlock the call box....

Wentworth shoved the window open swiftly, and began to lower the body of the Evil One. He payed out the rope hastily, trying to keep the captive from hitting against any window which might be below.

Someone was calling, "O Kong Gai! Is all well? You have opened a window!"

Wentworth could not trust his voice now. Without replying, he went over the sill, and began to slide down the rope.

Halfway down, he heard a scream above him.

He mustn't look up! He hadn't counted that some device would signal the opening of a window to the doorguard of the lair.

Wentworth caught a snatch of Chinese: "Do not cut! The Master is at the end!"

And then he heard a white man cry:

"The window, Sergeant?" and, without waiting for impossible reply, Officer Crawford's gun roared, directed at the heads so high up, while with his left hand he jammed down the indicator in the call box which was already setting the gong in Headquarters to blaring!

Riot call! Box 114-C... Chinatown!

What happened next Jimmy Wentworth hardly remembered. Somehow he must have cut loose Kong Gai, so that the Evil One fell to the awning. Somehow he himself let go, and his heavier body ripped through the canvas, taking Kong Gai's bound body with him....

Somehow he was on his feet again, back to back with Crawford, and over the prone form of Kong Gai, they were fighting off the disorganized attack of the Brothers of the Snake, whose numbers were being augmented every minute....

And then there was a scream of siren, and the roar of automatics and clatter of the police choppers—a bedlam of noise.

It was all hazy to Jimmy Wentworth; all hazy until the physician in Headquarters put something pungent under his nose, which cleared away the dizziness. He knew now that he was sitting in Captain Dunand's chair, and that the old gray-haired veteran's eyes were wet.

Standing beside the desk was Kong Gai; he had really caught him! Kong Gai, with handcuffs still circling his wrists!

The end of the chase. The peril of Chinatown, of the entire city, ready to go behind the bars at last.

"You did it, Jimmy," Captain Dunand whispered. "What a tale it must be!"

The physician pleaded, "Not a word now, Captain. Tomorrow. Not before."

"You're O.K., Sergeant?" Commissioner Jerome, hurriedly summoned, demanded. "You've done a remarkable thing. We'll make it up to you! We'll—"

Wentworth said hoarsely, trying to sit erect, "A drink of water... couldn't lap with... snakes... couldn't...."

"What a story this must he," marveled Jerome.

Jimmy Wentworth managed to grin as a glass was held to his lips. He supposed that he should stand in the presence of the commissioner, but he was too tired... and, anyhow, everything was going round... and round... and round....

FOUR MONTHS LATER, in Captain Dunand's office, at exactly ten o'clock in the morning, Detective Sergeant Wentworth (who had been awarded the police medal for valor) sat quietly beside his chief.

Dunand's watch lay on the desk. The room was so still that every tick sounded like a hammer beat.

"He's going up the thirteen stairs now," Dunand said slowly. "They're putting the black hood on his neck, lad…."

"The hood of Kong Gai," whispered Jimmy Wentworth. "He's dying like a Hooded One."

"Aye, son. The world will be a better place with him gone."

Wentworth said nothing. How strange it was, to think of Kong Gai doing his dance of death at San Quentin. Kong Gai—the Evil One, who had murdered, stolen, done every horrible crime. Kong Gai—the hooded King Cobra. Caught in his own lair.

"Ten eleven," muttered Dunand. "I've heard the most evil men take the longest in dying. D'ye think that's true, Jimmy?"

"I don't know, sir. Only, this waiting is horrible."

Nodding, Dunand said, "Maybe there was a hitch. But he couldn't escape the death cell. Guards all around. Nor could he take his own evil life—"

The telephone rang sharply.

"Dunand," the captain said. "Yes, Warden?" He listened closely, saying gravely at last, "Thank you, Warden." Turning to Wentworth—" Kong Gai is dead. When he was dropped through the trap, the hood was knocked off… a horrible sight, the Warden said. It's all over. The Evil One is dead."

The two detectives, gray-haired captain and youthful sergeant, sat in silence. Softly the bell of the old cathedral announced the quarter hour. *Bong... bong... bong....*

Wentworth wondered suddenly if Kong Gai, leader of the hooded cobra brotherhood, had ever looked at the words on the bell-tower:

> Son, Observe the Time
> And Fly from Evil.

The last note of the bell fainted away.

Captain Dunand said slowly, "Peace. Peace in China-town." He remained motionless behind his desk a long time, and then he said, "A terrible man. A terrible man. We must forget about him and his deeds... Take the day off, Jimmy. Go somewhere—in safety at last—with your girl. Now, when I was courtin' my wife, it was always to the beach we went, on a day like this—"

"And," grinned Jimmy Wentworth, who had heard the story from another source, "you poured sand down her neck and she almost married a fireman! That's what Mrs. Dunand told me, anyhow."

"Get out of here," roared the old captain. "Have I not enough to do without listening to the idle words of a lazy young scamp who ought to be patrolling the Children's Playground in the Park? Out with you, Jimmy Wentworth!"

Jimmy saluted smartly.

"Yes, sir," he said.

The two men laughed. Dunand's arm was about Went-worth's shoulders as the pair walked together out of the office.

www.ingramcontent.com/pod-product-compliance
Lightning Source LLC
Chambersburg PA
CBHW051139030726
47504CB00004B/954